Walking on Sea Glass

A Sea Glass Inn Novel

Julie Carobini

DOLPHIN GATE BOOKS

Dolphin Gate Books
Trade book ISBN: 978-0-9862292-9-9
Print Edition

Cover photos from Shutterstock.com and Dreamstime.com
Cover design by Roseanna White Designs

Julie Carobini writes novels set by the sea. *RT Book Reviews* says, "Carobini has a talent for creating characters that come alive." Julie lives in California with her family and loves all things coastal (except sharks). Learn about new releases and download freebies at www.juliecarobini.com

"To your health"
… "Love you"

Chapter One

✳

EVEN AS A CHILD, Liddy believed the sea could heal.

She remembered being seven years old, crammed into a van with cousins and a couple of stray friends. Her mother drove, while her Aunt Clarice played navigator, her round nose inches from a map. Her aunt looked up occasionally, her face a knot of concern, until the lines around her eyes brightened like a light going on and she jabbed a finger toward one of the green highway signs looming over them.

"There. Merge into that lane. Don't miss it!"

Before that, the ride seemed to go on forever and ever, the humid air of children—the pungent aroma of *boys*—blanketing them all. They lived about an hour inland, but the way her mother drove intently and her aunt fussed and the air hung so heavily, you would think they were days away.

And right about the time it all became too much, it happened.

The starkness of Interstate 10 through Los Angeles, its concrete walls dingy grey, its curves hard and etched from time's abuse, belied what lay like a pot at the end of the proverbial rainbow. That curve in the road … the black tunnel in the distance. As they barreled toward that dark and seemingly endless tunnel, a mix of wonder and surprise caught her breath. They would make their entrance, the tunnel's windowless walls shutting out the famous Southern California sunshine, rocket around a bend, then—and this is the part she remembered so well—the darkness would open up to the vast and deep blue sea.

Funny how a stray memory like that could show up unannounced, like a sudden thunderstorm, without a hint of where or why it had come ...

"Liddy?"

Liddy stared straight ahead, unmoving. She wanted to respond, but somehow couldn't.

"Liddy?" her friend Meg called out again. "Are you okay?"

Liddy blinked hard and took in a gulp of dry heat. She slid a glance at Meg who sat in the shade beside her, fanning herself with a copy of *Forbes* magazine. "Sorry. I don't know what came over me." Liddy's cheeks grew warmer than ever. "Guess I got lost in thought."

Meg eyed her suspiciously. "Well, sure. It *is* stifling out here—even in this shade. No idea how you can stand living in the desert."

"Were you saying something?"

Meg's expression calmed some. "I was saying that it must be tough working and going to school again."

Liddy shrugged, glad her moment of confusion had dissipated. It was late September, and a storm had blown through long enough to lower the temperature to a comfortable 85 degrees. "It's not easy, but there's so much more I want to learn, so much I didn't appreciate when I was younger."

"It has to be strange being back on a college campus again,

though, with all those babies around."

Liddy laughed. Those so-called babies were only a handful of years younger than her. "Well, yes, to a lot of them, twenty-five is ancient, but every once in a while when I'm eating lunch in the 'caf,' a group of girls will sit down with me, like I'm one of them. Total opposite of high school—thankfully."

Meg flipped the pages of her magazine. "And how's Shawn handling having you around campus so much? Do you have to call him Mr. Buckle—or worse, Professor B?

"Please. He's fine with it. Although ..."

"Yes?"

"Nothing. I'm just seeing Shawn's life from a different angle now."

Meg did that thing with her mouth, letting her tiny pucker pop open, then quickly shutting her lips together—as if suddenly thinking better of what she had intended to say.

"One student calls his cell all the time with incessant questions. She's in his Geography class and apparently still thinks the world is flat."

Meg looked at Liddy full force now, her fingers bookmarking a page on women in marketing. "Isn't that kind of inappropriate? Calling Shawn like that?"

"What are you suggesting?"

Meg's voice turned pointed. "I'm just saying that a coed should not be regularly calling a married man."

Liddy leaned back, tilting her chin up toward the clearing sky. "I met her, actually. That's what I meant by seeing my husband from another angle. I stopped into the library's tutoring area and they were at a table together going over some flashcards. Shawn introduced me."

3

"Good."

"What do you mean 'good'?"

Meg paused. "I just meant that, otherwise, she might have mistaken his attention for something ... else."

"Oh brother."

"So what did he do? Say 'Here's my gorgeous wife, Liddy,' then give you a kiss?"

Liddy paused. "Actually, he just said, 'Kyra, this is Liddy. Liddy ... Kyra.'" She winced a little at the memory. "I remember thinking that I should mention that I'm the wife, but then thought better of it. Of course, she knew who I was."

"Hmm."

Liddy turned, scrutinizing her friend's face. Meg rarely held back. "What?"

"That must have bothered you."

Liddy waved her off. "It didn't. It's no big deal, really."

Meg pursed her lips again, then let them pop open with a fat sigh. She let the magazine slide from her lap and onto the paint-chipped deck. "If it didn't bother you, then you wouldn't have mentioned it."

Liddy frowned. She shook her head slowly before moving her gaze back to the sky. "Well, then, let's forget I ever did."

THINKING WOULD COME LATER. Beau gripped the steering wheel and sped through the night, the streets lonely, empty. Minutes before, he had pulled into the driveway of his home after another long day at the hospital, unable to recall a time when the muscles and sinew that wrapped his bones had ever ached from fatigue quite so much. He had turned off the engine, pulled the key from the ignition, and allowed the door to swing open as he gathered his briefcase, a stained coffee mug, and Anne's favorite sweater from the passenger seat. It was green and matched her eyes.

Beau hoisted himself out of the car, careful not to drop anything, and stepped around the door intending to pop it shut with his hip. Before he could, the cell phone in his pocket rang. He froze. Fear snaked around his heart and squeezed vise-like. Anne had programmed the sound of birds chirping into his phone's memory the first time she had to stay in the hospital. "Hear that, and you'll know to come running," she had kidded him.

He watched the screen light up, watched the familiar name flash across it, and listened to the odd twittering of birds against the moonless night. "Anne?"

"Beau, this is Pam."

Not Nurse Jones or Nurse Pam. The woman on the other end was simply "Pam." She'd been assigned to Anne's care so often that she had become more like family. The family member who, though you hated to be the one to point this out, always seemed to hustle into the house with an assortment of unwanted baggage.

He could hear her sucking in a breath. "I'm so sorry, but you need to come back." She paused. "Now."

Beau's grip tightened on the handle of that mug. His jaw clenched and something other than fear quickened his heartbeat. A sharpness like ice burned through his insides. He paused, fixated on the mug in his hands, wishing to calmly take it inside the house and set it in the sink as he had planned. In the next instant, he pitched the cool vessel to the ground, watching it shatter on impact.

For several seconds he stood in the quiet, exhaling roughly and staring at the shards that littered his driveway. He would need a broom to clean them up. Probably the push broom would be best. He kept it in the shed out back ...

He lifted his chin toward the stars, allowing his breathing to slow. Heat returned to his insides. He turned toward his car, tossed his briefcase into the backseat where it had lain most of the day, dropped Anne's sweater on top of it, and slid back into the driver's seat.

Pulling strength from some invisible well, Beau put the car in reverse and headed back to the hospital. He continued through the black night, unable to shake a prickling of his senses. The sensation began in his gut, climbed up and through his chest, then spread web-like over his throat, strangling him. He forced himself to breathe, to focus on the road and on getting back to the hospital ... before it was too late.

Chapter Two

Two Months Later

LIDDY TWISTED THE KEY IN the lock of her rental, a condo far away from every dry and dusty trace of the home she had once shared with Shawn. Four years of marriage—two-hundred-and-eight weeks—and she found herself living alone. If someone had asked her if she had ever expected this, she would have reacted with shock. Living somewhere else, perhaps, and with a boy or a girl—or both—in tow, but never, ever this.

Moisture seeped through the bottom of the bag nestled in her free arm. She hurried inside and plunked the mess down next to the voice mail box with the message light blinking. Three messages. She hardly knew anyone in this up-and-coming beach town, but something about that blinking light made her feel less invisible.

Thank God for Meg who had recommended her for a job in a new place, far away from her troubled marriage. Her best friend since childhood worked in sales and marketing for a chain of hotels, but kept her office at Sea Glass Inn, where Liddy now spent her days as a concierge.

Liddy stashed cream in the fridge and French Roast coffee beans in the cupboard. How lucky was she to have found a job *and* an apartment in such a short time.

She pressed the flashing red light on her answering machine.

"This is Dr. Grayson's office calling to let you know we can fit you in next Friday at 2 p.m. Please call us back to confirm."

Another thing to be thankful for: a doctor who came recommended, and who could see her on short notice. She glanced at the calendar and made a mental reminder to confirm the appointment. Maybe the doc would finally have some answers for her.

Beep.

"Hey Lid, it's Trace."

She wrinkled her nose at the nickname that one of her new coworkers had picked up on after Meg had lapsed into using it on occasion.

"It's a real yawn around here today—occupancy's way down—so I'm gonna leave early. Will leave you some notes under the volcano."

After less than two weeks on the job, Liddy had learned about Trace's obsession with garage sale "must haves." A ceramic volcano had made the list.

"Oh, before I go," she said, lowering her voice, "have you seen anything weird going on in the restaurant? There's some … talk. Anyway, let me know. 'K, bye."

Okay, then.

Beep.

"Liddy, it's Shawn."

She frowned.

"… I found your skis and boots in the shed. Look, it's no big deal to me, but if you want me to get rid of them for you, I can do that. Call me."

Strange. Liddy's soon-to-be ex-husband had not cared to call when she did the lonely work of dividing a home. Or bothered to tell her when one of her credit cards showed up at the house—*their* house. She'd found that out on her own when she learned he had charged it up to its limit. Meg had nearly booked a one-way ticket to the desert when she'd heard. "I'm going over there to key that loser's car now!" her friend had proclaimed. Liddy had stopped her, of course, but not without thinking about it for longer than she should have. Odd that now, when Shawn had found something of potential value that Liddy had left behind, he decided to call.

She grabbed the towel that lay on the kitchen counter and began wiping down the spotless surface. She circled the cloth over and over and over the smooth granite surface, each stroke stemming the tide brewing behind her eyes. How had it come to this? In a matter of minutes, she replayed the last few months of their marriage in her mind, carefully sifting the clumps of memory that exposed themselves to her scrutiny.

The more she thought about it, the more she worked that towel over the shiny surface, and the duller her thoughts became. Shawn probably figured that he would get points for mentioning it, that she would then ask him to do the work of selling her things—and that the proceeds would make it into his bank account. The reality of that thought settled inside her gut, reigniting her already tender emotions, the ones that threatened to hurl her into the abyss of depression every time they surfaced.

Stop being so melodramatic.

Shawn had left her. His girlfriend—an eighteen-year-old

college student—was pregnant. And with this knowledge in hand, she had moved hundreds of miles away from them. (So he couldn't ask her to babysit, for example.) She shook her head. Didn't Shawn know that with their divorce pending, and his life already being reshaped by his choices, that her future and how she lived it was off-limits?

With a sad little groan, she pitched the overworked towel into the kitchen sink. Then she reached across the counter, and like a leg reacting to the sharp tap of a plessor on the fleshy part of the knee, Liddy punched "delete."

BEAU CLIMBED THE STEPS TOWARD HOME. Anne had been gone more than a month already, and though he had been back at work for almost a week, the evenings were the hardest. Work hadn't helped him forget his loss, but it had kept his mind occupied with something other than his grief.

He stepped into the foyer, winced at the echo of his own footsteps, and bent to scoop up the mail spread across the tile. Arms loaded, he wandered into the kitchen to dump his briefcase and mail, then grabbed a Corona from the fridge. He stood in the center of the small room and drank it, the fizz going down like a cold burn.

He spied the highlighter-yellow flyer in the pile and plucked it from the bunch, scanning it for details. *Single Mingle*. His head rocked back and a gasp escaped from his lungs. He stared at the ceiling, wondering just whose sick idea it was to invite him to the church's singles group ... already.

The phone rang and he straightened, cracking his back in two places. He reached to answer it, but not before crumpling the neon flyer into a wad and pitching it into the garbage. "Yeah?"

"Rough day?"

Beau sighed and shook his head in the empty room. "Hey, Taylor."

"Well?"

"Well, what? It is ... what it is."

"What's that—Shakespeare?"

Taylor's wit brought a smile—albeit a small one—to Beau's face. First one he'd experienced all day. "You know what I mean."

"Maybe I do and maybe I don't. See? I can quote literature too."

"Right."

"Is that a smile I'm hearing?"

"You can't *hear* a smile."

"You can if you have super powers like mine."

Beau smiled widely this time. Taylor and his wife, Ginny, had been by his side for months, ever since Anne entered the hospital for the last time. He was a goofball with a heart. *Isn't that what Anne had called him?* He stepped out of his loafers and sank onto the couch. "Why are you bothering me again?"

Taylor blew his nose into the phone, the sound reminiscent of an off-key trumpet.

Beau loosened his tie. "Man, that's horrible. How does your wife stand you?"

"Are you kidding me? Robust nose-blowing is a sign of virility. The first time she heard that, the woman was hooked!"

Beau laughed, but the sound of it soon died away.

"So. You want to talk about it or do I have to blow my

honker again to get it out of you?"

"I'll pass." Beau pushed himself deeper into the couch cushions, attempting to allow the day's stress to ease its way out of him. "Right before you called I was checking the mail and found that the church had sent me an invitation to a singles event." He paused. "Can you believe that?"

"That they sent the most eligible bachelor in the church an invitation to the singles potluck?"

Beau coughed out a shocked and somewhat tortured laugh. "You agree with this?"

"Hey, I'm not saying I agree. Just look at the facts, though: You're not ugly, you drive a nice car, and you're employed. My friend, you are the freshest meat that group has seen in a while. Why wouldn't they invite you? Kudos to the genius who thought of it."

Beau shook his head and groaned, yet was unable to shake away the odd smile that Taylor's ridiculous theory brought to his face. It was strange on the church's part, really, thinking that he would be ready to wear a badge that said "I'm available" quite so soon. And yet, Tay's assessment had entertained him right into considering forgiveness. Likely it had been the idea of the church's kindly pastoral care assistant, Tessy, who never liked to see anyone sad.

He released a sigh and cradled the phone against his ear as he relaxed into the couch. "So this is why you called me? To harass me about meeting women?"

"That and to see if you want to meet for a burrito on Friday. That is, if you don't have a date by then."

"Oh." Beau eyed the ceiling, and for a moment experienced déjà vu. He had spent many nights like this, staring up at the ceiling as Anne slept in the other room, hoping for answers. He still hadn't received any.

He sat up, digging his elbows into his thighs. Friday night was coming and his calendar was clear. "Sure," he said. "I'm in."

Chapter Three

THE NEW NORMAL.

That's what people called a change so drastic, so unanticipated and unwelcome in a person's life that it actually needed a
moniker as a reminder of his or her new "situation."

Kind of like finding one's name and address on the singles'
mailing list.

Why had he been so taken aback? Beau had always prided
himself on his ability to reason, to plan his future in an
organized fashion. He'd taken to Excel like a dog takes to
water, for example. And so it should not have surprised him
that someone at church, too, had exercised their own naviga-
tion skills through the murky waters of logic.

Anne was gone, and he was single. Hence, he had become
eligible to join a new club.

Taylor's raucous laughter volleyed in his memory, saving
him from another go at a pity party. Though he had been
momentarily tempted.

Beau shoved a naked foot deep into the sand and began to
trudge along through the morning air. One foot in front of the
other until the steep, dry drifts flattened into packed wet sand.
His mind turned in another direction, tumbling with a to-do

list that seemed as far and wide as the sea itself. Email to answer, clients to reply to, bills to pay. And yet, none of it felt all that important anymore. Necessary, yes, but no longer important enough to skip a walk by the sea on a crisp morning. He stopped and gazed out toward the horizon, a hazy glow sent from the east forming over the water. For the first time in months, it occurred to Beau that he hadn't had to remind himself to breathe.

He continued moving along the shoreline, allowing the lapping waves to lick at his feet. The icy water made his toes throb. Sandpipers skittered out of his way, and gulls gave him a haughty glare before they, too, scurried out of his path.

He smiled. "Chickens."

One particularly fat seagull let out a bark-like cry, as if taking offense at Beau's remark. Beau watched it fly away, his eyes settling on a solitary figure jogging from the opposite direction. The woman in black running pants and a sleek long-sleeved jacket moved swiftly toward him. Then she slowed before stopping abruptly, as if spooked by something in the water.

He glanced out to sea, but saw nothing amiss. No fins or troubled swimmers. By the time he returned his gaze to her, she had started up her jog again. She moved tentatively at first but picked up speed on approach, then dodged around him as she passed by. In that brief instant of hair flying and limbs pumping, their eyes met—hers were dark and intense—and he found himself smiling at her.

Beau continued his walk along the shore, drawing steady breaths from the sea and contemplating his plans for the day. Maybe, he thought, his new normal was finally sinking in.

WHAT *WAS* THAT? Liddy gulped the wet air, her body running on autopilot. If she stopped long enough to contemplate the suddenly odd and disconcerting behavior of her own body, she very well might never run again. One second she was jogging along, her mind ping-ponging between trivial matters, and the next, her legs refused to move forward as they had been trained to do.

Everything about this morning had been normal. She had pulled on her running pants and top, yanked her hair into a ponytail, and laced up her Nikes. She had set out, allowing the morning to drench her with its salt-infused air. She jogged slowly at first, then sped up, her breathing measured and her body adjusting to the pace.

Just like normal.

As she ran, her mind wandered to the all-sorts-of crazy Trace had left her under the volcano yesterday, to that cute bellman with the floppy hair at work, then to the vastness of the sea, and back again. She could always count on using her morning runs to sort out the mental to-do list that seemed so mangled when she awoke each day. Without her daily jog, she might not remember to apply mascara to both sets of eyelashes and wear matching shoes. Exercising in the morning, she had long ago decided, was better than espresso—though she always downed one of those before work, too.

Was this all in her head? Workout over, Liddy crossed the street to her condo complex, narrowly missing the bicyclist in her path. He flashed her a sign that let her know exactly what he thought of her. Whatever. She had worse things to worry about. Like why, as she ran along the sand this morning, her feet suddenly would not cooperate. Why they wanted to go in another direction, even though her mind was telling them to continue forward. And why her left arm had a distinct shake to it as her mind battled to get her feet and legs to cooperate.

This blip in her usually event-free morning workout passed as quickly as it had occurred, leaving behind nothing but confusion and worry. She'd had a similar occurrence months before, but less dramatic than this one. Back then, she had attributed the oddity to "nerves." Shawn had just announced that he was leaving her, so when she had experienced momentary confusion one day while walking to the store she figured that stress was the culprit. An unanticipated divorce could do that to a person. Couldn't it?

Now she was far less convinced. Liddy climbed the stairs to her rental, replaying the moments that she still could not define. When she had snapped out of her confusion on the beach—had been able to convince her body to do as it was told—she vaguely remembered a man walking toward her. He may even have looked at her as she passed him by.

He must think I'm crazy...

Liddy unlocked her door and slipped into her home, aware of the rivulets of sweat running down her back and the lingering fog dulling her mind.

The test results she hoped to get later this week couldn't come soon enough.

BY NINE A.M., THE MORNING'S STRANGE episode was behind her. Liddy bustled past the valet desk and several bellmen wheeling carts, caught a wink from Thomas who worked most shifts that she did, and strolled in through the sliding doors leading into the lobby—uncharacteristically quiet for the moment. " 'Hey, Trace," she called out as she took her place behind the concierge desk.

Trace glanced up from her seat at the desk. "Hey, yourself. Glad you're here. If I have to order up one more harbor cruise, I think I'll puke."

Liddy plunked her bag in a drawer. "Where's your sense of adventure ... your longing to connect our guests with the sea?"

"The only thing that connects me to the sea is the railing I spend most of my time leaning over."

"Ah. Hence the puke visual."

Trace nodded, her smile evident as Liddy's phone rang from behind the concierge desk. "It's all yours, girl."

Liddy watched as Trace grabbed an overly stuffed purse from beneath the desk and padded away, her high-heeled sandals smacking on the tile. She picked up the phone. "Good morning, concierge desk, Liddy speaking."

"Hi. My family and I are in room 202. What time does the lunchtime harbor cruise leave?"

Like she'd been booking local cruises for months instead of weeks, Liddy entered a reservation within minutes, reminded the caller to bring windbreakers and barf bags for his family— just in case—and hung up the phone. Since moving to this lesser-known stretch of the coast, Liddy had learned that although air temps were cool, the sun shone bright and the days were crisp and comfortable in the fall and even into winter. Visitors could stand on the beach and make out many of the identifying shapes of islands off in the distance. No wonder Trace had been taking calls about cruises all morning ...

The voice mail light on her phone blinked, and a line had begun to form in front of her. A wispy-haired elderly man wearing a beret and pulling a golf bag behind him barked at her. "Need a ride to the course."

"Certainly, sir." Liddy raised two fingers into the air, letting Hannah, the bell captain, know she needed assistance at the desk.

"This is Thomas. He'll take you in the shuttle." She glanced around the lobby, searching for more signs of collared shirts and comfortable pants of the brightly colored variety. "Does anyone else need a ride to the golf course?"

A couple more golfers came forward.

"Looks like you have a full shuttle, Thomas."

"Great." He paused, raising two sandy-brown eyebrows as if a question hung on his lips. As he tipped his chin, a lock of his hair flopped over one eye. "I'm taking lunch downstairs at 12:30. Join me?"

She shrugged. "Sure."

The duffer in plaid pants grunted and Thomas turned toward him. "Yes, sir. Follow me."

Three hours passed without a break. As guests checked out, some needed help with rental cars, while others, as if soaking up the last precious moments of their vacation, lingered in the lobby to ask for directions and restaurant recommendations. Meg had called once from the road giving her some much-needed girl time, not to mention a hilarious recap of some of her cold calls. Who knew an organization existed to help prevent animal obesity? By the time help arrived for her to take a lunch break, Liddy was famished.

She wandered down to the employee area known as "the Galley," a euphemistic term, really. For while the name may conjure up an image of a gleaming brass seaboard kitchen, the Galley was actually located in the bowels of the hotel, far away from the polished lobby and halls. There employees could graze on leftovers from hotel events.

Thomas sat at a table, his thumbs working over his iPhone, and two plates piled high with chicken à la king in front of him. Apparently, the hotel chef had overestimated the demand for creamed chicken at the previous night's banquet.

He barely looked up. "Says here there's an event at that church of yours."

"That so?" Liddy slid in beside him. Considering she had only visited the nearby church a couple of times, she hardly thought of it as her own.

Thomas peered at her over his phone. "Some kind of documentary."

"And you'd like to go."

He shrugged. "There'll be a guest speaker."

She waited.

"Cody Kent."

"Aha!"

He grimaced. "What?"

She shrugged back. "Who's Cody Kent?"

Thomas plunked his fist on the table, still clutching the phone. The right side of his lip curled upward with force, as if he were a fish on a hook. "You're kidding. You don't know the name of the greatest pitcher that ever was? Or at least ... that ever was in our lifetime?"

Liddy poked her fork into the unappetizing meal on her plate. She twirled the beige mess in front of her. "Sure, I do. Thought maybe it was some other Kent."

He stared at her until she laughed, then he took a bite from his own lunch, groaned, and slid the plate away from him. "So?" he said. "Will you go with me?"

"Why? You don't think they'll let you in on your own?" Liddy laughed and added, "Sinner."

Thomas slanted her a look. "Actually, I was hoping to spend some time with you outside of"—he looked around at the windowless room, then back at her—"outside of this miserable place."

Liddy set down her fork and considered the man in uniform sitting across from her. Not a line anywhere on his face and his grin sizzled—like he was cooking up a secret behind those baby blues. She and Thomas were likely close in age, and yet the experiences of the past few months had aged her. She sensed it in her body, but worse, in her mind too where clear skies battled continually against the presence of a persistent, hazy grey cloud. Despite physically distancing herself from the pain of her breakup with Shawn, she had yet to fully embrace the laid-back lifestyle of her new surroundings.

Maybe Thomas would help change all that.

"YOU'RE THE LAST ONE HERE."

Beau's chin jerked upward. His assistant, Jill, hovered near the doorway to his office. How long had the older woman been standing there?

"Beau?" She spoke quietly, almost motherly. "Those documents can wait until tomorrow. Go home. Get some food in you."

Jill paused and he knew she would find a way to stick around until he turned off the light and wandered down the stairs to his car. Despite the fascinating spreadsheet in front of him, Beau nodded at the woman who had a family of her own to tend to, and he pushed away from his desk. "I think I am getting hungry. Thanks for the reminder, Jill."

But when he reached his car, the little white lie he had told—the one about being hungry—became ever more apparent. Instead of food, he needed something to wake him from the fog that had crept into his thoughts long after his quiet beach walk this morning. Food, however, was of no interest to him.

On his way home, he remembered the hoopla announced again at church last week about baseball pitcher Cody Kent showing up at a midweek service, no less, to talk about living right both on and off the field. A worthy, charitable event, not to mention a good excuse not to head home quite yet. As he sat at the stoplight, his mind wandered to good times before Anne's illness, to the early days when Saturday afternoons meant a cold beer and watching his favorite team.

At the green light, Beau made a U-turn back to town, all the while thinking that baseball season couldn't come soon enough.

HE SPOTTED HER JUST AFTER taking the last open seat on the aisle of the third row of the church hall. It was much easier to find a spare seat for one, he had found. She was talking animatedly with a guy next to her—maybe they'd arrived early—her hair pulled back much like it had been this morning when they'd passed each other on the sand. She wore red well.

A slap on the back by Taylor broke his concentration. "Hey, Beau."

"They let you in?" he shot back, over his shoulder.

Hands in his pockets, Taylor gave Beau a good-natured smile. "Had to. I hung the lights for this blowout." Tay glanced around, his chin bobbing. "Man, there are a lot of women here. No idea so many of 'em liked baseball."

Beau smirked and looked away, his gaze landing again on the mystery woman in the red sweater. The guy next to her playfully bumped her shoulder. He forced himself to listen to Taylor's banter. "Baseball. Yes, I'm sure that's why they are all here." He answered his friend without looking at him.

"Oh, I get it. You're here to see all of *them!*" He swept an arm toward the people in the crowd, many of them female.

Beau nodded. "Right—" He whipped his chin back toward Taylor. "Hey—what?"

His friend stood there nodding, a Cheshire-cat-sized grin on his mug. "Want me to help you pick one? You have a penchant for blondes, right? Saw one over by the exit and I don't remember her having a ring on her finger."

Beau shrank back. "You looked at her hand? You are one strange dude."

Taylor placed a forceful hand on Beau's shoulder, his smile sheepish. "I consider it my job to look out for you, friend. You can count on me."

Beau shook his head and laughed. "I've no doubt about that. But I'm not here for ... for anything other than to hear the speaker."

"So you're in need of some inspiration."

Beau considered the past ten hours, most of them spent with his eyes staring at a computer screen, analyzing marketing data for clients who had been waiting for answers. His mind still exploded with figures and charts, many of them meaningless to him now, but still enough clutter in his head to keep him from dealing with his new life. He knew that wasn't good, but the alternative—dwelling on how he wanted his future to play out—made him weary.

Instead, he nodded at Taylor and simply said, "Some inspiration is good for the soul. Wouldn't you agree?"

Taylor's grin faltered, and Beau realized just how much his friend wanted to keep smiling on his behalf. "Then you're in the right place."

After Taylor wandered off Beau took his seat, the hall still bustling. The rumble in his belly told him he probably should have stopped for a sandwich on the way. He was contemplating this menial thought as one of the elders strolled up the aisle with a woman close beside him. They stopped right next to him.

Beau stood again, wondering if perhaps he should have not made that U-turn tonight. "Hello, Rex," he said.

Rex shook his hand and quickly stepped aside. "Beau, I'd like you to officially meet Wendy Wilkes. She's part of our new member's class and quite fascinated by art, like you and … well, like you are."

No doubt he was staring blankly at the petite woman with the stick-straight hair and kind smile peering up at him. Rex had said "officially," which probably meant that they had already met at some previous time. There was nothing particularly familiar about the young woman, though, and Beau had no recollection of ever speaking to her before now. Inwardly, he held back a sigh. Anne had often chided him about forgetting faces and names, for that matter.

He stuck out a polite, if not overly friendly, hand. "I'm Beau. Welcome to the church."

She shook his hand. "Thank you. I'm glad to be here."

Beau glanced at Rex for more, but found him looking off into the distance. The elder flicked a look at Beau. "Would you excuse me, please?"

Beau opened his mouth but shut it quickly, realizing that Rex was likely running off to chase after a fictitious church member in need. The image of that yellow singles' group flyer burned in his mind.

He caught Wendy contemplating him. "I understand that your wife passed away recently. I'm truly sorry for your loss."

He nodded, and quickly swallowed. "I appreciate that."

"Sorry if Rex put you on the spot. I moved back into town recently after being away for school. My grandparents still live here—maybe you know them? Kat and Steve Wilkes?"

The granddaughter of the Wilkeses? "Yes, we have met a few times," he said. Her grandfather was a retired judge, and her grandmother, a retired lawyer.

"Anyway," she continued, "when Rex heard that I had studied art, he seemed to think you and I would have a lot to talk about."

Beau forced a smile, willing to give Rex the benefit of the doubt. At least for now. "I can't say that I know that much about art, but any interest I've taken in it is a direct result of

Anne ... my wife. She was an artist in her own right."

"Then she must have been a compelling woman."

"She was," he said, remembering the times she had cajoled him into accompanying her to various museums, both at home and abroad. It was through her influence that he had become fascinated by the physical manifestation of what an artist had conjured up in his or her own mind. "She saw things that most of us would miss, whether a distinct color or an image or even the artist's intent."

"If you're interested, there are a few nice galleries down-town. Maybe we could visit them together. There's even an Art Walk we could attend." When he didn't answer right away, she touched his shoulder. "I promise I won't bite."

His insides froze at her boldness, but then again, her tone was easy-going, too. He found himself smiling, and considering a change of pace. It wouldn't hurt to have a reason to leave the house more often, would it? "Sure," he said, as the lights in the hall began to dim and the crowd took their seats. "Let's do that sometime."

Chapter Four

✳

THE AIR HAD TURNED BLUSTERY and cold and on one uncharacteristic lull in early December, Trace, who had straightened and dusted her collection of kitsch for the umpteenth time, let out a sigh. "Feast or famine, now isn't it, Liddy?"

"I'm okay with the downtimes," Liddy said. "Always something to do." For her part, Liddy had determined to make herself useful, so she used the occasional lulls to gather a collection of her own: namely, operation manuals from other parts of the hotel. She figured that if she better understood the duties of various departments, she could better carry out her own.

Trace didn't seem to care whether or not Liddy improved her knowledge of the inn's operations, but she had quickly learned that her co-worker was not one for allowing a good lull to go to waste by allowing it to pass by without filling it with conversation. So Trace had filled the silence of the morning as often as possible, asking questions about Liddy's life, some that felt too personal and uncomfortable to talk about still. It wasn't that she had anything to hide, or that she didn't like Trace— she did, very much. But though she had long accepted her new normal, sometimes the familiar things of the past were still too raw to face.

"I brought you something," Trace said, sidling up next to her. "Here."

Liddy carefully took the "snow" woman ornament from Trace's hands. The sculpture had been made to look like as if formed from sand. "This is so cool." Liddy laughed at the pink hat and ruby-colored lipstick on the "sand" woman's face. "Oh my gosh ... those are flip-flops dangling from her, aren't they? Where in the world did you find her?"

She expected Trace to tell her she had found the treasure in one of the thrift stores that dotted the area of otherwise tony boutiques—or at least some trying to be. Instead, she said, "I ordered it online."

Liddy flipped a glance at Trace, who wore a satisfied smile.

"I was on Facebook when she popped up on the screen and I thought, now there's something that has Liddy written all over it."

Liddy continued to cradle the ornament, touched by the gesture. In the several months they had known each other, Trace had never once shown off something that she had purchased new. And here she had done just that ... only she had given it to her. "It's ... Trace, it's perfect. Thank you so much."

"Do you have your tree up yet?"

Liddy swallowed the growing lump in her throat. She lowered the ornament. "N-not yet." Would she even bother this year? She considered the expense, especially since she had dashed from her home with Shawn in too much of a hurry to bring even one strand of tinsel. First she would have to buy a tree, then all the trimmings. She exhaled. Maybe the rotund gal with the floppy hat and pink flip-flops dangling from strings would bring her enough cheer for the season.

"Speaking of the holidays," Trace continued, "what *are* you doing for Christmas?"

"Again. Not sure yet," she replied.

Liddy knew she could drive to her parents' home about an hour south on Christmas Eve. But that would mean sleeping on the couch, since her brother took over her room years before. She had never been in this predicament before. Liddy had gone from the luxury of living in a teen-sized bedroom, its walls coated with concert tickets and selfies, to the cabin in the desert with her then-husband, to her new, well-worn place up the coast. It had not occurred to her, until now, that she had never woken up to an empty house on Christmas morning.

"Well, you could always go to church in the ballroom on Christmas Eve."

Liddy frowned. "Is that a thing?"

"You don't know? That church you and Thomas have been going to—"

"Once. We went together *once*. And I've only visited a couple of times on my own."

"Whatever. Anyway, they rented the ballroom out for Christmas Eve. Do you not read the Daily Bulletin?"

Liddy's expression must have looked as blank as a freshly painted wall.

Trace whipped out a copy from her desk drawer. "Says here the church is holding one big service here at 6 p.m." She looked up. "Be here with bells on."

"It does not say that."

"Well, then, maybe it should. And then you can sleep in and come have Christmas with Agatha and me."

"Agatha?"

"My cat. I named her for Agatha Christie, you know, the mystery writer?"

Liddy nodded, remembering her mother's stacks of the mysteries around their house growing up. She took the bulletin from Trace and offered her thanks for the invitation. She'd weathered her first Thanksgiving without Shawn and had survived, but the memory of a rather desolate Black Friday continued to haunt her. She and Shawn had made it a tradition of sorts to rise early the day after Thanksgiving, brew a Thermos-full of coffee, and hit the stores with a list that covered not only their parents and a few friends, but things they had saved for all year long. Kind of like their own personal holiday.

She swallowed a sigh, willing herself to keep her chin up. Truthfully, she didn't miss her marriage. Was that okay to admit? The painful way it ended notwithstanding, there had been myriad troubles, and though she would have fought to fix them—or died trying—she reasoned that it took more than one person's will to fix a two-person problem.

The loneliness, though, had burrowed itself a little deeper lately. For the past several years, she had commented wistfully to Meg about her friend's abundant travels, wishing now and then that she could tag along with her. She had pictured herself sunning on the terraces of various resorts while her friend toiled to fill them, then meeting up for glasses of wine and nonstop chatter. Meg would laugh at those images, and more than likely she would have given Liddy work to do while she waited for sundown—make calls, map out travels—you know, the kinds of tasks she now got paid for.

Liddy slipped the Daily Bulletin into her purse, along with Trace's gift. Then she pasted on a smile, urging herself to act hospitable. Guests would be approaching the desk soon, and it was her job to make them feel cared for and welcome ... and anything but alone.

AS TRACE HAD BOTH SUGGESTED and predicted, Liddy found herself in the hotel ballroom some weeks later on a starlit Christmas Eve. She marveled at the frenetic pace of music and people who all seemed to know each other. How odd to be so alone in a room where everyone else was not.

"May my children and I sit here?" a woman asked.

Liddy nodded.

Two young children, a boy and a girl, scurried onto the seats next to the woman. The girl laid her head on her mother's lap. On her other side, a couple probably younger than she was, held hands. She pulled her gaze away, instead keeping her eyes focused on the altar. Or was it a stage? The ballroom twinkled with lights and red poinsettias and towering, decorated trees, like it had all month long. She supposed this was as good a setting as any to worship the Christ child on the eve of his birthday.

The service began and as it did, the empty spot directly in front of her was taken by a familiar-looking man in a suit the color of deep charcoal. He was slim, but not skinny, his dark suit expertly fitted to his average height. A crisp white collar folded over at the base of his neck, his hair thick and deep red, almost brown, landing just above it. She bit her lip. Was it inappropriate to admire the man in front of her while in a house of God? Or was the fact that this cavernous room could boast years of snake-like conga lines in its history reason enough to let her eyes linger on the man in front of her?

At greeting time, he turned and wished her a "Merry Christmas." His smile lit up his eyes and the spattering of freckles across his nose—a grown man with freckles!— captivated her. But it was the dimples, drawn long and deep and friendly on either side of his face, that made her stare. Not to mention the warm, comforting, and strangely electric pulse to his handshake. When her lack of verbal response (read: tongue-tied) became awkward, she broke eye contact with the stranger. And then the music began again, and the moment passed.

For the next hour or so, Liddy watched as a string-bean of a guy on the front platform—the youth pastor it turned out— scooped up his fussy daughter and led the congregation in singing anyway. He was followed by another pastor, this one delivering a sermon on the gift that Christmas brings and how His presence is meant for every day. The dry crevices of her life, the ones that had formed and cracked deeper over the past year, received more than a sprinkle of nourishment from that message and, as if by some kind of miracle, she forgot all about the divorce and the fact that her doctor, after not finding one thing amiss in her blood test, had urged her to get a CT scan sometime after the new year.

She would do it, of course, but for now, as she wandered with a light heart out into the wide sky of Christmas Eve, all Liddy wanted to do was celebrate.

BEAU HAD CREPT INTO HIS parents' home early in the morning after catching a red-eye from LAX, but had yet to really sleep. Outside, powdered snow blanketed the morning of this Colorado town where his parents lived. As if Norman Rockwell planned it himself, however, the inside of the house smelled of maple and bacon and coffee so bitter and strong that his father handed him a mug along with an apology.

With one arm, Beau easily pulled his four-year-old niece up onto his lap. Unlike his nephews who wiggled and kicked their way through their young lives—smelling really foul doing it— little Madi sat doll-like against him. She probably weighed less than one, too.

Madi peered up at him with doe-like eyes, her miniature fingers tapping his fleshy chin. "Are you happy now, Uncle Beau?"

The din of chatter around the family Christmas table halted and all eyes veered to him.

He cleared his throat.

"Madi," the girl's mother, Ally—Beau's sister-in-law— chided. "Don't bother your uncle."

Beau shook his head. "Of course she can ask. And yes, I'm happy today because it's Christmas!" He curled the girl's petite hand in his, and kissed it.

Madi pulled it away from him, her laughter like wind chimes. "Your face is sharp!"

Beau's dad, who himself sat grizzle-faced at the far end of the table, said, "That's nothing. Come over here, and I'll give you sharp!"

Laughter filled the old dining room. Just like old times.

Except, instead of his mother seated at the head of the table across from his father as usual—she was buzzing around the kitchen—her seat had been bestowed upon Beau. Years ago, his dad had custom built the long wooden table for gatherings like this, even though Beau lived across the country on the west coast. Whenever Anne and Beau had flown out to snow country for holidays, they would sit side-by-side on one end of this ancient, beat-up table, much like his siblings and their spouses did today. Until this year.

Still wearing PJs, young Toby and his big brother Maxson bounced from foot to foot on the creaky floorboards next to their respective parents. Those kids laid the guilt on thick. "Please? Can we open more presents? Please!?"

How exactly had the two children showed so much restraint this long anyway? When Beau and his siblings were all kids, they would wake up on Christmas morning and tear into every last shred of wrapping paper until they hit the floor. Those same impatient kids had grown up to be "responsible" parents, and had somehow taught their own children to wait until after breakfast.

This parenting thing was all a mystery to him, and for the slightest moment Beau wondered if he would ever have a chance to unravel it for himself.

Madi hopped down from his lap and wrapped her fingers around his pinky. She pulled at him. "C'mon, Uncle Beau. Let's play with my presents!"

He marveled at his tiny niece's sudden strength, then grinned at his brothers still chomping on bacon. "Sorry, guys. How can I resist?"

For the next half hour, he sat cross-legged on the floor surrounded by his niece and nephews and mounds of torn wrapping paper. He found himself laughing at their antics—including gasps of delight and choruses of "just what I always wanted!" And for an instant the fissure in his heart began to show signs of closing up.

And then he craned his neck at the sound of snickering. Beneath his mother's traditional mistletoe stuck firmly to the alcove with a piece of clear tape, his brother Curt embraced his wife, Jen. In that instant, no matter how hard he fought off the pathetic image, Beau took on the role of "Dan" from the movie *Dan in Real Life*, standing there as a forlorn, solitary figure in the midst of happy couples.

He disliked that film.

Worse, he disliked feeling sorry for himself.

Anne, on the other hand, loved the film—she had even cajoled him into watching it with her more than once. He had always questioned that, although not out loud, thinking her fascination of it odd considering all that she faced.

Beau's mother interrupted his musings. "Here you go, honey." She handed him a gigantic trash bag.

He looked up at her, his brows arched into a question.

"For the wrapping paper," she said with a hearty laugh. Then she tweaked him on the nose like he, too, was still a boy.

The last few months had brought nothing but unwelcome change, but as he filled the garbage bag with paper of gold and red and green Beau thanked God that some things had not.

Chapter Five

SHE HAD SPENT NEW YEAR'S EVE curled up on her couch with nachos, a cozy mystery, and not a drop of champagne. So when Thomas leaned over Liddy's desk that morning announcing that "something shady was definitely going on in the restaurant," intrigue wooed her. Would be nice to do something interesting for a change. Not that she wanted to appear desperate or anything. But sniffing out a nice mystery might shake away the doldrums.

"Tell you what," Thomas whispered, taking note of her enthusiasm. "Let's grab drinks in the bar after work and check it out."

Liddy grinned. Maybe Thomas wasn't exactly "the one," if that was even a possibility for her anymore, but he was cute, in a surfer-dude kind of way, and she enjoyed his company. At least she would have company. "Well, if there is some kind of criminal activity happening over there," she mused, "don't you think it'll be suspended while we're enjoying a nice wine flight together?"

Thomas winked at her. "I don't do girly drinks," he said as a hand landed on his shoulder. He straightened in a hurry.

Hans, the hotel's operations manager and resident worrywart, hissed in his ear. "Guests are arriving. Guests are arriving."

The sky is falling!

Thomas gave the boss a serious nod. "Yes, sir. On it." He backed away and pointed at Liddy, mouthing, "You and me. After work."

She grabbed the little white flag of surrender from her desk—Trace had bought it at a 99-cent store—and waved it at him. Hans frowned at her with his perspiration-lined face, so she quickly placed it back in its holder.

"Anything I can help with?" she asked him.

He glanced over his shoulder, then looked back at her, his spy voice on. "Listen, my wife's going to drop by in a while and I'm not sure where I'll be."

Liddy watched him, waiting.

"You understand?" he said.

She didn't. Was he asking her to cover for him somehow? She wouldn't lie, if that was what he was asking. But why would she need to?

He blew out an exaggerated sigh. "I'll need you to text me when she gets here, all right? I've got two groups in breakout rooms this afternoon and the chamber mixer to get ready for tonight. Not to mention all these people around here today."

"You mean the guests?" She smiled teasingly.

He rubbed his hands over and over across the counter. "You know what I mean!"

Liddy laughed. "Relax. You've got this. And yes, of course I'll text you when Misty arrives. No problem."

Hans exhaled. "Wonderful. Thank you." He began to walk away, but suddenly turned back to face her. The thumb and one finger on his hand pointed into the air. "You haven't heard anything from Mr. Riley, I presume?"

Liddy recalled the name, but barely. Was he an ultra-important guest? Had she taken a message from him? She grimaced. "Sorry, Hans, remind me who Mr. Riley is again."

Hans's expression turned peevish. "Only the big kahuna around here ... when he's in town, that is, which is rare these days. He's one of the owners of this chain of resorts—I would have thought you knew that—anyway, if you ask me, he's the one in charge so it would be a good idea to memorize his name."

She made a mental point to do just that.

As it turned out, Thomas had to ask Liddy for a rain check on the bar espionage he had planned for them later that evening. Hans was short on servers for the chamber mixer and Thomas had willingly agreed to help out, something about the need for more "ca-ching" in life. This was something she clearly understood.

An hour later, she was half-glad that Thomas had canceled since she could feel her energy waning. Maybe this had not been such a great night to stay out anyway. Trace had been busy all day, bustling from conference room to conference room with various assignments. She showed up now with a pile of folders and a whole mess of calls to make.

Trace blew a puff of air out of one side of her mouth to dislodge a straggly strand of hair, the motion only a temporary respite. "Help me with these?" she asked.

Liddy grabbed half of the stack. "Happy to," she said.

Sometime between opening the second folder and reaching for the phone to call a guest, Liddy froze. Her mind stayed awake enough to tell her that something felt off, but her body wouldn't follow any direction she attempted to give it.

"You okay, Liddy?" Trace asked.

She wanted to answer, but for what seemed like eternity—or at least several torturous seconds—Liddy could not form the words. Nor could she turn her head.

Trace's hand landed on Liddy's arm then, and gently helped her put the phone down. Slowly Trace turned Liddy around in her chair, the pitch in her voice higher than usual. "What's got you spooked?"

Liddy blinked hard. She gulped air, and tried to settle the erratic thumping of her heart. She took in the worry lines framing Trace's eyes. "I'm so sorry. I don't know." She forced out a tiny, hollow laugh. "I guess I'm just tired after this long day."

Trace's eyes remained on Liddy's, her frown intensifying. "Maybe you should stay away from that Thomas."

Liddy gave her a quizzical look.

"I know you don't talk about it much, but divorce is hard on the soul. My parents fought all the time, so you would've thought a divorce was the right thing. But dating other people took its toll on them. They both look older than Methuselah."

Yes, well, he's dead ...

"Don't give me that look—I know he's dead," she snapped. "All I'm saying is that you need to take care of yourself. Go do yoga, for heaven's sake. You seem really tired."

Out in the parking lot, Liddy thought about what Trace had said. *Had these strange sensations really been about the divorce all along?* She had mentioned to the doctor that her life had changed course almost overnight. And he had agreed that her bouts of nervousness *could* be related …

But he hadn't looked all that certain.

With a sigh, Liddy slipped inside her Jeep and made yet another mental note to make an appointment for that CT scan. She started it up and with more than a little irritation noticed a new rattle as she pulled out of her space. The car was gently used, a classic, she'd been told, so why should an unfamiliar sound spook her? Good thing her condo by the beach was just a straight five-mile shot along the shore. She would be home in less than ten minutes.

She blinked against flashing lights at the L in the road. Just two more miles on the straightaway, and she could be home. But a large orange detour sign blocked her way. "Oh, come on." Her mind ticked along. She could probably zip around the sign and fly home faster than the authorities would notice.

But could she afford the ticket if she was wrong about that?

With a groan, Liddy turned left and followed the detour road away from the beach and through seemingly endless fields of newly planted crops. She turned up the sound on the radio and laughed at herself. "First-world problem, Liddy." It's not like she had anyone waiting for her at home, nor any matter of urgency that made the extra minutes of her commute all that dire.

Her first inclination that something was wrong happened about the time that she noticed one field of light soil morphing into another of dark, a sure sign that something amazing would surely be growing out on that expanse of land soon. She barely noticed the rattle; it sounded like a friendly tumble under the hood of her car, like a rapping on her front door. After one particularly loud knock, she turned down her music to listen more closely, continuing to make her way alongside the dirt-filled fields.

That's when she heard the hiss and caught sight of the temperature gauge shooting upward into red. "Crap!" By the time she pulled her car to the side of the road, next to a ditch, the hood was bouncing like a heavy load of towels careening inside too small of a washing machine. She switched the key to off, listening as her Jeep shuddered in relief.

Dead.

And the day's glow was fading fast.

She groaned and rubbed at a slight pulsating above her right temple. Surprisingly, few cars had followed her onto this lonely road. She thought about that. How lucky was she to have avoided a freeway commute each day? Still, this was no place for a breakdown. The more she considered her options—there weren't many—the more her focus narrowed. It was as if her mind had begun to spiral from the stress and she had to hold her eyes steady so as not to be crushed by it all.

She pulled herself together, and then she called AAA and waited. And prayed. Her newfound interest in prayer hearkened back to the hotel church service she had attended on Christmas. That's how she thought of it … "hotel church."

A minivan pulling a trailer passed her, causing the Jeep to shift and groan from the gust. She thought back to the wide-eyed abandon when it came to the prayers spoken on Christmas. Those people all seemed so … so happy. Or maybe just peaceful. But she knew better. The woman next to her, for instance. She wore no wedding ring but had two young children to care for. How easy could that be? And the handsome man in front of her. She had tried not to eavesdrop—

well, at least not too obviously—but several people had come over and hugged him and asked him how he was doing, as if he had recently met with some kind of difficulty.

She let out a sigh. "God, thank you that despite this trouble, you are with me. Please help me to be able to handle whatever comes out of this." It wasn't eloquent or particularly long, but the prayer had somehow eased the rising sense of dread as she waited.

Eventually, the tow truck driver reached her, assessed the situation—a blown water pump that had damaged the radiator—hoisted her car onto the rig, and drove her to a gas station some three miles up the road. She was now even farther from home.

She tried not to dwell on the fact that she could have been sipping an oak-scented Chardonnay right now. Instead she waited some more as the driver handed off her car to the mechanic, who was now preparing to deliver the harsh news to her, i.e., an estimate of repairs.

"Had a little trouble on the road, I see," the man in a grease-soaked shirt said.

She teetered. The acrid smell of carburetor cleaner overwhelmed her, invoking a memory of when she was little and her brother and friends spent Saturday afternoons taking apart their cars. "A little," she answered. "Can it be repaired?"

He nodded, his eyes fixed on the clipboard in front of him. He jotted some things down as she stood there in the night, waiting. Traffic provided a blasé shutter of background noise, impervious to her bad news. Goose bumps began to rise on her skin in direct correlation to the night's drop in temperature. She hugged herself for warmth, and maybe a bit of comfort.

Nothing could have prepared her, though, for the sense of panic that slammed into her at precisely the moment she was finally handed that clipboard.

It started like paralysis. The mechanic was saying something to her as she clung to that clipboard, its sharp ridges digging into the undersides of her fingers. His words, like butterflies without a net, resounded in her ears, but her mouth could not—would not—allow her to respond. Her left arm shook then, a trembling with no distinct starting point. Just a steady and strong tremor that spread through her hands, and swiftly lit her left leg on fire. In a blink, her body collapsed under its own weight, and she landed in the arms of the attendant.

She couldn't recall being carried inside and deposited onto a less-than-stable vinyl chair in the tiny gas station office, but she remembered the crying. Sobbing, really. Later she would joke about how violently she had reacted to the estimate of car repairs.

Oddly, the attendant said nothing other than, "Would you like to borrow a phone?"

Twenty minutes later, Meg careened into the lot to pick up Liddy, her face knotted with concern. "My god, what happened to you?"

"I-I think I may have epilepsy!" The flood opened again, releasing the tears she had managed to hold back while waiting for her friend to arrive.

Meg drove her Beemer with one hand and patted Liddy's shoulder with the other. "Oh ... oh ... it's okay. My cousin has that—and she's fine. You'll be okay, too."

With everything she had, Liddy dearly hoped that in her

case, her friend's words would ring true.

"HAVEN'T YOU HAD ENOUGH OF Google Analytics yet?" Jill peeked in through the doorway of Beau's office. "Your trip back home did absolutely nothing to slow you down."

He leaned back against the leather desk chair and folded his arms at his chest. "You know it."

"Give it a rest already. Really, must I always have to keep after you like this?" She tsked, tsked. "You are like my children."

"Which one?"

Jill laughed heartily. "All of 'em, darn it. Not a one listens to me anymore."

Beau switched off his desk lamp and stood. "Oh, come on now. Can't be that bad."

She wagged her pointer finger at him. "One day, you'll see."

He looked away as he gathered his things. Would he, really? The way things were going it wasn't likely that Beau would find himself being called "Daddy" anytime soon. He swallowed a saturated sigh.

"I'm sorry."

Beau jerked a look up to find Jill back at his doorway. "Sorry?"

Her expression was grim. "Sorry to remind you of something sad. If it helps any, I believe you will find love again, Beau ... even though it's probably not my place to say so."

Beau shook his head. "Don't be silly. You've been telling me what to do for nearly ten years now, even longer than I was married to ..." His gaze caught that of his assistant. "Well. Thanks for kicking me out of here. Sometimes I need to hear it." He flashed a smile. "Not always, but sometimes."

"Good night, Beau."

" 'Night."

In the dimly lit parking lot, Beau sat in his car checking his phone. It was Wednesday and if he were to leave now he could stop by the church for a midweek service. Hadn't been to one since Cody Kent stood in the pulpit proclaiming the benefits of living well.

Ten minutes later he arrived to find the doors to the sanctuary already closed. He shuttered his annoyance. For as long as he had attended this church, public humility had been his pastor's unmasked way of discouraging tardiness. Not that it had ever worked on him.

An usher approached him and with a quirk of his head said, "I can let you in over here." He led Beau to the front row— another procedure settled on by the pastor, as if doing so was akin to putting a kid wearing a dunce cap in the corner at the front of the classroom.

He never let it bother him, but this time, as he approached that front row, fourth seat from the center aisle, he slowed. The woman he had noticed out on the beach, and then the night of the Kent event, and recently at the church's Christmas service, sat next to the open seat. Seat three. The usher slapped him on the back and Beau quickly slid in next to her.

Her eyes were closed, but she was singing, her chin tipped upward, oblivious to his arrival. He gawked a second or two longer than necessary before closing his own eyes and opening his mouth to worship the God he had come to see. But as he sang, words of another kind filled his head. Words filled with hope about his future … concepts he could hardly wrap his mind fully around, and yet they were there. It was as if God himself had chosen this night to assure him that he had not been forgotten.

SHE ALMOST HADN'T COME. The past week had brought a flurry of tests, guests, and, unfortunately or fortunately, depending on how one looks at unexpected results, a diagnosis. After charging up what was left of her credit card, she got her car back from the repair station. And thankfully, the anti-seizure medication she was prescribed removed not all dark thoughts, exactly, but at least those associated with her future behind the wheel.

Gone also were thoughts of lingering wine dates with Thomas or anyone else for that matter. Not that Thomas would have obliged her anyway. For some reason, the minute he'd learned that she may have some kind of illness—even though at the time what had now been confirmed had not yet been—Thomas had seemingly lost interest in their friendship.

Whatever.

"Do you want me to go to that church of yours with you tonight?" Trace had asked earlier in the day at work. "I mean, I'm Catholic and all, but I don't think God'll strike me dead or anything if I went with you. If you need me, I mean."

She pressed her lips together and found some papers to shuffle about on the reception desk. "Thanks, but no. I'm fine. Not even sure if I'll quite make it tonight."

Trace stood there in the lobby, that overstuffed bag weighing down her shoulder. She'd filled it up at the dollar store with who knew what. "And you're sure you're okay to drive? The meds working okay?"

Liddy's nose prickled at the question, but she refused to cry. Trace's concern touched her. She had, after all, been on the desk next to Liddy when the neurologist's call had come through. The rims of Liddy's eyes grew damp. "Of course, of course. The doctor wouldn't allow me to drive if he thought there'd be a problem." She flashed a look at Trace, deeply appreciative for her quirky co-worker's concern. "Now, go home."

Trace nodded, her usual smile gone. She cinched the heavy bag to her side. "Call me if you need anything. I mean that."

Trace meant well; she knew that. But truthfully, Liddy would rather be alone than to have to sort all this out with someone she hardly knew. If Meg were in town, they would likely have sat in her tiny sunken living room with a bottle of wine and discussed her options. Chocolate would have been indulged in, too. But Meg was in Oregon tonight, and moving on to Washington tomorrow—not that she hadn't called incessantly between stops. So her options were to sulk at home alone ... or to visit the happy little church again and hope that answers would be forthcoming.

When he had sat next to her, she'd had to force herself not to acknowledge him. She was worshipping God at the moment after all, sold out in song to her Maker for the first time in her life, actually. Not that God would have been all that offended if she had glanced at the familiar man who had crept into service late; she doubted that he let such things as human inattentiveness get to him. But life had delivered her one confusing set of blows lately—and she desperately needed answers, not any more detours. She had to keep her focus.

"Tonight we're going to try something a little different," the pastor said once the music ended and all the musicians had taken their seats in the auditorium. "So instead of a sermon, earlier today I began to feel that there are some deep needs in our congregation—things that you and I know nothing about."

I'll say.

"So tonight, we pray for each other." He glanced about the room. "Who's first?"

Her heart plummeted. She had hoped to soak up something to help her with all she had to grapple with, to find solace in hopeful words. But he wanted people to shout out their problems to the entire congregation? She could not fathom it.

A woman in the back raised her hand and asked for prayer for her daughter who was having a baby. A man behind her asked for prayer for a work decision he had to make.

Really? You're not going to ask for prayer after what you learned this week?

A little girl at the far end of her row asked for prayer for her "boo-boo." Chuckles bounced around the room. A few other people spoke up, adding their needs to the growing list.

The pastor urged his flock to continue to come forward with their requests.

Liddy noticed that her hands had turned cold, clammy. They say that people fear public speaking more than death. Picturing people in the audience naked never worked either, because, let's be real, some things a girl just didn't want to imagine. The truth, though, was that she was the one who always felt naked when speaking to a group. Unclothed, vulnerable, and a little too round at certain corners. Worse, she feared that if she were to open her mouth and let her news tumble out, raw, uncontained emotion would follow.

So what?

She swallowed back a painful ball of unshed tears. Her heart began to race so much that she feared the man next to her could hear it beating against her ears. She hadn't signed up for this, but then again, if she stayed quiet, Liddy would go to an empty home with nothing more than the unknown to comfort her. So she raised her hand, and when the pastor nodded for her to speak, she found herself saying, "I just found out that I have a brain tumor."

BEAU TIGHTENED BOTH HANDS INTO FISTS. He couldn't believe it. How old was she? Twenty-three? Twenty-four? A puff of wind might have knocked him over if the blister of heat throttling his insides hadn't made him so angry. Another young woman hit with a dangerous illness. God—please! He wished he could shout, but what good would that do?

Instead, he bided his time, and after all the prayers were said and most of the congregation had filed out—some stopping to give the young woman a squeeze of encouragement—he turned to her.

He had a million questions, but didn't want to overwhelm her, so he simply stuck out his hand. "I'm Beau."

She smiled shyly. "Liddy Buckle."

"Tell me more about what you're facing."

Her eyes darkened. Had he scared her? Or was that fear? His fist clenched again. What was he thinking, of course it was fear. He reached out and touched her elbow. "Here," he said, motioning to a seat, "can we sit for a minute?"

They sat close to each other. She looked him right in the eyes. "What do you want to know?"

"For starters, who is your doctor?"

"Grayson."

"Great. He's good, solid."

"You know him?"

"We've met. My company handles marketing for a number of doctors and hospitals in the area."

"Oh, so you know which ones are good—and which ones need a good dose of PR."

She'd caught him off guard with her joke and he found himself smiling at her. "Something like that."

"I'm new to the area, and from what I can tell I hit the jackpot when I found Dr. Grayson. I've been feeling strange for months and ..."

He both did and did not want to hear what she had to say about her illness. For years he'd dealt with diagnoses and treatments, but for the past few months he'd had a reprieve. To be honest, he'd hoped it would be for far longer. Why, then, couldn't he pull himself away from her?

She continued. "The good news is that the doctors believe it's benign."

He nodded, relieved.

"The bad news is I'm told it must be removed or it will continue to give me problems, like seizures. Brain surgery wasn't exactly on my bucket list, but ..."

"So that's how you knew you had a problem."

She nodded. "Focal seizures at first, then another that was

more, uh, adventurous."

"I'm sorry."

She stood up abruptly then, brushing a stray hair from her cheek. "Anyway, thanks for your concern. I appreciate it."

"Liddy, let me give you this." He pulled a card from his wallet. "It's got my cell phone number on it."

Her brows dipped and she opened her mouth to speak, but shut it quickly.

"My wife, Anne, passed away a few months ago."

She gasped. "Oh, I'm … so sorry."

He swallowed. "Thank you. She and I had many decisions to make regarding her treatment, and I know it's tough. If you ever want to run anything past me, call me." He pressed the card into her hand. "Please."

Out in the parking lot, he watched her drive away in a rattling old Jeep. As he opened his car door, he heard his name called. Marty, an elder from the church, walked briskly toward him.

"Hey, Marty," Beau said. "Did I forget something?"

"No, nothing like that. I was just noticing you talking to the young woman … with the tumor."

"Liddy."

"Yes. Do you know her?"

"Not really. I've seen her here before, but we just met tonight."

Marty nodded, his mouth grim. "Well, some of us are concerned, Beau."

He felt one of his eyebrows raise on its own volition. *Some of us?* "How so?"

"You know, it's natural to want to make new friends after

going through a traumatic time, but maybe you should think about easing yourself into things. In fact, I was going to ask you if you'd join our men's softball team."

Beau held his car door open. "Wait ... you think I shouldn't talk to her, to help her in some way if I can?"

"No, no, of course that's not what I'm saying." He folded his hands in front of him and let out a gust of a sigh, like he regretted being forced to say what had really caused him to chase after Beau. "You two were sitting very closely. Our concern is that you might become too attached to this young woman ..."

"Liddy."

"To Liddy." He paused. "You've already been through so much."

Beau eyed the longtime church elder whose white knuckles told him this conversation was as comfortable as having a cavity filled. He let the door fall closed with a click. Didn't Marty understand that he had something to offer Liddy that might help her in the days to come? Beau hesitated, then spoke quietly. "I don't enjoy the idea of remembering, you know."

Marty reached out and placed a palm on Beau's shoulder. "I understand."

"Do you?"

Marty's frown showed him that he was trying.

Beau looked up into the dark sky. "I will never understand why Anne died young, why she ... had to go through what she did, and why I had to witness it." He swung his gaze back to Marty. "But I remember it all, and when I sat in there next to Liddy hearing her story, all I could think of was that, maybe, my experiences could somehow help her. Is that wrong of me?"

"No, no. Of course not."

"Do you understand what I'm trying to say then?"

Marty nodded. "I think so. You want to be someone she can talk to. But Beau, maybe you're the one who needs a friend right now."

He looked directly at Marty. "I'm grateful if anything good can come out of something so ... so wretched."

On his ride home, Beau replayed the night in his head. Except for a warning to "be careful," Marty seemed to have accepted his position, and Beau had let it go at that. He had people around him who cared, he reasoned. Not everyone could say that. That sort of protective care was the simple reason Marty had approached him in the first place. Frankly, if he ever thought a friend needed a good talking to, Beau would likely do the same.

But would he really? Beau tightened his grip around the steering wheel as he sorted through a mental disheveled load of experiences from the past. He wished those thoughts could be banished from his head forever, but they never would be truly gone, would they? His nerve endings swelled, a mixture of frustration and anger melding together to urge him not to accept the status quo when it came to the issues in life where he just might be able to help someone else. One evening church service had made that mighty clear.

As Beau turned the corner toward home he could not get Liddy, and her problem, out of his mind.

Chapter Six

"WHAT KIND OF PICK-UP LINE is that? 'Hey, baby, who's your doctor?'" Meg laughed at the absurdity, but the tension in her face was unmistakable.

"I know, right? But he was cute."

"Cute, huh?"

Liddy sighed. "All right, darn handsome. You happy?" And he smelled heavenly, though she kept that tidbit from Meg. For now, anyway.

"Liddy, this whole thing sucks."

"I know."

"I spent the last flight Googling benign brain tumors, and did you know Mark Ruffalo had one? And look, he survived just fine. He's been nominated for an Oscar."

"More than one, I think. And yes, I had heard that. Sheryl Crow, too."

Meg shook her head. "I wish I didn't have to fly out to New York tomorrow, or I'd go to the hospital with you for all those stupid tests."

"Seriously, you just got back from your whirlwind up north—what am I saying? Don't give it another thought. Please. My mother wanted to accompany me too, but I convinced her not to take the day off because I have my e-books loaded up and all I plan to do in between needle pricks is read."

"You sure?"

"Yeah. Can't wait."

"Liddy ..."

"Really," she said, with friendly force this time. "I'll be fine."

The next morning, Liddy set out to the university hospital in a large city about an hour away for a day of pre-op prep. "You have a cyst in your brain," her neurologist had said. "And inside of that cyst, a pinky-sized, active tumor, which we believe to be benign."

Believe to be benign.

The tiny tumor, she'd been told, was resting next to a motor strip in her brain, and the hospital in the small beach town she lived in—up and coming as the local tourism board touted it to be—did not have the kind of equipment that would (nearly) guarantee no slip-ups.

"Without more precise equipment, the surgery itself ..."

"Yes, doctor?" she had asked at her consultation.

"Liddy. The surgery could cause paralysis. I'm recommending we transfer your file to a hospital that can better handle this delicate surgery."

Which is why she now found herself in this bustling hospital. She moved from room to room, giving blood for her own use should she need it, taking this test here and that test there, and "relaxing" as best she could in between. And for a while, the tale she delved into on her e-reader about an aging minister and his artist wife living in the south kept her spirits elevated with its whimsy.

But whimsy could only go so far. She hadn't eaten much all day, had no appetite at all. If she ever wanted to lose weight, she would get a job in a hospital. Food lost all its attraction when it shared space with vinyl tile and antiseptic. Today, however, was not the day to skip out on nutrition. She knew this, intellectually. Yet she couldn't seem to force even one bite.

Liddy had just entered the office of her fourth appointment of the day when she came upon the very real possibility of ending up face first on the corporate-patterned carpeting. The smell hit her first. The room tilted one way, then the other. It wasn't a seizure; it couldn't be—she had taken her meds that morning.

"Excuse me. Can I help?" A woman with white hair and translucent skin crooked her arm through Liddy's and led her to a chair. An *elderly* woman. "There. Now, how about I get you some water?"

Liddy glanced up, afraid that if she were to do so too quickly, she would become further disoriented. "I-I'm not sure if I can have any right now."

"Shall I ask the nurse for you?"

Liddy nodded.

The woman returned with a paper cup of water, the flimsy kind Liddy's mother always kept stacked next to the mouthwash. She downed it quickly. "Thank you."

"Liddy Buckle?" a woman in scrubs called her name from an open doorway.

Already?

"Shall I have them fetch you a wheelchair?"

Liddy forced herself to look up at the elderly woman with

white set curls hovering above her and realized she was wearing pink. A pink lady. She swallowed. There was no way a woman older than her grandmother—God rest her gentle soul—would be pushing her in a wheelchair. Though the offer had been sweet.

"No, thank you." Liddy pulled herself to standing. "I'll be all right. You've been kind. Thank you again."

"My pleasure. You take care of yourself."

Liddy took a seat in the cold room, laid her arm across the narrow drawing table, and waited for another needle to pierce her skin.

The phlebotomist tightened a latex band below Liddy's elbow. She poked her glove-covered finger around the area. "Hmm. Having trouble finding a good site."

She made the stick anyway, but it didn't work.

Liddy looked away and blew out a breath.

"Let's try this again, shall we?"

If we must.

The technician muttered to herself. Something about needing a good vein ... she tried the stick again. And again. Both times failing. Then she heaved an exasperated sigh.

Since this ordeal had started, Liddy had chosen not to allow herself to fall over the edge of despair. This time, though, as multiple attempts were made to plumb her veins for blood— how many times had a similar procedure occurred today in this very arm?—she more than teetered on that edge. And when the procedure failed for the umpteenth time?

Liddy lost it. She pulled her arm away. "I'm done."

The phlebotomist sat up straight. "Not yet."

Liddy slid out of the chair. With one hand she untied the

band strangling her other arm and tossed the latex into the trash. "I've had it. Not one more prick."

"But … but we need this last one. Just one more try."

Liddy turned her back. "Not happening."

By the time she reached the hall, the tears she had rejected since her first step into this black hole of an experience fell without any regard for her pride. When she arrived back at her Jeep, her cheeks and neck were drenched. She slammed the door shut, inhaled to calm herself, and when that didn't work she began to slap the heck out of her steering wheel.

A groan so deep and mighty emerged from her. She barely recognized her own voice.

She didn't know what to do next. Part of her wanted to forget about the surgery and the aftermath. When she was prayed for by church members the other day, some asked for healing, as in maybe she wouldn't have to go through with this after all. Liddy had never thought of that, really. She figured they would likely ask that the tumor not kill her—that kind of prayer she actually encouraged—and that she would go on to run a marathon or something. But heal her? Was that even a thing?

The idea of taking a leave of absence from her job and flying to Hawaii for a month to wait it out was suddenly very appealing.

Liddy fished around inside her purse for the ticket to give to the parking attendant and pulled out Beau's business card instead. She rubbed her thumb over the embossing of his name. *Beau Quinn.* Would it be too stupid to call him right now? She set the card down, found a tissue in her glove box, and blew her nose. He would not have given her his card if he hadn't meant it, right?

She cleared her throat, then dialed his number. He picked up on the second ring.

"Beau? You might not remember me but this is Liddy ... from church."

"Of course I remember you." He paused. "How are you today?"

She wagged her head, though there was nobody with her to see it. "Been better."

"Understood. You're in a tough place."

"Can I ask you something?"

He didn't hesitate. "Ask away."

Her heart rate had picked up at the sound of his voice. It had this softness to it that thrummed against her heart. She took a breath. "I've been confused ever since the other night at church."

"You mean, about the things I said to you?"

She smiled. "No, you were great. It's just that a few people prayed that I'd be healed and there's a part of me that wonders if going through with the surgery is somehow ignoring those prayers."

"I see. You mean, does it show a lack of faith?"

She thought about that. She hadn't known it, but yes, that was exactly what she wondered.

"Not at all. Anne and I had this discussion many times when well-meaning people tried to keep her from moving forward with her treatments."

"May I ask ... what did you do?"

"Well ..." She heard him sigh into the phone. "We prayed a lot. And we listened carefully to her doctors, even getting second opinions when necessary. I won't lie—it was hard. I often wished we could book a trip to anywhere rather than have to deal with all of that."

Hawaii would be beautiful this time of year ...

He continued, "In the end you have to go with the path you are given. Who's to say God doesn't work through doctors? I certainly believe he does. I saw it many times with Anne."

"Thanks. It's just ... difficult right now."

"No doubt. I'm sure it's overwhelming."

She drew in some more much-needed oxygen. "Thanks for the talk. I just had a rough time today. Too many needles, you know?"

"Yeah, I do."

"Thank you so much, Beau."

He didn't answer right away, and then, "Does that help at all?"

"You have no idea."

He chuckled, and she liked the sound of it. "Oh, I'm not so sure. Call me anytime, Liddy. I mean that."

She hung up knowing that he certainly did.

A WEEK AFTER THE SURGERY, when she was home recovering, her mom and a couple of aunties taking turns doting over her like a princess, Liddy noted that she had not heard from Beau. Not like she expected him to show up on her doorstep or anything. But she wondered.

After another week had passed, and sprouts of hair had begun to dust the area that had been shaved for surgery,

Liddy's mother drove her across town to Shear Dreams one evening after the salon had closed.

Missy, the owner of the shop, unlocked the door to let her in. "Okay, let's see what you've got."

Gingerly, Liddy sat in the chair and pulled off her head covering, a little purple turban-like number one of her aunts had found at the hat store over by the harbor.

Missy gasped. "Well, okay then."

"I call it Frankenstein chic," Liddy said. She peered into the mirror, aghast all over again at the unevenness of it all. One side of her head hung with limp, unshorn hair, and the other? Not so much.

Her stylist frowned. "I wonder why they didn't just shave your whole head."

"Well, they tried. Two orderlies came in, one to shave my hair off and the other to catch it, I'm guessing." She smiled at her attempt at humor, although it ached to do so. "They were so shocked when I swatted one guy's hand away and told them only to shave off one section. They argued with me, but I told them, hey, I have a hairdresser all ready to perform a miracle, so do as I say!"

"And they did!"

"Honestly, when I woke up with my head wrapped, I didn't care anymore. I was just so happy to be alive at that point."

"Yeah." Missy was quiet for a moment, then took a breath. "So bleach and curls maybe?"

"Definitely. Do it."

For the next hour and half, Liddy tried to stay awake as Missy fussed over the one section of her hair that had been left intact. At times it hurt to keep herself upright.

"You doing okay?"

"Yeah, just tired."

"Hope this isn't too much for you. Can I get you something?"

She shrugged. "Not unless it's a bed."

Missy sighed. "Sorry. I'll try to get you out of here as soon as possible. Did you not get a lot of sleep in the hospital either?"

Liddy laughed a little then. "True story: On my last night, they made an old Russian woman my roommate and her screaming kept me awake. I begged them to find her another room, but the hospital was full. So halfway through the night, I was pretty delirious and wrote a cranky note to my doctor and slid it under the door to his office."

Missy chuckled.

"And then I disappeared for a while."

Missy stopped working. "You what? Where'd you go?"

"I wandered around, first falling asleep in the nurses' lounge—a nurse chased me out of there—"

"Wait. A nurse told you to leave?" Missy grunted out her disgust. "Didn't she at least ask you where you belonged?"

"No. It was weird. So I kept walking and found the sleep lab."

She scoffed. "You did not."

"Did. And I fell asleep there. When I emerged, I learned there had been some kind of all-out, panicked search for me."

Missy spun her around and looked her in the face. "You must've been scared out of your mind."

Liddy flicked her chin up. "Not really. I was rested and

happy, but the floor doctor—actually, he was a resident—kept apologizing over and over. Then they found me a new room and gave me a cupcake. It was hilarious."

Missy shut her eyes and shook her head. "You are the weirdest girl I've ever met."

By the time she left the salon, the left side of Liddy's face was framed with loose blonde curls. She wore her hat cocked to the right side, and the curls spilling out the other ... like some kind of fashion statement.

Unfortunately, fatigue overtook her for days and few people, except some sweet visitors from church staff, her co-worker Trace—chattering away with hotel gossip—and, of course, Meg, saw her new 'do.

"You have the nicest friends," her mother said one day while changing the water for a burst of flowers that had been delivered days earlier. "By the way, Meg called. She wanted to know if you would like to visit your church for a midweek service."

Liddy sat up in bed and reached for the compact mirror on her nightstand. She inhaled deeply, then snapped it open and allowed herself a look at her face. Her gaze avoided her hairline and instead zeroed in on her right eye where a yellowed bruise had settled sometime after surgery. Thankfully that little treasure had now gone, but she still looked so tired. She could tell by the less-than-robust color to her skin and the droop in her eyes. Still, the thought of getting out of the apartment, even for a short while, appealed to her.

"You know," her mom said, taking a seat on the bed, "I'd be happy to drive you to church and leave a day later."

Liddy shook her head. Her mother had missed work and

seeing her father long enough. It was time Liddy eased herself into some kind of normalcy on her own. "Mom, thanks, but I think I'm strong enough now to get back into life. I appreciate everything you and Dad have done for me."

Meg showed up a few days later with enough energy for the both of them. "Let's go praise God or something."

"I'm not even going to ask what the 'or something' could be."

"Okay so my halo's a little tarnished these days. If this church thing works for you, I'm all for it." Meg glanced around Liddy's living room. "Dang, look at those gorgeous flowers. I don't suppose those are from the hotel?"

"The church."

"Nice. Let's get going already."

Liddy's nerve endings convulsed as she walked into the church service on this busy Wednesday night. So much to take in—bright lights, well-wishers, children weaving through the halls. Her heartbeat picked up the pace as she attempted to take it all in after weeks away.

And just about the time she longed to find a seat, a steady hand cupped her elbow. She turned to find Beau watching her, his smile almost shy, his eyes crinkling at the corners.

"You look good," he said, still holding her arm at its bend. He didn't wince at her hat nor the fact that she wore cottony clothes so comfortable they could moonlight as pajamas. "I had hoped to see you here soon."

"Th-thanks." So it wasn't poetry? He had rendered her speechless. Or maybe it was the meds. She let her eyes swoop over his expression of genuine concern. Nope, it was all him.

Meg, however, had no such problem. She reached out her

hand to him. "Meg Whitson. And you are?" The sudden lilt in her friend's voice was unmistakable.

Beau politely shook Meg's hand and introduced himself, but before she could comment further he turned to Liddy and hugged her gently. "No doubt you'll be running down the beach again soon." He paused, his gaze piercingly intense. "Maybe I could join you."

When he had gone, Meg eyed her. "I can see why you like this place."

Liddy laughed. "Shut up." She wouldn't admit it to Meg, but in the last few minutes her walk had gained a bit of a lift.

MORE THAN ONCE DURING THE SERVICE, Beau let his gaze wander over to where Liddy and her friend huddled at the end of one aisle. She looked fragile yet not sickly, like she had triumphed over her diagnosis but still could use plenty of rest. He was glad to see her; to know that she had not only survived the ordeal of brain surgery, but was, quite obviously, gaining back her strength. A tinge of regret traveled through him—and not only because he had missed the past few minutes of the pastor's sermon.

He hadn't visited Liddy in the hospital, even though the idea had crossed his thoughts more than once. The thoughts, when they occurred, were usually hunted down and destroyed by dark musings. She would never know how much her call to him in her time of crisis had meant, but other than that, they had only spoken to each other a few times ...

Would she think me impulsive?

Prying?

A stalker?

In the end, Beau chose to observe Liddy from afar. He had asked about her condition, and upon hearing that all seemed to have gone well, he waited (sometimes impatiently) for her to wander back into church. And now that she had, he couldn't decide what to do about it.

As it turned out, he wouldn't get the chance to do anything at all. When the service had finished, he intended to grab his coat and perhaps say goodbye to Liddy and her friend out in the parking lot. But first he had to avoid, once again, one of the women who had been systematically chosen for him by the elders who ran this church.

They meant well ...

Beth strode toward him, her smile wide, and her focus on him uncomfortably pointed. He swallowed back his own knee-jerk criticism and tried not to allow his gaze to sprint too quickly toward the exit. He wanted to avoid the woman—not insult her.

"Beau," she sang out.

He said hello, painfully aware that his light skin was unavoidably turning a shade of pink.

"I hear you and I are supposed to be getting married."

He let Beth's words sink in. The impish quirk of a smile on her face gave her away and he laughed into the rafters.

"Don't worry. I'm not into you either." She paused. "No offense."

He wagged his head, the laughter lingering. "None taken." If only everyone he met could be this forthcoming.

"Seriously, Beau. I hope you're having some real laughs these days. Life bit you in the rear for a long time."

"Doing my best."

She nodded once and socked him on his upper arm. "Good to hear it." Before she left, she leaned in. "Beware, though. I think they've formed a committee to find you a woman. Ha ha ha."

Out in the parking lot, Beau slid into his car, buckled up, and sat in silence. Maybe Beth had done him a favor. He felt inexplicably drawn to Liddy so much that, if he were asked, he would not have been able to recount much of tonight's service. But another question continued to daunt him, one he had not allowed too much of a voice yet, but it nagged at him anyway.

Namely, did he want to find himself in a relationship with someone who had so recently fought off a serious illness? Wasn't that too much to ask?

Maybe those who had counseled him—without any prodding from him—had been right. He should play it safe. Date a variety of women. Avoid commitment for now.

Still, he cringed at the idea that a committee could be created for the sole purpose of finding him said women. Of course, Beth had been kidding about that (right?). He'd loved well before, and even he admitted to himself that a gaping hole now existed in his chest.

He groaned, the sound of it reverberating through his car. If he were to utter that romance-novel notion to anyone— Taylor included—he would never hear the end of it.

Chapter Seven

FUNNY HOW ATTRACTIVE SOLITUDE SOUNDED after many days of being hassled by highly energetic folks on vacation. That was the thought that occupied Liddy's mind on this too-quiet morning. Sometimes on those harried work days at the hotel she craved alone time more than her morning coffee. But isolation? Not so much. Especially now during her leave of absence from work. Each day she perked up when, through her second-story window, she spotted the mail carrier weaving through the complex and stopping at the set of grey metal boxes that held the mail. Had he always been so cute? So tall? And where had that swagger come from?

Had it really come to this? Stalking the mailman?

Plus there was the issue of ongoing fatigue, the kind that brought with it mysterious plunges with alarming irregularity. The more she sat alone in her apartment debating whether she had the energy to, well, to get dressed and gobble a snack, the more tired she became. Or maybe she had just settled into some kind of blasé lifestyle feted by sleeping in and all-you-can-eat leftovers. The church folk had no doubt been conspiring to make her fat.

"Come on, Liddy," she admonished herself. "Pull yourself

together. You're twenty-five—not ninety-five!"

With a sigh and a not-too-feminine grunt, she made up her mind to pull on a pair of yoga pants and take a soothing walk along the beach. It was only across the street—surely she could handle that on her own.

The breath of air and stillness of the sun met her on the way down the stairs, along the winding path out of the complex, and toward the beach. When her toes plunged deep into the sand, comfort blanketed her, overwhelming her with its warmth. She rolled her head in a loop, releasing tension from her neck, grateful for the swoosh of rolling waves that provided the music to her walk. She should have done this days ago, her body and mind both needing to move away from the four walls of her recovery. But a trickle of something that felt an awful lot like fear had stopped her cold each time she had considered venturing out. Liddy, her father always said, was as independent as they came, always able to pick herself up after setback, and with little to no help from anyone else.

But things were different this time around. She had been pushed beyond the posted danger signs and had stepped closer to the perilous edge than even she felt comfortable with. It had scared her, in a way, and caused her to over think every step forward since.

She drew in air and took a tentative step toward the slow lapping of water onto shore, allowing her body to relax as she expelled her breath. As she made her way slowly toward the water's edge, she noticed a man about her age, creating the most luxurious sandcastle she had ever seen. The multiple turrets, the moat—even a drawbridge—every part of it made out of sand and stunning, really.

"She's beautiful," Liddy told the man.

He acknowledged her with a nod, continuing to sculpt the fairytale, his long, graceful fingers shaping a window at the top of one of the towers.

"Aren't you concerned that the tide will be rolling in soon?" she asked.

He turned his eyes upward, shading them with one hand. "Her beauty is fleeting, but her memory will draw me to create again."

She smiled. "Aw, that's a sweet sentiment."

He returned her smile. "Amazing what can happen when you sit out here and let your mind go unfettered, like that tide you are so fond of."

Liddy slid her gaze out to the ocean where in the distance a paddle-boarder lofted along silky layers of sea. She returned her attention to the shirtless sculptor on the sand, his long blond hair tangled in wispy threads. "I guess you're right. Walking the shoreline can do that, too, I think."

"When I'm out here, nothing else matters. There are no worries. No causes for concern." As if to prove his point, he lifted a frosted sliver of glass and skipped it out to sea.

"Don't do that!" Liddy lunged for the treasure, scooping it from wet sand seconds before it would have been carried away by the tide. She rubbed the piece of white sea glass with her thumb and brought it back to the man. "Here," she said, tossing it onto the sand in front of him. "Your princess will need a window in her castle, won't she?"

He flicked a smile up at her. "I suppose you're half-right."

She raised her brow.

"This castle's built for a prince. ... though I suppose there is room enough for a princess."

The fuzz on her arm stood on end. "Ah, I ... I see." Her laughter sounded nervous in her ears. "If not, you could always add on another turret or something, you know ..." *Was she blushing?* "... for when they've had a spat."

"Now there's a word you don't hear every day."

She rolled her eyes. "Sorry. The best I could think of." She didn't add: *considering the recent brain surgery and all ...*

He laughed. "As I said before, no worries."

"Well," she said, with another nod of appreciation toward his artistry. "Enjoy your day. You're very talented."

She took a couple of steps toward the water when he called out to her. "Stop by my booth across the way sometime, over in the lot. You'd like the paintings I do."

She gave him a wave. Perhaps she would.

"BEAU? YOU HAVE A CALL on line seven," Jill said from the doorway. "Wendy Wilkes."

Beau stared at the blinking light on his phone. He hadn't spoken to the young woman that Rex introduced him to since the night of the Kent event. He shut his eyes, trying to retrieve the contents of their discussion. A twist of a memory remained elusive. Hadn't they planned to meet somewhere for something? Had that day already passed?

Jill stuck her head through the door again. "Line seven?"

Beau swallowed a sigh and answered the phone.

"Hello, Beau? This is Wendy ... from church? I know we haven't talked in a long time, but I'm calling because the Art Walk is coming up later this week."

That was it.

"So ... would you still like to go with me?"

He sat up and pressed his lips together, thinking. They had talked about his wife's love of art on that night when he had driven around, trying to get the bearings of his newfound normal. He had not seen her around much—maybe they had attended different services, or maybe she hadn't been back. No matter. She had been nice enough. Rex thought so, anyway. "Sure," he finally said. "When is it?"

"Friday." She sounded relieved. "Can you pick me up?"

Beau glanced at his calendar, acknowledging that though the day hours were booked, his night stood free. In the next breath, he was asking for her address and filling up all available white space for Friday night.

"THINGS ARE REALLY HEATING UP HERE, Liddy. There's talk that it's all gonna come down soon. So bummed that you're missing out."

If Liddy had not pulled herself out of her funk and hit the beach earlier in the week, chances were she, too, would be bummed right about now. Not that a week of beachcombing had cured her curiosity about the goings-on at work—in reality, she did feel a little left out when it came to water-cooler gossip. But the walks along the beach had rejuvenated her in ways that only fresh air and a bump of good blood flow could.

"Has anyone been caught yet?" Liddy asked.

"Well, no, but the other night a food supply truck showed up in the middle of the night—a housekeeper spotted it. Pulled right up to the back entrance of the restaurant. Who delivers lobster tails at three a.m.?"

Liddy opened her mouth, but Trace kept talking.

"No one, that's who. Oh, and Hans was here all night I heard. Makes me nervous thinking that he's somehow involved. His poor wife and kids!"

"But maybe the truck really was delivering, um, lobster."

"That's the thing … it's not even on the menu."

Liddy weighed that truth. "I suppose …"

"So anyway, how are you? Coming back soon? I'm pulling an extra shift tonight, but I don't mind. The extra dollars will come in handy."

She breathed in, noting the flapping of flags on the boats out in the harbor on the other side of the peninsula. "I'm feeling better every day. Not sure when I'll be back; I'm just waiting for clearance from my doctor." And for fatigue to stop nipping away at her when she least expected it.

"Well, phew on both accounts. I miss you desperately. Nobody else here puts up with my inventiveness!"

Inventiveness was Trace's code word for hoarding and the transformation she made with all of her "finds."

"But," Trace continued, "we don't want you back here until you are completely well. Capiche?"

Liddy smiled. "Thank you. I'm sure it will be soon. Keep me up to date, okay?"

With a "will do," Trace hung up and Liddy turned her attention to her calendar. It mocked her with its lack of entries. She grabbed her phone and texted Meg.

Hey.

Hey, yourself.

Want to grab a pizza with me tonight?

Aww! Wish I could, gf. On my way to Portland. Grrr.

Okay. No big.

When I get back, okay? I'll buy the Chianti!

Liddy texted back a series of emojis and tossed her phone onto the couch with a sigh. At the counter, she sifted through the mound of junk mail. She couldn't stand the sight of it, but also could not bring herself to toss any of it away without first examining each and every piece.

A glossy postcard with impressionist-like brush strokes caught her attention. *Art Walk Weekend*, it said. She glanced at the clock. A little makeup and an espresso would do her good.

The Uber driver dropped her off near a pink-and-brown bakery, the cool night air surprising her with its brisk force. The sidewalk teemed with couples wearing leather jackets and boots. She ignored a twinge of envy, and instead focused on the twinkling white lights that made the downtown area sparkle.

After picking up a map at the information table on the corner, Liddy followed behind other art enthusiasts. Unlike times in her past, she was in no hurry. Paintings, photography, and sculptures were tucked into stores, many of which offered appetizers and sparkling wine to visitors.

She meandered through a jewelry store whose walls had been transformed by a local artist's paintings of the sea and listened to piped-in classical music. One particular painting of a family building rudimentary sandcastles together on a windy day at the beach reminded her of the artist drifter she'd come upon earlier in the week.

Her stomach began to grumble, so Liddy stepped outside

again and considered her options. She watched as a couple holding hands wandered up toward the taco bar. The idea of Mexican sounded ....

Liddy stopped. She heard an intake of breath and realized it had come from her own lungs. Beau. She recognized him when he turned his chin to speak to ... well, to speak to whomever it was that he was holding hands with. She stared for a beat too long, unfortunately. The way he turned then and spotted her happened nearly in slow motion. Their eyes met and though she tried to avert her gaze, she didn't. Couldn't.

Until she did pull away. Her eyes landed on the bustle of traffic, and then on passersby, many of whom wore lingering smiles and expressions of reflection. She assumed that Beau had continued on. As for her? Liddy no longer felt hungry. Instead, she found the Uber app on her phone and ordered up a ride home.

SHE HAD TAKEN HIS HAND, and for reasons he could not quite figure out, Beau had let her. It was only for a moment, a way for her to pull him along to see something in a shop window. He remembered the foreign feel of her touch. Her fingers against his weren't unpleasant, but they weren't quite comfortable either.

"What do you think of this brass sculpture, Beau?" she had asked when he turned toward the window. It was of a sleek dog, standing tall, its tongue hanging out of its mouth. He supposed it would look nice in a library laden with books and ebony-stained wood.

He answered her, but he had no idea what he actually said.

Something vague, most likely. What caught his attention wasn't the sculpture or any of the other art pieces on display, but his reflection in that store window. Hers and his. Together. Wendy was kind and sweet, and most of all, healthy. He couldn't ever recall a time in the past when he had considered a woman's health as a criterion for dating, but the thought reverberated so clearly in his head that he almost thought he had said it aloud. As he stood there, his thoughts conflicted, an obliging smile on his face while gazing into that window, Beau realized that Wendy Wilkes would make the perfect mother for the kids he hoped to have some day.

But could he love her?

Perhaps there was truth in the notion that a person could *feel* eyes upon them, could sense their draw. Beau would never know why he chose that instant to turn his head away from the window, but when he did, something jolted inside of him. Liddy stood on the sidewalk not far away, her stance in mid-stride, as if she had intended to move in his direction, but for some reason had stopped.

Their eyes met. He was sure of it. But something like pain had come over her face, and she quickly turned away.

"Beau?"

He flicked a gaze at Wendy, who stood much shorter than him, her earnest eyes gazing upward.

"Are you hungry?" she asked. "I was thinking about the taco place up the street."

He nodded. "Sure. Sounds good." When he glanced back down the street, Liddy had vanished.

Chapter Eight

SO BEAU HAD A GIRLFRIEND. Good for him. Liddy didn't know much about his wife's illness, but certainly he had gone through a lot of pain watching her suffer. He deserved happiness now. Still ... hadn't he said something about wanting to walk the beach with her?

Liddy shook away the memory, threw the covers off, and pulled herself out of bed. He was just being kind. Making pleasantries. Isn't that what nice church boys did?

Or maybe ... maybe Beau was uncomfortable around her. She considered this as she washed her face and got dressed. Maybe in the shock of the moment that night at church, when she'd told the entire congregation about her condition, he'd risen to the occasion because, well, he'd been unlucky enough to be seated next to her. Poor guy. Gentlemen don't run, even when they want to (which he probably did). Instead, he stayed beside her and offered her an ear.

He was very kind.

But it was time to think of something else. She spun around ... well, more like a not-terribly-slow turn. She groaned. The plain, cream walls of her rental were beginning to bore her. Color. She needed color. Maybe this was a sign she was getting better? Whatever the reason, she had to get out of the apartment. She applied concealer under her eyes, scrunched her half-head of curls with gel, and strategically placed a straw bowler hat with a bow over the black-brown virgin hair that had continued to grow in on the other side.

She stood in front of her floor-length mirror. "There," she said, to the nothingness around her. In her fitted cotton top and deep purple sarong, not to mention that straw hat hiding her shock of stubble, strangers might think of her as some sort of trendy beachcomber with nothing but time and money to burn.

Unless they looked closely.

Truth was she was nearly broke. Disability income barely covered her rent, so Liddy was relying on her meager savings to make up the rest. Her parents had already helped her with her medical co-pays, so she couldn't ask for more. How fun would it have been to recover without this kind of added pressure? Or with someone by her side to help pick up the slack?

She groaned again. First, she had to heal. So she pulled on a sweater, then grabbed her key and slipped out the door.

Thankfully, the sun poked through the fog and Liddy could pad along in flip-flops as if she truly were free of cares. Living on a peninsula presented soul-soothing options. She could wander out to the sand and watch the waves roll or walk along the harbor's edge where seagulls fed just as hungrily.

She chose the latter. Maybe she'd run into that drifter she'd met on the beach the other day. He hadn't seemed to notice or care about her somewhat-fragile state …

The booth he'd mentioned was nothing more than a lean-to near one of the storage areas in the vast parking lot that the local boaters used. Why hadn't she noticed him there before? She found him painting the face of a girl onto a narrow fence board.

He smiled at her briefly before continuing his work. "Thought I might see you again."

"You did?" She watched his graceful hands as they worked.

"You had wanderlust in your eyes."

"Hmm. Well, maybe that was just fatigue."

He stopped for a moment and looked at her, his eyes dropping down her length. A curdle of a chill ran through her.

"I'm Zack," he said.

"Liddy."

His appraising smile reminded her of the look on her own face when she viewed a gleaming case of fresh-baked pastries. Carbs, apparently, didn't bother him either.

She cleared her throat. "Beautiful day."

"That it is. I'm going to take a break now over in the tavern. Join me, Liddy?"

Hitting a bar at lunchtime. With a stranger. So ... rebellious.

"They have burgers there, in case you're wondering."

Okay, so she *was* wondering if there'd be more than beer available. "Why not?"

He dunked his paintbrush into a bucket of water and cleaned off his hands with a wipe from some nondescript holder. "Let's go."

They took the long way to the tavern, strolling along a path that offered a crystal view of pleasure boats, their stalwart masts holding firm against the breeze. Occasionally, a pelican soared overhead, spotted its prey, then spiraled into the water with a "whoosh" to catch its lunch. She had noticed the bar before. Its lights seemed to stay lit longer than most other restaurants' did in the area. Music often streamed out of its doors, occasional notes reaching her condo deck on a fogless night.

The inside was brighter than she had expected, although still rather "rustic," with rough-hewn split logs for walls. Dated, worn serapes hung from the logs in no particular order. They grabbed stools at the bar and in view of the picture window overlooking the harbor channel.

"What'll you have?"

A mimosa tempted her, but considering the amount of medication running through her veins, she opted for a Perrier instead.

He looked at the bartender-waiter. "Add a couple of burgers to that, and a beer on tap for me."

"So," he said, a smile reaching the edges of his eyes, "tell me about the girl on the beach."

"That's a rather vague question."

"Okay. The hat. Tell me why you wear hats."

She nodded. "Do I have to have a reason?"

He weighed that. "It is my experience that a woman always has a reason for the things she does."

"You spend time analyzing women, then."

"I spend my time creating and, in that time, deeper thoughts come to me." He shrugged. "It's a gift."

Liddy laughed. "You're teasing me."

He winked. "Maybe. A little. I've noticed you around, you know."

No, she hadn't. "Really? How so."

"I'm staying with a friend in the same complex. Every

morning, right after the mail carrier leaves, you come down-stairs and fish out your mail."

"Doesn't everybody?"

"Most people just have bills, so why would they? My guess is that you have love letters in there."

"Okay, now you're flirting."

He took a sip of the beer that the bartender had placed in front of him. "Is it working?"

She was tempting fate, and she knew it. But it was fun. The most fun she'd had since … when was the last time she'd done anything worth celebrating? She sipped her Perrier. "I'd say yes."

He laughed into his beer. "Well, okay then."

She was pretty sure that her parents had warned her against strangers, but they'd never met one as a charming as a chisel-chested artist who could wrangle a paintbrush over an old fence the way Zack could. Nor one who could cause her skin to tingle in a good way by one sweep of his eyes (you know, compared to the medicine-inducing kind of tingling she had more recently grown accustomed to.)

After feasting on burgers, they walked together for at least a half hour, until she could no longer deny her need for a nap.

"You doing okay?" he asked as she leaned heavily upon a railing overlooking a yacht named *Valentino*.

She pushed herself upright. "Yes, fine."

"You ready to tell me about the hat?"

She peeked at him through downcast lashes. "Is it obvious?"

"That you've suffered?"

She waved a hand at him. "It's not that traumatic."

"Then it won't be hard to say it."

Liddy sighed. "I had brain surgery and I'm wearing a hat while the rest of my hair grows in. Simple."

Zack grew quiet. He neither looked shocked nor indifferent; instead, he reached for her hand and gave it a squeeze. "I'm sorry," was all he said.

He walked her home after that, and though he didn't say it, Liddy knew she would see him again.

"FIRST, THE GOOD NEWS."

Meg cradled her goblet of Chianti. "Tell me."

Liddy curled up on the couch in her living room, the gas fireplace snapping in the background. "The doctor has given me the go-ahead to drive."

"Yes! That's great. You really are looking marvelous. Something about all that walking in the fresh air has helped your recovery, I'd say."

Liddy sipped her sparkling water. She could have told her friend about meeting Zack, but really, she knew so little about him still. And if she wanted to be truly honest, she felt protective of his sudden and somewhat ethereal presence in her life.

"And I guess there's more good news coming, actually," she continued. "The divorce papers should be here any day now."

"Finally!"

"Yeah. It'll be good to move forward. Officially, anyway."

"Don't look back, girlfriend."

"So," Liddy said, "what about you? Sick of all the traveling yet?"

Meg signed. "Oh, you know, it's fine. It's not like I have a man at home to worry about."

"Aw, you will."

Meg looked away.

Liddy paused. Meg was ever ready to talk about Liddy's love life. But her own? Not so often. In fact, Meg often changed the subject whenever the topic of men in her life came up. When she'd made a comment about not having a man at home, Liddy thought maybe things had changed. Liddy took another sip and smiled, intending to lighten the mood. "Hey," she said, "maybe you'll meet a pilot, with all the air travel you do."

Meg nodded, a mischievous grin lighting her face. "Now you're talking. Maybe he'll let me wear his captain's hat while we, you know ... fly."

Liddy laughed so hard she inhaled sparkling water, the sensation burning her nose. She crumbled forward, trying to breathe.

Meg slapped her on the back. "Sorry. Didn't mean to incapacitate you."

Liddy threw herself backward against the couch, sighing into the air. "I needed that!"

"Oh, hey, there's more stuff going on in the restaurant at work. Wanna hear?"

Still prone, Liddy slid a glance at Meg. "Spill."

"I was in the sales office the other day when Sally—you know her, she's the executive assistant."

Liddy nodded.

"Anyway, Sally pulled a fax off the machine and then I heard her rant to the comptroller about unauthorized expenses coming from the restaurant."

"Like what?"

"Not sure, exactly. She shut the door, of course, but apparently Chef's been ordering up some pretty expensive stuff. I think I even heard the words pufferfish and duck embryos bandied about."

"Gross. But wait … pufferfish, I think, is poisonous."

Meg screwed up her nose. "Double gross."

"Chef Franco? Did he have an explanation?"

"That's the thing. He showed up a while later, grousing that the invoice was all some big mistake and that the items he purchased had been mislabeled."

Liddy shrugged. "So there's the answer."

"I don't know. Word in the 'hood is that those items were code for drugs."

"I don't unders—wait. You think that Chef is buying drugs in the restaurant?"

Meg nodded solemnly. "Buying and selling."

"Oh … my …"

"It might explain the late-night shipments, the various staff members hanging around even after they've clocked out. It's all very clandestine, and of course, nothing's been proven yet."

"This is all so sad … I suppose Thomas has still been going over there?"

"That's what I heard. I'm afraid things are going to be changing at the hotel soon. I just hope …"

"Hope what?"

Meg sighed. "There's something I haven't mentioned to you about hotels, Liddy, but basically, this industry is notorious for sending in suits to take over properties, usually cleaning house when they do."

"And you think that's what's going to happen at Sea Glass?"

She shrugged. "No idea. It would be strange since this hotel chain has been owned by the same family for years, but you never know. They could keep ownership, but just bring in someone else to manage it. Happens all the time."

"And staff loses jobs."

"Sadly, yes."

Liddy hadn't even made it back to work yet and already change was in the air. She experienced a thump of sadness at the thought of losing a job she had barely started—and one that she enjoyed more than any other before it. Not like she was in a big hurry to work full days again soon. (Well, other than the fact that her savings had shrunk like cotton fabric in hot water.) But why did life have to keep changing?

The next morning, Zack showed up at her door wearing paint-streaked shorts, a wrinkled button-down, and carrying a handful of wildflowers. *Be still my heart.*

"Thought I could walk you to your mailbox," he said.

"Charmer."

Liddy doubted that he could have known what waited for her inside that metal box. She pulled out the large, white envelope, and just stared at it a few seconds.

"Something you've been looking for?"

Liddy slid a glance at him. "Divorce papers."

He nodded once. "Ah." Then he turned her away from the mailbox and grabbed her hand. "C'mon. Let's drop that off at your apartment and take a walk."

The divorce had long been decided, and Liddy had anticipated the delivery of the final declaration. She'd even contemplated various ways to celebrate the package's arrival—fancy dinner out (too expensive), cruise to the islands (too cold), skinny-dipping in the sea (still thinking about it).

In the end, she felt content to wander aimlessly on the beach with the mysterious Zack. Maybe he was exactly what she needed to accelerate her healing. She'd never met someone so obviously *not* in a hurry. By the time they made it back to the condo complex, they had traversed more of the sand than she ever had on her own.

The sun warmed her face as she leaned back against the rubber-slatted lounge chair on the pool deck. She'd never seen a soul swimming here since she moved in, but she supposed that could be because it was still winter. Although winter in California was a bit of a joke, really.

"I've got a bottle of champagne chilling at home and my roommate's nowhere to be seen. Wanna celebrate tonight?" Zack asked her as they contemplated the sky.

She turned her head in his direction. "I would love to."

And that's how she, a brain surgery survivor, ended up in the arms of an artist on the evening that her divorce became final.

As HE SLIPPED IN THROUGH the back door to his office late Monday morning, Beau could hear the counselor's voice in his head. Not that he'd actually gone to see one, but if he *had* sought counseling for his lingering grief, he felt quite sure the words "do what makes you happy" or "take a vacation" or even "bury yourself in work" might have shown up in the mix.

What he didn't think he would ever hear was "grow a beard." He rubbed his hand across the grizzle or "sharp" feel of his skin, as little Madi might say. After the poor child nicked her tender skin on his face, he'd shaved and kept it up each morning. Unlike his brothers and father, Beau spent Christmas week beardless.

But today was different. The weekend had begun nicely enough with a stroll downtown after work ... he shook his head. No time for memories. If he didn't have so much work to do, he'd pack a bedroll and some food and head into the wilderness of Yosemite. A man could get lost for a good long time in those sacred mountains.

As luck, or lack thereof, would have it, he had more work on his plate than he knew what to do with. Great for business—and burying oneself—but not so much for mindless meanderings in the great outdoors.

Jill leaned in through the doorway. "Good," she said. "You're back. I just dropped off a stack of messages and four proposals for you to sign."

He dropped his satchel onto the floor and kicked it under his desk. "Got it."

"So, you'll do those soon?"

He sank into his seat and began logging into his computer. "Uh-huh."

"Beau?"

He didn't feel like it today. Jill's nagging. Loved the woman as an assistant, and as a friend, but he feared that if he were to tear his eyes from the screen, she would clearly see "get out of my face" flashing in his eyes.

Jill was now standing right behind his computer screen.

Harsh taskmaster, that one. Sometimes he wondered who employed whom.

He sighed. Of course, she was right. He had let the messages pile up. And though he had worked his butt off on all those proposals, he'd yet to finalize even one of them. Reluctantly, he was thankful for Jill. And her nagging self.

"Are you going to look at me?"

He glanced up.

She scrutinized him and nodded succinctly. "Huh."

He frowned. "What?"

"You're growing a beard."

He touched his face.

"It's kind of patchy, but the girls will like it."

"What girls?"

"Oh, you know, the young ones who go for that sort of thing. Makes you look rugged," she said with a gravelly growl and he had to hold back what tasted like revulsion. He had never imagined Jill as the growling type.

"I'd thank you for the compliment, but my guess is that you didn't mean it that way."

Jill laughed. "To each his own, Beau. If you suddenly want to become a mountain man, then that's your prerogative. Who am I to say? We will need to have the photographer come in to take a new profile photo of you, of course. You know, for LinkedIn, your website, etc., etc."

He rolled his eyes.

Jill smiled at him in that "I'm glad you're finally listening to me" way of hers. "So you'll sign those proposals?" she asked sweetly.

"Sure thing," he said. "After you deliver my coffee."

"Touché, boss."

When she'd gone, he sat back and surveyed the fan of documents across his desk. He had a lot to be thankful for, and the first at the moment was all the business coming his way.

His eyes caught sight of one of the messages Jill had left. From the local physician's association. He'd been invited to their annual beach picnic, but had not RSVP'd. He ran a hand through his hair, scratching his wrist across his cheek as he did. He couldn't miss this event ... it was too important to his business. In the past, Anne attended with him.

Jill delivered a mug of coffee, black, and left without a word. Beau glanced at the RSVP card again. Sure enough, there was a spot for the number of guests. He picked up a pen and allowed it to hover over the card, then he tossed the pen back down and watched it roll off the mound of documents and onto the floor.

He gulped down a swig of the hot coffee not bothering to let it cool first. Really, he didn't need the caffeine today. He was antsy enough without a drop of it. He hauled in a breath, rolled one shoulder, and then the other.

Beau stood, and marched over to the small closet on the other side of his office door. He swung it open and stared at the stack of paintings leaning up against the inside wall. His breathing reverberated in his ears. His memory took over, bringing with it the smell of paint and solvents. And color. So much color. That's what he was missing.

He glanced around his office, taking in its bland walls. He'd always let the bank of windows on one side provide his art, as the view was decent enough. Oh, he had always wanted to hang some of Anne's work, but perfectionist that she was she had not allowed it. Instead, she'd given him a stack of unfinished (her word) paintings and then presented him with the task of choosing one or two for his walls. She had promised him she would finish her work.

He had never taken the time.

Or maybe he'd always preferred the thought of her having at least "one more project" to complete.

With a surge of his heart, he lifted the bundle of paintings and began to go through them slowly, one by one. Each of them held a memory of its own. The profile of her face as she concentrated ... the tinkling of classical music that served as background ... the changing light that flowed through westerly windows, constantly frustrating her efforts.

He expelled a breath of surrender and plucked one from the bunch, a forest scene with unexpected bursts of spring color.

Chapter Nine

✱

A GREY-TINGED CLOUD FLOATED IN front of the morning sun as if Eeyore himself had pulled it along with him. Or maybe that was a remnant from too much celebrating the night before. She yawned, tucked strands of uncooperative hair behind one ear, and fought off an odd niggling of … what? She couldn't define it. All she knew was that for a woman who had been given her freedom, she felt anything but unencumbered.

Liddy shrugged off the malaise and padded down the stairs to pick up the mail, half-expecting to find Zack waiting for her. He wasn't. Inside her mailbox, though, she found an unexpected invoice from the hospital. "Great," she muttered.

"Everything okay?"

Liddy pivoted around to face the person who had heard a comment for her alone. "Fine," she said, biting her lip.

"You're Zack's … friend. Aren't you?"

Liddy flicked another glance at the man. He wore jeans and a button-down shirt that bulged midway at the buttons, offering her a view of way too much body hair. Frizzy shoulder-length hair gushed from beneath a clean painter's cap. "How do you know Zack?" she asked.

"He's been living with me for a few weeks." The man

pointed in some vague direction over her head. "Although I've been in and out of town myself."

"Oh, of course. You're his roommate ..." Did she even know his name?

"Bob."

She nodded, her mind a dazed swirl, most likely from one too many sips of last night's champagne. "Hi."

"Yeah, hi." He shifted. "Hey, I'm glad I ran into you this morning. Zack's snoring like a freight train back at the condo, but his wife left a message on my machine this morning. She's decided to pop in tonight on her way down the coast. Thought it would be awkward if you two, you know, ran into each other."

Liddy blinked. A catch in her lungs made it difficult to breathe. Her mind began to spiral, the sensation too raw, too horribly familiar. "What did you say?"

He raised one eyebrow. "About Zack's wife or what?"

"Zack ... has a wife?"

Bob straightened and pushed back his cap, recognition first reaching his eyes and then his mouth pursed a couple of times before he spat out, "Figured you knew."

Liddy shook her head slowly. "I-I, no. I didn't." She looked down, scuffing the sole of her flip-flop against the cement walkway. "And you're sure?"

He frowned. "I'm not some liar."

His harshness delivered deep color to her cheeks. She could feel it. *He must think I'm ... I'm some ... oh no ...* Liddy lifted her chin and hugged her stack of mail to her chest.

"Well?" he cut in.

"Uh ..." How had she not known, not seen? Thoughts of

confusion, anger, and bitterness rioted in her mind and without another word, Liddy pivoted and briskly walked away. When she reached the bottom of her steps, she ignored him further when she heard Bob call out, "What am I supposed to tell your boyfriend now?"

Inside her apartment she dumped the mail on the floor and collapsed onto her sofa. A rush of tears clawed their way through her insides, scratching her raw. Her sobs came out in sharp gasps.

She grabbed her cell and called Meg, who she knew to be on her way to Florida. "I let him touch me!" she said when her friend answered. The din of airport sounds rattled in the background.

"Liddy? What happened?"

Liddy told Meg about the drifter she'd met, how he complimented her when she felt uglier than a dog that had long needed a bath. "Oh, and last night—"

"I don't understand," Meg interrupted. "When exactly did you even find time for a new boyfriend?"

Liddy continued her rant into the phone. "Last night, we drank champagne until so, so late …"

"You drank champagne, Liddy? Even with all your medication …"

"You're right! I'm so stupid and dumb. And irresponsible."

"No, you're not. Stop it. I shouldn't have said that—*I'm* the irresponsible one. Let's start over." Meg's voice hung with unshed tears. "Are you okay? I mean, he didn't do anything to you … physically."

"Nothing … it was nothing. You know what? I'm fine. Just feeling ridiculous." She paused. "Oh no! I'm the other woman.

I feel like I've done to Zack's wife what Shawn's bimbo did to me. I hate myself!"

"You didn't know."

Her heart raced so hard in her chest she thought it might leap into her throat and out of her mouth. *And here I thought Zack was an answer to prayer ...*

"Liddy, hear me. This isn't good for you. You need to focus on gaining your strength back, on healing. Stay away from that guy. Promise me."

"Are you kidding? You think I'd go out with him now?"

"I didn't mean it that way, but he sounds like a guy who might try to sweet talk you when you're especially vulnerable. I wish I could be with you tonight so we could tear him to shreds over a pizza, but I can't." She groaned into the phone. "It's just that I know guys like him. He'll probably show up with flowers and some kind of explanation about his wife not 'understanding' him—and he might even be able to pull off that kind of cliché!"

"You know what? No. That's it. I'm done."

"Wha-what do you mean?" Meg's voice rose in pitch.

Liddy clucked her tongue. "I'm not committing suicide, but I *am* done with men. Forget it! Even if I were to find one who wasn't totally horrible, I'm no good at relationships anyway." Her voice became rueful, jagged yet quiet. "I think I've proven that."

"Liddy? Today's Wednesday, isn't it?" Her friend spoke gently. "Shake it off and go to that church of yours. You always seem so much better off after one of your prayer meetings."

She scoffed. "Just what I need ... to hang out with perfect people tonight."

Meg giggled. "Uh, honey? I saw some of the outfits those women were wearing … Birkenstocks and skirts? Trust me—they ain't perfect."

"I've never seen that." Liddy's heart had settled into a more reasonable rhythm now. "Maybe you're right, though. If I stay here I'll probably eat a half-gallon of ice cream. And then where will I be?"

"A plus-size clothing store?"

Liddy pressed her eyes shut. It was only mid-morning and already a nap beckoned. "Thanks, friend. I'm going to get some rest, and if I can pull myself together, maybe I'll try the church thing later."

"Okay. Love you."

AS IT TURNED OUT, she'd been unable to sleep. By the time evening had fallen and she had eaten more dark chocolate than she cared to admit (it is the best kind for you, after all), she longed to get out of the apartment. Too tired to drive, she called for an Uber driver to drop her off at service ten minutes late. That way she wouldn't have to talk to anyone. She slipped into a seat in the back row, miraculously avoiding the glare of an elderly usher who prided himself on seating rule-breakers such as her up front. Even after brain surgery, she was faster than that old guy.

The evening itself was uneventful, but calming. And she needed it that way. The only hiccup was the twist in her gut when she noticed Beau walking in the parking lot after church with the same woman she'd seen him with downtown. Though she had become slightly fixated on the swath of fine bristles on his face, thankfully, he hadn't noticed her, too.

During the service, when her mind was able to parse through the events of the past week, Liddy realized she needed to take charge of her life again. She had been allowing circumstances to toss her about, but no more.

"Tomorrow," she said under her breath as the Uber driver pulled up to the curb outside of her complex, "I start over."

HE'D NOTICED HER. She wore red … how could he not notice? Beau pulled into the driveway of his home and threw the car into park. It lurched to a stop and he hesitated to open his door and see which of his neighbors noticed his less-than-smooth parking job.

He grabbed the basket from his front seat and stepped out into the cool night. The sky was clear. Perfect night to put his feet up in front of the fire and watch something on ESPN. He glanced at the basket of baked goods. Wendy apparently thought he needed to add a little around his middle.

A grimace tugged at his mouth as he entered his home. Wendy was sweet enough, and she was pretty. If Rex had his way, she would be wearing a ring and choosing a date on the church calendar for their wedding. Beau shook his head. As he removed his collared shirt, swapping it for a sweatshirt from his alma mater, the only face he saw in his mind was … Liddy's.

Chapter Ten

LIDDY AROSE THE NEXT MORNING, pulled on her yoga pants and a long-sleeve tee, covered her eclectic mess of hair in various stages of growth, and walked across the street to the Farmer's Market. She had decided to start her "new" life small. There she wandered among the throngs of people vying for non-GMO veggies and fruit. If she ran into Zack, so be it. She had nothing to hide.

Still, the thought of seeing him inflamed her gut and she tried very hard not to think of him again. A sad, lingering commentary left behind was that her dalliance with an artist who'd snowed her, had, unwittingly, brought to mind memories of her recent divorce. It still irked her that she was so terrible at choosing men.

She glanced out to the marina and the boats and the lapping blue seawater … anything that could possibly make the pain go away. When she felt sure that she was able to take on the next challenge, she hoisted her bag of fresh items over one shoulder and headed for home.

"We meet again."

His voice crept like a thorn-bearing vine up her back and she winced.

"Liddy. Turn around."

She threw a glance over her shoulder. "Get away from me."

He gave her an ethereal smile like he was about to follow it up by quoting some kind of sonnet. She pressed her lips together. How could she have fallen for that crap?

"I've got to go," she said.

"Where to? I'll walk with you."

She stopped and turned around. "Why don't you go find your *wife* and leave me alone?" Tears brimmed in her eyes and she hated herself for it. "You've done enough damage."

"On the contrary, I set you free. You were wasting away up there in your tower, coming down only to pick up mail. And now? Now you're a feisty woman on the way to healing. I'd say I did you some good."

Her breathing had become leaden and she willed herself to stay upright. He took a step toward her and she recoiled. "You are such a creep." As she pulled herself away from his prying gaze and moved swiftly toward home, she had to block out the unmistakable sound of him chuckling.

"That's it!" Inside her apartment she dumped her items in the fridge and fished around for the key to her storage closet. Back outside she threw a wave to her across-the-breezeway neighbor Brandon, charged downstairs, unlocked the door to the closet and pulled out her bike. She had not ridden the thing since the desert, but at this moment all she wanted to do was feel the sea breeze coursing through what hair she had left, to inhale the saltiness of the air.

Only she would be responsible for her recovery. Not Zack ... not anyone.

The route alongside the soft-sand beach was dotted with

side-by-side beach shacks and mansions, kind of like life. They all just had to get along or be bulldozed. She rode past a home at one end of the beach that rose into the sky like the Queen Mary, and at the other end, she coasted past a tiny cottage surrounded by walls embedded with oddities. Down at the turnaround a dive bar held court next to a realtor's office. Fishermen caught their supper, tossing guts to passing seagulls. By the time she returned home, Liddy's cheeks stung from the relentless force of salt and sand and raw air.

Too tired to take her bike to the storage closet, she locked it to the staircase outside of her condo, and inched her way up to her front door. Her extremities—toes, hands—creaked from a chill, as if the day's wind had lodged itself into her bones. She sank into the sofa and pulled a blanket around her, not recalling a time when she had ever felt this cold. Or this tired. The heavy cloak of fatigue weighed on her so that her fingers cramped, making it so very difficult to grasp the ends of the blanket that she had buried herself in. She hated to admit it, but finding a way to feed herself tonight might just take a miracle.

Her cell phone rang and she groaned. If she didn't answer, though, Meg or her mother, or whoever it was on the other end, would probably call the police. Hmm … if she weren't so exhausted and so done with men in her life, she might have let her mind fantasize a moment about a strapping police officer breaking down her door …

The phone rang again. She let out another groan. "Hello?"

"Is that you, Liddy? This is Beau."

Her mind swirled, but her heart sank. "Yes. Hi, Beau."

"Are you feeling okay?"

Well, let's see. She'd had brain surgery just weeks ago, carried on with a married man, and then tried to shake it all off by riding her bike for over an hour. And now she could barely move. But instead of all that, she answered, "Yes, fine."

"You sound … tired."

"I am ridiculously fatigued at the moment."

"Are you alone? Would you like some help?"

"It's not like that." She kept her eyes closed. "I've just had a tough week, that's all."

"But your prognosis is good, right?"

She allowed herself a deep breath before continuing. Oh, she was tired. "Yes, yes. The doctor says they got it all. As he suspected—the tumor was benign." Something leaped inside her heart at repeating this news. If she'd had any strength left, she would have used it to smile.

"Beautiful." He said the word with a slight accent, like he was from some far off region of the United States, the sound of his voice moving from anxious to warm and low. For the first time, she wondered if he was from around here.

"I noticed you last night at church, but didn't have a chance to say hello," he said.

Maybe your new girlfriend had something to do with that? Meow.

"I was glad to see you," he continued. "You looked well."

"Thanks."

A beat of silence passed between them. Beau was the first to interrupt it. "Well, I'd better be going. Glad to hear that you're on the mend, Liddy. I'll see you soon, all right?"

"Sure," she whispered, and dropped her phone to the floor.

BEAU MET TAYLOR FOR DINNER at their favorite burrito stand in midtown. Nothing like beans coated in lard to heal the hurts of the day. Taylor took the steps in one long leap all the while carrying on a conversation through earbuds.

"Yes, honey, I got it. A quesadilla for Tiffany and taco salad for you—hold the sour cream. Sure you don't want chips and guac?" Taylor listened to his wife while making faces at Beau. When Taylor grabbed the cords of his headphones and wrapped them around his own neck like a noose, Beau grinned. "Okay, hon. Gotta go. Beau says hi by the way."

"In a hurry?" Beau asked after his friend had yanked the earbuds out of his ears and buried them in his back pocket.

"Nah. Ginny's got Tiff in a ballet class, so I'll order their food on my way out. I'm starved—let's eat."

They ordered two stuffed burritos, the tortillas stretched thinly around the beans and cheese, and a couple of sodas. Taylor took a huge bite. "It's better that Ginny doesn't come with me here. Turns up her nose at the size of these babies anyway."

Beau couldn't muster much of a response.

"You're quiet."

He shrugged. "Yeah."

Taylor waited a beat. "Bad day?"

"Not really." He shrugged. "Something like that."

"Schedule's out. Want me to pick up tickets so you can watch the Rockies get a pounding from the Dodgers?"

Now Beau smiled. "We both know the Dodgers are getting spanked this year."

"You wish." He took another bite and spoke with his mouth full. "Wager?"

"Sure. Winner buys the burritos next time."

Taylor let loose a high-pitched giggle. Always sounded a little weird, but oddly fitting coming from his gentle giant of a friend.

"So," Taylor started, "what's going on with you in the female department?"

Beau took a swig of cola. "Nothing."

Taylor lifted one brow. "Don't lie, bro. Everyone's talking about you and that Wilkes girl."

"I don't believe you. She and I have made no commitment to each other." *Yet.*

"Actually, let me retract that. Ginny heard about a couple of others who've sharpened their claws around you lately. And what's going on with you and Beth? Someone heard her tell you that you guys are supposed to get married?"

Beau snorted. "That was a joke. Honestly, lately it feels as if I'm the punchline of a slew of them."

Taylor frowned. "How so?"

"Do you know Liddy Buckle?"

"The woman with the tumor. Yeah, I heard you'd been seen talking to her."

"See? That's what I mean. Who's been saying this stuff?"

"C'mon, people just worry about you. Forget about it. What's up with Liddy?"

"I called her last night, you know, to check on her."

"Uh-huh."

Beau sighed and ran a hand over the stubble forming on his face. "She said she was fine, but she didn't sound like it. She sounded sick to me, frankly."

"Because you're a doctor."

Beau snapped him a hard look. "Because I know what sick sounds like."

Taylor plunked the rest of his burrito onto the table. "Okay, I get it. And you're worried about her or something?"

"Let me ask you … has God ever spoken to you?"

"You mean like the time he told me to suck it up and hold my wife's hair when she barfed during labor?"

"That was a nurse talking."

Taylor shook his head vehemently. "Whatever it was, it sure put the fear of God into me." He paused. "I take it you're talking about something else."

Beau puffed out his cheeks and blew out a long, slow breath. "Remember that night Liddy told the congregation about her surgery? That night I was running late, and the usher seated me right next to her in the front row."

"Well, you *were* late …"

He shook his head tightly. "I don't know, Tay. I remember walking toward her, and sensing—well, more than sensing— that …."

"That what?"

Beau looked his friend in the eyes. "That she was my future."

"Why? Because God told you that?"

"Can you think of anyone else who would put us together?"

Taylor sat back, his face grim. "No one."

"I had planned to ask her out that night and thought that for once, my late arrival had worked in my favor."

"But then she made her announcement."

"Could've knocked me over with a feather, to borrow a cliché. Ever since then I've been questioning myself." He wagged his head. "Maybe the upheaval of the past year has messed with my mind."

"If that's the case, why do you keep thinking about her? And why did you call her last night?"

"What do you mean? I told you. I wanted to see how she was doing after the surgery."

"Bull."

Beau's laugh sounded incredulous. "You think I have some ulterior motive? What's wrong with you?"

Taylor grinned at his friend before taking another bite. "You're an idiot. Of course you did."

Taylor, Beau had learned, had a way of cutting through the layers that he often stacked up between himself and his troubles. One night a couple of years ago, he and Anne had invited Tay and Ginny to dinner to celebrate. He remembered well the smile on his wife's face as she sat across the dining table from Ginny and relayed good news about her prognosis. She glowed. Thinking back on that moment wrenched Beau's heart in his chest until he thought he might bleed.

Later that same evening, as the girls went into the kitchen to talk and dish up dessert, Taylor collared him. "You're scared out of your mind, my friend. I can tell."

His mouth had dropped open at Taylor's pronouncement. Had he been that transparent?

Tay had been a steady hand in his life, both then and now. He recalled the way he pulled him aside as they prepared to leave that night. "I've got your back. Just wanted you to know."

Now as Taylor finished off his burrito, Beau ruminated on his friend's accusation about him having some kind of ulterior motive. He really did want to know how she had been faring …

Taylor pitched his wrapper into the waste can and slapped the red-painted table. "Now put us both out of our misery and ask that girl out."

Beau wadded up his own wrapper and pitched it into the trash, too, knocking Taylor's onto the floor. He grinned. "Maybe I will."

MEG WOULD NOT ALLOW LIDDY to forget her recklessness of that day. At least she had the decency to take her to task over cupcakes and iced coffees at a beachside café with floor-to-ceiling chalkboard menus, drifts of salty air, and plenty of sunny outside seating.

"I could kill you for what you did—you could have died!"

Liddy shrugged. "Might have defeated the purpose, don't you think?"

Meg's voice softened. "You've always had an independent spirit; I've loved that about you. But following after some loser drifter and then drowning your sorrows in some relentless show of strength?" She shook her head. "It's not like you. You're too smart for that."

Tears pricked Liddy's eyes and nose. Meg was right, of course. She'd spent most of the last week in bed, ignoring the phone as much as possible. That seemingly simple bike ride about did her in, so much that she had frightened herself. If it hadn't been for sweet Tessy from the church popping in with a lasagna "just in case," she might not have had anything other than chips and salsa for meals. As it happened, she ate squares of that lasagna all week long—often cold. And she still lost weight.

"It's behind me now."

Meg peeked at her from beneath the brim of her hat. "Consider yourself dutifully warned that it had better be."

"Yes, ma'am. New subject. Tell me about what's going on at the hotel. Will you be in town for a while?"

"As a matter of fact, yes. The hotel's been very busy lately. Occupancy is way up, as are site visits. You do know there's a Male Heartthrob Impersonators Convention coming in next week."

"You didn't?"

Meg wrinkled her nose and bit her tongue. "Booked the whole thing. Now somebody has to stick around and manage all those ..."

"Heartthrobs?"

Meg laughed. "Don't knock it. They paid big for the entire ballroom."

"Guess this is a good time to tell you that I've decided to go back to work next week." Liddy laughed. "Just in time."

Meg tilted her head. "Isn't it a little early for that? It's one thing to take care of the daily basics, but working? You have to be 'on' all the time ... I don't know."

Liddy sighed. "I know what you mean, but I think I need to. For one thing, I'm a little bored and I don't have the funds to really do anything fun. Disability just doesn't cover much more than the rent so my savings are, like, what savings?"

Meg cringed. "I'm so sorry. I didn't know."

Liddy shrugged. "No big. Anyway, I'm glad you'll be around next week. And all those handsome pseudo-celebrities ... sounds like some wicked fun."

"Yeah, well, you'll have your hands busy directing all those fan girls to the ballroom."

Liddy laughed and held up her iced coffee for a toast. "Well, then, to fan girls for keeping us both employed!"

Meg clinked her glass against Liddy's. "Here, here."

Chapter Eleven

"YOU LOOK POSITIVELY DEAD ON your feet," Trace said, peering at Liddy through her latest thrift store find: a pair of Warby Parker glasses. They weren't her exact prescription, but "close enough"!

"Gee, thanks, friend."

"I'm serious, Lid. You've worked three full days in a row after being gone for how long? Shoot, I'm exhausted after coming back from vacation. Can't imagine having gone through"—she gestured toward Liddy's head—"you know."

"Brain surgery?"

Trace grimaced. "Yeah, that. Seriously, go take a break."

Hans showed up at the desk just then, key in hand. "Here," he said. "I'm leaving this room unoccupied for you for the next week, well, unless we get one-hundred-percent occupancy, and when does that happen?"

Liddy frowned. "I don't understand."

Hans handed the key to Trace. "Gotta run. You explain."

Trace let out a succinct sigh. "It's for you to take catnaps, whenever you need them." She pushed the key into Liddy's hand. "C'mon, don't be too proud to take it. If you won't go home, then take a nap. Now."

Reluctantly, Liddy acknowledged her need for a break and took the key. "Thanks. I'll set the alarm and be back in a bit."

She stood inside the neat-as-a-pin guest room at the end of the west hall. What the room lacked in updated decor, it made up for with a crispness that earned them high praise on Yelp. That and the forever sea views. Hans had chosen a room for her far away from ice machines and elevators and stairs. She let out a sigh. He was a good guy, and she sure hoped he wasn't somehow connected to the mystery involving the chef.

As she lowered herself to the end of the bed, a dark shroud descended on her. Her eyes drooped on their own volition, but she fought to keep them open. Had she known that she was this tired? She glanced into the mirror on the wall across from her and removed her hat, laying it on the bed next to her. The blonde curls that framed one side of her face contrasted sharply with the soft, nearly-black hair that had filled in her other side. From where she sat, she could see the deep-set circles that had formed under her eyes.

Trace—and Hans—were right. She needed sleep. And so she crawled beneath the crisp, bleached white sheets, and fell into slumber.

Sometime later, she awoke to the muscle-jarring ring of the phone next to her bed. She had not owned a house phone in year—hardly anyone she knew did anymore—so the impact of the screeching in-room menace rankled her nerves. She groaned and picked up the receiver.

"Oh, thank God!"

"Hmm?"

"I thought you were dead or something!" Trace hollered into the line.

Liddy furrowed her brow and squinted at the clock, its bright red symbols glowing in the darkened room: 6:30. "Wait, what?" Through the gauzy sheers, she could see that night had fallen. "Oh, I overslept."

"I'm just glad you're not dead!"

Liddy sat up. "Sorry to have scared you. Must've set the alarm for a.m. or something. I'll be down in a second." She glanced around for her hat.

"No worries. Actually, your shift is over, so go on home. Do you need a ride?"

Relief flooded her. "No, I'm good. Thanks, Trace. This helped."

Even though she was checked into this room for the next week, she made the bed and fluffed the pillows. No sense in housekeeping staff thinking she was a slob. She shut the door behind her and made her way down the hall toward the parking lot, her clothing rumpled from the last few hours of slumber. Hopefully those who passed her by didn't think she was taking a walk of shame.

Outside, she shivered in the chill of the night. She slid into her Jeep and drove out of the lot, passing by the back of the restaurant on her short jaunt home. A familiar figure had slipped in through the double back doors of the hotel restaurant. Hans. He was still on-site, and his shift had long ended.

With a groan, Liddy hurried home, anxious for dinner and more hours of sleep.

IN THE WEEK THAT HAD PASSED, Liddy had seen more fan girls over the age of forty—and more heaving breasts—than she cared to think about. Housekeeping had been busy cleaning up too-many-to-count spillages of Chardonnay on the indoor tile floors, not to mention the array of thongs flung from various balconies. What would these women have done if the men parading through the lobby for several days had been the real deal—and not just impersonators?

"Score!" Trace showed up for the night shift wearing a vintage cap.

Liddy tapped her chin with her index finger. She didn't want to hurt her co-worker's feelings, but that hat did not match her outfit at all. "A new thrift store find?" she finally asked.

Trace laughed. "You wish. No, it's a replica of Noah's newsboy cap. Matilda in Housekeeping said it was left behind in one of the guest rooms after the fake heartthrob convention, so she saved it for me."

"Noah?"

Trace's eyebrows rose. "Ryan Gosling? From *The Note-book*."

"Ah. Now I get it."

Trace swooned. "The most beautiful movie hero that there ever was. They don't make them like him anymore."

Liddy laughed lightly. "Good thing you have someone looking out for you." She stood then and hooked her purse into the crook of her arm. "With that I guess I'll take off for the night."

"I have to say, Lid, you're looking so much better than you were last week. Sweet hat, by the way."

Liddy tried not to wince. "Really?" Today she had worn a flimsy black hat that her mom had bought her the weekend before, when she and her father had come for a visit. Her hair had been growing in well lately, but it still stuck straight up in the air like from electric shock, and so she'd had to become more creative with her appearance in public. At the beach, she didn't care—all kinds of weirdness on the sand, so she fit right in there. But here, in the public eye, she conceded that she needed more polish.

"Maybe not as cool as mine," Trace said, preening over her own find, "but darn pretty, if you ask me."

"Thanks. See you tomorrow," Liddy called out as she headed out the door. It bugged her how much she needed that compliment right now. She was woman! Hear her roar! Okay, seriously, it was more of a whimper right now. But a downright healthy one, at least.

Who was she kidding? She was headed to church and, just in case she ran into you-know-who, she didn't want to look like a freak. Last time he called her, she certainly sounded like one.

She turned in to the church parking lot, adjusted her hat, and stepped out of her car.

HE WAS THERE. And he was alone. Not that she had noticed during the service. She was paying attention to God (for heaven's sake), offering up whispers of thanks for the silver linings in her life. Home – check. Food on the table – check. Health – double check. Regardless of the dips in the past year—and they were plentiful—Liddy knew that all had not been lost. In fact, much had been gained. Well, okay, *some* had been gained.

And for that she was thankful.

Liddy was so deep into contemplating her newfound gratefulness that as she made her way toward the church's exit doors she nearly ran into Beau.

She stopped short. "Hey."

"Hi." His eyes swept across her face.

"Nice service," she said, knowing immediately how lame that sounded. Everybody knew that describing an event as "nice" meant you couldn't think of anything else because you had not paid one whit of attention to any of it. You need to say something specific, such as the pastor's message on forgiveness stirred you to seek out all those whom you have offended sometime in your lifetime. Or maybe something less cheesy.

"You look ... beautiful."

She blushed. She couldn't see it, of course, but she could feel the warmth all the way to the tip of her hat-topped head. She managed to keep eye contact with him, however, and answered with a simple, "Thanks."

"The beach must be treating you very well. Are you able to take walks and enjoy the sunsets?"

He had this look on his face that made her think he had more to say but that, perhaps, something was keeping him back. "Yes, I do take walks," she answered him. "And I've also been back to work for a week." The banter was banal at best, yet strangely cozy, too, like they were the only two people left in the sanctuary when, really, several elders hovered nearby. For his part, Beau didn't appear to be in a hurry to run off, even though service had already ended.

"Wow, you've made great strides in what, six weeks?"

She nodded, fully aware that it had not exactly been a smooth time for her. She had made plenty of cringe-worthy mistakes in regards to both her mental and physical health. Still, she seemed to have turned a corner. "I'm back to cooking my own meals again," she said. "Feels good."

"Ah, so you're a good cook."

She laughed at this. "Hardly. My idea of a good time is organic pasta with some simple homemade sauce that I usually eat standing up over my sink. I'm just happy I can do that again."

He nodded. "Sounds perfect."

Liddy leaned her head to one side, considering him. "Would you like to join me at the sink sometime?" She hadn't meant that to sound like such a come-on, but somehow it did. She could tell by the surprised smile that so quickly alighted on his face.

But instead of answering her question, he said, "What are you doing right now?"

The hovering elders had wandered away. Except for the lone custodian straightening chairs at the front of the sanctuary, the church was now empty. She didn't know what to say in response to Beau's question.

"What I mean is ... why don't we grab something to eat right now? Would you like to?"

She hesitated. Her head tried to grasp more than one thought, like dangling strings. Why now? And what about the woman she had seen him with on occasion? She couldn't read Beau, and it unnerved her. Would it make him feel weird to sit across from her with her blonde locks spilling out from beneath the brim of her hat? Would it make her feel weird, too?

Despite her awful divorce, then her awful mistake with Zack and the subsequent pledge to forget about men, this moment felt safe, and she couldn't help but answer, "Yes."

Chapter Twelve

"WELL?? IS HE ... *INTERESTING*?"

Liddy gasped at Meg's question about her impromptu ... what was it exactly? Not a date, really. Casual meet-up? Rendezvous? She gave her head a tight little shake in exasperation as she and Meg walked side by side on the paved road after sunset, listening to waves crashing in the night. "What do you mean? Of course he was interesting. And so, so funny."

"Okay, so, that I don't see." Meg's pace sped up as she talked. "Handsome as all get out—I'll give you that, but the guy I met that night at your church was intense. Really serious."

"He lost his wife, Meg. Life's been rough on him, but—" Liddy released a breathy sign into the night air—"I don't know, we just sat there in this old coffee shop talking for forever. I'm almost embarrassed at how I talked the poor guy's ear off, but he looked amused the whole time."

Meg glanced at her. "You're happy."

She wrinkled her nose. "Well, I don't want to read too much into it—it was just coffee and pie."

"True. You did talk the guy's ear off, after all." She paused. "Just how much did you tell him?"

Liddy ran the memory through her mind all day at work, and now as Meg asked the magic question, she wished she hadn't said quite so much about herself. Hopefully, she hadn't nauseated the poor guy.

"We didn't talk much about the surgery," Liddy said. "I was relieved about that, really. I'm pretty sick of retelling it." She shrugged one shoulder and continued. "But I could have been a little less regaling with stories from my married days."

Meg hummed a groan.

Liddy slowed and turned toward a beach access break between houses. The moonlit pocket of wave caps darted in and out of view. "I know," she said, staring out at the dark sea. "He just kept asking me about my life, and I don't know … I spent most of my adult years with Shawn so things about that time kept, you know, coming up."

"How did he react?"

"He laughed mostly."

Meg paused. "So you kept the ugly stuff out then."

"Yeah, pretty much. Now that I think about it, I told him about my house renovations gone bad, and how freezing the desert could get at night. He asked how I ended up here and I told him that my mom used to drive us out from our home in LA to Santa Monica to play in the sand and that I never wanted to leave, so it was natural to find a place by the sea after my marriage ended." Liddy dipped the toe of her shoe into the sand, reveling in the soft landing. "He's got this …"

"This what?"

"He's got this laugh that's contagious, you know? It's deep and hearty, like stew, and I kind of wanted to eat him up."

"You're in trouble."

"Am I?"

"You just said you wanted to eat the guy up, like he's some kind of thick, rich soup." She wagged her head. "Never heard a woman say *that* before."

Liddy could feel pink encroaching on her cheeks. She lifted her foot out of the sand and gave it a good shake before continuing on their walk. "I did let him get a few words in here and there," she said. "He's a Rockies fan, for instance."

Meg weighed this news with one hand. "I guess we can forgive him that. You'll have to wear blue on game days, of course."

"Of course."

"And he likes to play tennis, so I told him he could use the courts in my complex."

Meg slowed again. "I hate to be a downer, but—"

"But what?"

"Well, aren't you going a little fast? I mean, you've always gone for the dark and brooding type. Beau's more like a ginger, a handsome one, but my guess is he burns easily in sunlight."

"What … are we in high school again? Beau doesn't fit the criteria that I once wrote inside a cootie catcher, so we can't be friends?" Liddy dipped her chin. "Tell me you don't think I'm that shallow, Meg."

"I'm not saying that about you, but in all fairness, you may get tired of taking spoonfuls of ginger. Since he's not exactly your type, I mean. My point is … where will you be if you've already committed to free anytime admission to your tennis courts?"

Liddy kept moving forward, her arms crossed at her chest. After everything that had transpired over the past year, wasn't it time for something positive in her life? A real downer would be to live a life of valleys, and for once, it seemed, she'd reached a tall, green hill.

Then again, Meg had one thing right: Liddy moved fast. Often too fast for her own good. That's how she'd ended up married to Mister Wrong in the first place. She'd followed him out to the desert, where he wanted to be, and her existence there became a living metaphor. Her dry, dusty reality.

And she didn't care to think about her stupidity with a married drifter. What possessed her to go off with a stranger? She hugged herself a little tighter. When he had appeared on the beach like some kind of alluring kindred spirit, she'd been intrigued. And when he'd looked at her like a slice of watermelon on a blazingly hot day, especially so soon after her surgery, well, he had found her kryptonite. Until then she had felt ugly and weak, but his attention managed to help her forget her truths. Now, all she felt was shame, a constant mental flogging that would be her undoing, if she let it.

"Liddy," Meg said. "I'm sorry. I didn't mean to hurt you—"

"It's fine. You didn't. In fact, you're probably right."

"Not if you think that I meant you were shallow." Her friend's voice quivered. They had reached the end of the pavement that gave way to the harbor mouth and soon they would have to turn around. In front of them, a lone fisher boat chugged out toward the open, blackened sea, a harsh spotlight guiding its way. "I'm afraid for you, Liddy. That's all this is."

Liddy cut her a look. "You don't have to be. The doctor says my prognosis is good. I'm feeling better all the time."

"It's not that. I'm worried that you'll lose your heart to this guy."

"Don't."

"Maybe he's not ready for a whirling dervish like you."

Liddy laughed. "What?"

"Oh, I've no doubt he could fall in love with you, but what happens when he begins to worry about your health? He's already been through a trauma." She let out a worried sigh. "Maybe he'll never be able to commit to you or maybe not to anyone. And you deserve someone who can."

Liddy exhaled and began walking again, turning toward home. She had not considered Meg's dire prediction, nor had she focused on her illness much. It was, after all, behind her. "Let's not get ahead of ourselves, okay? Right now, Beau and I are just getting to know each other. He's funny, and I enjoyed his company last night. No need to start obsessing over what may or may not happen in the future. Can we at least agree on that?"

Meg linked her arm through Liddy's. "Yes, we can. But I swear, Liddy, if he hurts you he'll have me to deal with—and you know I'm not kidding one iota. I'll do it!"

Liddy chuckled, thinking back to that night a few months ago when Meg threatened to key her ex-husband's car. "Yes, I believe you will."

SUNDAY MORNING, AND DUTY CALLED. A large group of seniors from Arizona were checking in—taking advantage of the hotel's Sunday through Wednesday discount. The men were there to play golf (no surprise there), and the ladies all wanted to have their hair set. All twenty-one of them. Trace came in early to help Liddy make the calls to the private cell phones of shop owners all over town. Had to make special arrangements for Monday appointments, since most of the salons would be closed.

"Whooey," Trace said when she'd hung up the phone for the last time. "Was worried the town would run out of rollers."

Liddy laughed hard, releasing an un-ladylike snort. "I could almost feel Javier rolling his eyes when I begged him for a spot. And for a Monday, too."

Trace gasped. "Did he give you one?"

"In return for a voucher to the restaurant, yes, he did."

"Well, you're slick. I crossed him off my list a long time ago because he told me he threw out all of his rollers."

"He told me that, too, but amazingly he found a stash of them when I mentioned the voucher."

"Ha. Well, hopefully the restaurant will still be kickin' when he wants to use it. Otherwise, you'll have to come up with some other kind of bribe. Cash worked just fine for all of my salon owners."

Liddy twisted her lips into a frown. "Things have been awfully quiet over there, haven't they? Maybe nothing is happening in the restaurant after all."

Trace shook her head. "That's not what I heard."

Liddy raised an eyebrow. Thankfully the lobby had cleared of grey hairs and oversized luggage. Two of the bellmen had stepped outside for a smoke, and from her spot behind the desk she noticed Hannah take a rather relaxed sip from a flask before stashing it below the counter. "Are you going to elaborate?"

"Well, Jojo over at Hair-A-Lot just told me that Chef was in for a face peel and had some things waxed."

Liddy wrinkled her nose. "Guys get those?"

Trace glanced around and lowered her voice. "Yeah, and she says he's lost some weight, too. And that he asked her to shape his eyebrows for him."

"No kidding."

Trace straightened and shrugged. "He *is* Italian."

"So he's part of the mafia now?"

"Maybe."

Liddy groaned. "Oh, brother. Maybe slow down on reading all those murder mysteries."

"Okay, you laugh, but *everyone's* been talking about weird things going on in the restaurant at late hours, and now Chef is suddenly having himself all smoothed and powdered like some kind of don." She shook her head. "I don't know about you, but I'm staying on that man's good side."

"Maybe he won't be back."

Trace stuck her face close to Liddy's. "You hear something?"

Liddy recoiled. "No, not at all. But you said he hasn't been around awhile and, I don't know, Hans was evasive the last time I even mentioned Chef's existence."

"Hmm. It *is* all pretty bizarre, if you ask me. When I'm here I keep one eye on the lobby and the other eye on the door, just in case the cops come bustin' in." She touched her purse, a little used number she picked up from Downtown Thrift that hung on a nail beneath the desk. "They show up and I'm grabbin' this baby and getting out of here." She leaned forward. "There's mace in here, if you ever need it."

The desk phone rang and Liddy answered it before she could react to Trace's offer.

"Liddy, it's Beau."

Her pulse quickened. "Oh, hey." With her tongue suddenly tied, it was the best she could do.

"I thought I might find you there. Are you able to talk for a minute?"

Considering all guests were apparently taking a nap, she said, "Sure."

"Great. I thought if you were going to the service this evening, you and I could grab a pizza afterward. Would you like to?"

She thought about this. He'd qualified his invitation with church attendance, but had he meant to? And did grabbing a pizza constitute a date? Maybe he just wanted to clear up any misunderstandings about last Wednesday night's coffee date, you know, that wasn't really a date.

Was she overthinking this?

Liddy glanced at the clock. If she left work on time, which she surely would, she would have plenty of time to freshen up in time for the evening service. "Yes, I believe I will be there tonight. I'd love to grab pizza with you."

"Great. I'll meet you there."

She hung up the phone. Did he mean meet you "there" as in at the church or at the pizza place?

"What's got your face all screwed up?"

Liddy blinked hard. "Huh?"

"Well, for one thing, you've got a strange look on your face … like you've just been asked to the prom. Not that I would know what that felt like …"

Liddy felt the red creeping through her skin. How dumb. "It was nothing."

"Okay, well then, here." Trace tossed a roster onto the

desk. "I'm leaving but wanted to give you this list of couples who would like wake-up calls tomorrow. And don't give me that look—if I'd had to teach them all how to program their phones, I would've gone mad, mad I tell you!"

Liddy chuckled. "Fine. No problem. I'll program them all before I leave this evening."

Trace hurried out the front doors, stealing furtive glances over each shoulder as she did.

As IT TURNED OUT, Beau was nowhere to be found at the service that night, so in between listening to a riveting sermon on the Beatitudes and greeting those around her, Liddy spent a good chunk of time resisting the temptation to dwell on being stood up. At church, no less. After all, she as well as anyone understood that last-minute emergencies do arise—say, a flat tire or broken heel or any number of unplanned and unwelcome events. At least she could say that she had spent the past hour plus in a healthy place, surrounded by people absorbed in prayer. Certainly this would make it easier for her to forgive Beau for this slight.

She made her way out of the sanctuary and into the crowded hall where she found Beau standing against the wall, watching for her. He wore a white tee shirt, jeans low on his hips, and a smile on his face. "Ready to go?" he asked.

Her mouth fell open, and her mind played backward. Maybe he hadn't exactly said he would be attending the service as well. She had assumed that. He stood in front of her, looking fit and tan, his hair windblown and ruffled as if he had just pulled up in a convertible. She wanted to run her fingers through its waves. When he reached out to guide her toward the exit, she thought she might melt at his touch. *So much for those worries of yours, Meg.*

"You know," he said as he held the car door for her, "you don't need to wear the hat on my account."

She had worn the black floppy one again because the time had changed and the sun would stay out longer—hazy as it may have been. "You don't like it?" she asked.

He slid into the driver's seat. "I just thought you might be more comfortable without it."

She watched as he put the car in first gear and started her up. Going out without her hat was not yet an option. Her hair continued to grow in well, but what if the wind picked up and poor Beau caught a glimpse of her scars? True, the hat may have been a painful reminder of his wife's illness, but what lurked beneath Liddy's virgin hair would take them both to an entirely different level of intimacy.

And she wasn't sure either of them was ready for that.

BEAU PULLED THE CAR into the lot behind Nocello's Café and hopped out. "Would you like to wait here while I grab our pizza at the window? They're usually fast."

Liddy nodded. "I would. Thanks."

He strode across the lot to the take-out window at the back of the café. When he arrived, the line was longer than he'd expected, so he glanced toward his car, hoping to catch Liddy's eye to let her know it might be a few minutes. He stopped short, and winced. Liddy was peering into the mirror and adjusting her hat.

He crossed his arms at his chest and stepped up the line. He'd wanted her to forget about her surgery, but somehow he had highlighted it instead. *Good job making her feel uncomfortable about the hat, doofus.*

After he'd paid for their dinner, he put a smile back on his face and strolled across the parking lot. Inside the car he handed her the pizza. "Hold this for us?"

She nodded, but was otherwise quiet. "I hope you're okay with eating at my house rather than at the restaurant—even though I don't live quite as close to the beach as you do," he said, attempting to pry away at her thoughts. "Figured you might like some quiet."

Liddy sighed. "How'd you know?"

"I've stayed in my share of hotels."

She laughed lightly. "It was crazy today. Fun, but crazy."

"How so?"

"Tour bus of octogenarians."

He laughed deeply. "Enough said."

Liddy wandered into his home ahead of him, slipped out of her shoes, and slid them up against the wall. "You don't mind, I hope? My feet aren't used to shoes."

"Not at all. Shoes are overrated anyway." He kicked off his own and plunked the pizza onto the table. "I'll grab some plates."

"I'll help," she said, padding after him into the kitchen that he had shared with Anne. He set two glasses on the sink and Liddy filled them with filtered water, as if she had always done so. As she carried them to the table, she stopped and nodded at the bottle of red next to his fridge.

He smiled. "What's pizza without a glass of Cab?" Beau

grabbed a corkscrew and a couple of wine glasses and followed her to the dining table. After he uncorked the wine and left it out to breathe, he went back to the kitchen for the plates and forks.

Liddy stepped out of the kitchen, and when she returned, her wide-brimmed hat had been replaced with a turban-like black scarf. Seated, Liddy held up the fork he'd given her, examining it. "You really are quite formal, aren't you?" she said.

"Wouldn't want you to think I was a caveman or anything."

She shrugged. "Hadn't really thought that. Now, if we were having, say, filet mignon and you hadn't brought out steak knives, well, then I might have wondered." She winked at him before picking up a slice of pizza with her hands.

Beau poured them each some wine and dug into the pizza himself. He'd hardly known how to anticipate this evening, though he had made the attempt. In the end, the idea of dating again after spending years rooted deeply in marriage, with all its mountains and valleys, had left him without a game plan. So he had decided to wing it. "By the way," he said, wiping his hand on a napkin, "sorry about the hat comment."

Her fingers reflexively found the crown of her head, which was topped by the flimsy fabric. Her mouth and eyes formed a penetrating look and focused it on him. "Sorry? For what?"

He took a deep breath and reached for the bottle on the table. He was so stupid. Why had he brought it up at all? Had he learned nothing? "More wine?" he asked.

She dropped her hand into her lap and gave him what seemed a self-conscious laugh. "Wait ... oh my gosh ... are you trying to ply me with alcohol?"

He straightened. "No. I wouldn't—"

She caught his hand as he set the bottle down. "I was kidding."

He grinned at her. "Oh."

She wrinkled her nose, still smiling at him. "I really don't have much of a filter sometimes," she said, obviously not too concerned about this. "In case you hadn't noticed."

"I see. And have you always had this affliction?"

She quirked her head to one side, those fiery eyes watching him. "Are you wondering if I was different before the surgery? Like maybe the surgeon cut out some of my good sense or something?"

He coughed. "No! I'd never think something like that."

"You are so fun to tease."

Beau sat back. In a movement that took all of 1.5 seconds, he wadded up his napkin and pitched it at her.

She laughed well and grabbed another slice of pizza.

Man, she was fun to have around.

They sat there and devoured the pizza, and the wine, and somewhere in the middle he switched on some smooth jazz to fill in the background. Together they washed the dishes and put them away, and then they found themselves sitting a respectful distance from each other on the couch.

"Tell me about your wife," she said at one point.

"She was an artist. She was beautiful." He paused, his voice thick. "She suffered ... I hated that."

"I'm so sorry," she said. "How are you doing now?"

"It was difficult ... seeing her weak one moment and full of life the next. I held onto hope for years, often becoming deflated in the process—or at least battle weary—especially those times when her health took a dangerous turn." A sigh escaped him from deep in his gut. "In the days after I lost her, I found myself becoming overwhelmed ... first by grief and then by a kind of relief. The guilt over that latter emotion was treacherous."

"I can't imagine, Beau. It must've been terribly difficult for both of you."

"Yeah." Years of education, and that was all he could muster. Yet it didn't matter. She didn't ask for more, and at the moment, he couldn't offer it.

Instead, they settled into the cushions, leaning more comfortably into each other, becoming engrossed in the music filling the space, and, he thought, in each other. At some point, he pulled her into his arms and she allowed herself to be cradled against him. He sat there, listening to the rise and fall of her breathing, wanting for nothing else.

Comfortable as they both were, he had no secret plans to ruin things by moving more quickly than was advisable. Beau liked Liddy. A lot. He'd known this for months—even sensing something special about her before they had formally met. Some might even have called it divine intervention.

Still, why rush a good thing? That had always been his motto, and as he leaned his cheek against her temple, he saw no reason to make a change.

Chapter Thirteen

IT WAS ALL HAPPENING SO FAST. One minute she was committed to a man forever, digging in to a life in the desert, far away from the dreams that had long lay dormant, and the next she was recovering from unthinkable surgery and falling for a man she barely knew. Liddy stared at the ceiling in her bedroom, unable to sleep. Beau intrigued her. He made her think of new dreams, ideas she had barely touched on prior to now.

Like having children someday.

She laid a hand on her heart. Mercy. She'd been married to Shawn for long enough to have conceived a child … but never did. Truth was, she never wanted to be a mother. Not until … recently. On the fourth morning of her hospital stay, something profound had occurred. Until that day, she had not been alone in her room. Not one time. Although she had moved in for the week, her roommates had all been day-timers, women who had come for their regular chemotherapy treatments.

She had never known a person with cancer before then. At least not very well. But each day a new patient would arrive and she, thankful to be alive, would chat with each of them. She'd tell these women about her surgery, and her budding faith, and often, they laid bare their deepest fears, and when they had gone for their treatments, she would pray. Unorganized, ragged prayers for women she had only known for hours.

And then one day, she was alone. No cancer patient to share her room, nor nurse to fuss about her. She was content. New friends from church had brought her books. Stacks of them. She longed to dig in, but headaches brought on by trying to focus on words on a page prevented her from doing so. Instead, she reclined in her bed, allowing the dusting of leaves along the glass windows to cheer her.

She heard a voice that day, clear and strong as the day was quiet, and she knew: she would be married again someday and have children.

Funny how she never questioned that voice she heard, nor found herself afraid of it. Funnier still was that she found herself warming to the part about having children when, until now, little buggers of her own had never been part of her plans.

She pushed the covers off the bed and padded to the sink for a glass of water, then made her way out onto the deck, exhaling into the night. The inky blue sky stretched out like a backdrop of velvet for diamond-studded stars. A cat molded itself to a downstairs neighbor's fence. A couple of bats propelled themselves over rooftops. Liddy breathed in the sea air again and thought about Beau.

Last night at her questioning, he touched on his relationship with Anne. Tears pricked at the back of her eyes as she recalled the things he'd said about her suffering, and the emotions that flitted across his face.

The women Liddy had met in her hospital room that week had all been afraid and yet so eager to delve into chit chat, as if their banter could somehow put off the inevitability of

treatment. The recollection caused her to shiver. She remembered the way their husbands tended to them. "Would you like
a pillow, darling?" "Can I open the window for you, sugar?"
Heroes, every one of them.

A voice pierced her thoughts. "You're up late."

At the sound, Liddy twisted her neck quickly, causing it to
spasm. Zack stood on the path below her deck, like some kind
of derelict Romeo standing in the moonlight. She only wished
she knew where she had stashed her poison ...

"Can we talk?"

Liddy shook her head, pushing away from the deck railing.
He'd interrupted her musings while they were still so foreboding. She would add that to the things she would never forgive
him for.

"I'm leaving. Just wanted to say goodbye."

She wanted to wave him away with a single finger, but why
meet him at his level? Her eyes had adjusted to the darkness of
the path below. He looked small and bent over like an old man
leaning on a cane.

"It's freezing out here," he called up to her, his roughened
voice scraping across her solitude.

Somewhere a window slid open. "Shh!"

Liddy rolled her eyes. "Hurry up." On her way through her
apartment and to the front door, she pulled a blanket off the
couch and wrapped it around herself. She opened the door and
let Zack in, watching as he limped toward a chair at her small
dining table. "What happened to you?"

"Too many hours spent leaning over a sandcastle. Kink in
my back became a pulled muscle."

Good.

"Doc has me on shots and muscle relaxers."

Liddy sat across from him, crossing her arms on the table. "Leave it to you to turn beachcombing into a lethal activity."

He eyed her, his expression pained.

She blew out a breath. Her ill-advised dalliance with him already seemed like a distant memory. "What're you doing here in the middle of the night?"

"Could ask you the same." He shrugged. "Why does the beautiful patient not slumber?"

Liddy shook her head. *Oh brother.* "Zack, where's your wife?"

"Waiting for me to come home."

"Then, go."

"Yeah. Not sure why she's taking me back, but God love her, she is." He sighed and gave her a self-assessing nod. "Anyway, I wasn't planning to bother you again, but I saw you up and thought this would be my chance to tell you that I regret having caused you pain."

Liddy tilted her head and watched him. He had weathered in the last week, and maybe that wasn't such a bad thing. She wanted to hate him, but somehow could not. She didn't like him all that much, though.

Zack braced a hand on the table—he was wearing a wedding band now—and pushed himself back up, groaning pathetically as he did. "And now I have said it."

Liddy continued to sit. "I found someone else, you know."

He turned to her. "I knew you would. Is he kind?"

"Very."

Zack nodded as he made his way to the door. "No doubt, next time I see you, you'll be with him." He stopped before leaving her apartment. "I'll steer clear. Wouldn't want your man to take me down in a headlock or anything."

"Get out of here," she said, only this time when she spoke to him her voice was lighter than it should have been. He looked like Father Time, for heaven's sake.

When he'd gone, she padded back upstairs, a million more thoughts in her mind. She'd told Zack that she'd found someone else.

But had she really?

LIDDY LEANED HER TEMPLE against one hand. Thomas zipped by on his way to pull a car around for a guest. "Hung over?" he asked.

"I wish." So tired. That's what she got for staring into the sky in the middle of the night. Insomnia had shot her with its arrow last night, taking her captive until light had come. And then, of course, she fell asleep for less than an hour before the alarm rang.

Hans approached her, his eyes agog. "Are you having a relapse?"

She straightened. "Not at all. Just tired this morning. What can I do for you?"

"Because if you're not feeling well, I'll call in Trace to help."

Liddy shook her head. "Absolutely not. I'm fine. Really." Truthfully, lack of sleep combined with her recovery made for a fragile landing this morning. She hoped her health wouldn't suffer from the day's precarious start. Her doctor had already warned her that she may have gone back to work too quickly.

Her boss blew out an exasperated breath. "I'm tired this morning, too."

"Insomnia takes no prisoners."

His chin lifted and he looked her in the eye, repeating the word "insomnia" as if unsure of what it meant. "Yes," he finally said. "Insomnia. That was it. Now, while it's quiet, call these guests and confirm their dinner reservations for tonight. While you're at it, see if you can get some of them to take a harbor cruise or something."

"Got it."

He skittered away, passing Thomas on his way back inside from the valet desk. Thomas slapped his hands on the counter in front of her and lowered his voice. "He looks like he tied one on last night, too. Hey," he shifted a look around, "you two weren't out together, I hope."

Liddy recoiled. "Get lost. I have work to do."

Thomas laughed and held up both hands in surrender. "It was a joke, Liddy. Saw Hans last night, over in the bar. He was still there when I left long after happy hour."

Fatigue was causing her vision to tunnel. "Uh-huh," she said, hoping he'd leave her alone to make her calls.

"You know, now that I think of it there was some other guy with him. Was throwing all kinds of money around. Didn't look like a local."

She kept working. "Most people around here aren't," she said. They did work in a hotel, after all.

"If Hans weren't married, shoot, I think he would've been really into that guy. Laughed at all the guy's jokes like he was a celebrity."

"Is that right?"

Thomas slapped the counter again. "Oh, I see. Liddy's suddenly too good to listen to gossip. Why didn't you just say so?"

Liddy leaned her head back and let out a sigh. "Thomas, I'm exhausted. Didn't sleep well last night and I have to be here when I'd rather be curled up at home." The phone on her desk rang and she brushed Thomas's hand away before he could answer it. "This is Liddy. How may I help you?"

"Good morning, Liddy. It's Beau. Not a good time?"

Her scowl vanished. "No, no. It is." Thomas backed away from her then, watching her with curious eyes, but she swiveled her chair away from his gaze. "How are you this morning?"

"Great. Although I'm concerned that you may be cold out there today by the water."

"Oh? Actually, it's no cooler than usual."

"Glad to hear it, since you left your coat in the back of my car last evening."

Hmm. Yes, she had. Not on purpose, of course. They had played musical cars last evening, leaving hers in the church parking lot while they went to Beau's home for pizza. By the time she realized she had left her coat behind, Liddy had already started up her car after Beau had dropped her off. She could have flagged him down again, but how silly would that have been? Besides, would it be so bad if she had left behind a little motivation?

"Oh, thanks so much for worrying about me," she said with a laugh. "Maybe bring it to church next time?"

"Or I could take you to lunch today. Are you busy?"

"No, I'm free." And suddenly quite energetic, too. "But I don't have a lot of time. Would you like to eat at the hotel restaurant?"

"It's a date."

They decided on a time and Liddy hung up the phone, fairly fixated on the fact that Beau had used the word "date."

UNFORTUNATELY, ALL RESEMBLANCE TO an actual date left the building the moment the chef could be heard shouting at the kitchen staff in a foreign language. From her vantage point at a window-side table, Liddy counted one-two-three staff members emerging from the kitchen in long, harried strides.

"Wow," Beau said, taking another roll from the basket. "You didn't say anything about a show with our lunch."

"Try working here every day."

He chuckled. "You live a charmed life, Liddy. What language is that, by the way?"

"Hmm. I think it's a hybrid between Italian and Spanish. Ital-span?"

Beau laughed his deep, hearty laugh and they finished up their salads—the steak salad for him, the Caesar with shrimp for her—and emptied the basket of rolls. Liddy fiddled with her napkin, aware that the dining room had grown quiet again with so many ears tuned to the kitchen.

She gave Beau a worried glance. "I really am sorry about this."

He smiled. "Don't be. I should be thanking you, since most of my Mondays are usually rather boring."

"Thanks."

"But I did want to ask you something. Would you like to go on a real date with me this weekend?"

She peered at him. "What do you call pizza last night?"

"I'd call that supper." He smiled and paused, eyeing her, as if watching for her reaction. "Liddy, I would like to take you to dinner at a French restaurant on Saturday night. Go with me?"

He asked her, not in a timid way, but with a confidence that she would say yes. Not that he was cocky, just downright forward and sexy, causing butterflies to brush at every one of her nerve endings. She wanted to lunge across the table and kiss him, but she managed to hold it together. (After all, the chef could be carrying a knife ...)

She agreed to their "official" date, and walked him out to his car in the parking lot, the air awash with the ocean's touch. He reached into the back seat and pulled out her coat. "You don't want to forget this," he said, draping it around her, then rubbing the fleshy part of her shoulders to warm them up. He made no move to close up the inches between them.

Liddy, however, couldn't wait. Or she wouldn't. Whatever. She pulled him toward her, asking if she could give him a "garlic kiss."

And didn't wait for his answer.

HOW LONG HAD BEAU BEEN staring at this screen? How far had his eyes wandered down the rows of data before he realized his brain had not engaged with any of it? Beau sat back in his office chair, stretching his arms over his head and linking his hands together.

Liddy had kissed him. Lightly, but brazenly. Right there in the parking lot. He couldn't get the taste of her out of his head. Dr. Buchold—an avid sailor with a boat in the harbor *and* his client—had ridden his bike through the hotel parking lot just as it was happening. And Beau knew … if not for that little interruption at the moment Liddy's lips had grazed his, he might have crushed her to him in wide open daylight. As it was, it took monumental effort for him not to do a cartwheel on the pavement once Liddy and the good doctor had each rounded the building, out of his sight.

"Well, that's some goofy grin on your face." Jill hustled into Beau's office. "I take it you've come up with some drop-dead amazing marketing plan for Seaside Medical Group?" She dropped a stack of messages on his desk.

He shifted his eyes toward that stack, then to his assistant. "I'm still mulling."

"Mulling, huh? Been a lot of that lately." Never one to ask for an invitation, Jill took a seat in the chair across from his desk. "Business has never been better, though, so I guess you can't complain."

He unhooked his hands and pulled himself closer to the desk. "I'll say. As you know, I'm booked with appointments for the rest of the week. Lots of reputations to represent out there in the medical community."

She gestured toward the messages she'd left on his desk. "And even more in that stack. Doesn't leave you a lot of time for … mulling."

He knew Jill well and she was prying. In her own way, of course—ever since he had begun working for this company as a new recruit. When he purchased the company from the man who had started it years earlier, Jill stayed with him. He always admired the way she could adjust to bullet-fast changes in the industry.

Yet he often cringed inside at the way she could read him. She would peck at him, like a mother hen, until she uncovered what she believed to be true.

He grabbed the wad of messages. "Guess I had better attempt to call some of these folks back before my next meeting," he said, trying to deflect her fixation on the word "mulling." Surely she read more into his statement than he was willing to divulge.

Jill nodded. "You should. Especially the one from Wendy."

Beau raised an eyebrow. "Oh?"

She stood and leaned against the door frame, her mouth frowning, her voice coaxing. "Let her down easy, Beau." She turned and walked away, her stride clipped, almost formal. With a sigh, Beau picked up the phone.

Chapter Fourteen

THE AFTERNOON BEGAN INNOCENTLY ENOUGH. After lunch, Liddy wandered back into work to finish out her day. Adrenaline from Beau's company—and the kiss—kept her going until late afternoon.

Then about an hour before she was due to leave the inn, Hans called together the concierge staff, including bellmen, valets, and others, for a meeting in the conference room. The bell captain would cover all three desks.

Thankful for some time away from the frenetic pace of guest services, Liddy strode into the conference room and took a seat at the large oval table next to Trace, who had just arrived. There was water and donuts for everyone. Yes to the water, but no thank you to the sugar-encrusted fat pills.

Hans arrived with several thick binders, which he slid onto the table. "Pass these out. There aren't enough to go around, so share with the person next to you."

"What are they?" one of the bellmen wanted to know.

"SOP binders. Standard operating procedures."

One of the valets whistled. "Exciting stuff."

Laughter punctuated the airspace in the room.

"All right, enough of that," Hans said. "We're going to

147

crack open these babies and read through each of the points. That way no one can come back to me and say they don't know proper procedures around here."

Laughter turned to groaning. If Hans didn't hurry, he'd have a room full of defectors soon.

Liddy breathed in a deep pocket of air and pulled her shoulders back. So many people in the room. She looked over at the binder open in front of Trace, but the words were so tiny. Why would their boss use such a small font?

Two more staff members slid into their seats, filling the room to capacity. Liddy rolled up her sleeves. The room was becoming so warm.

She glanced at the others. No perspiration on foreheads anywhere, or people fanning themselves. Instead, yawns and expressionless faces surrounded her. Liddy turned back toward the binder, her eyes narrowing as she tried to focus on the page. Was this the beginning of a headache? She pressed a finger to her temple, willing away the start of the uncomfortable sensation.

One more hour, one more hour ...

Hans was pointing down the line of employees, expecting everyone to participate in this read-a-thon. They were all in second grade, going around the circle during reading time. One guy read, then another, and then a front desk clerk. Trace was up next.

Liddy fought to keep her head upright. Her peripheral vision was nearly lost, crowded out by a whammy of pressure along the outer edges of her eyes. When was the last time ...?

The room began to spin at the recollection of the last time Liddy had experienced another odd and unwelcome sensation.

The doctor had called them focal seizures, and she'd had them for months before realizing what they were. Barbed fingers of fear threaded through her. Surgery was supposed to have ended them forever.

Trace began to read.

"Excuse me," Liddy said, abruptly pushing away from the table. She stood, ignoring the sudden upward dart of chins and what sounded like a murmur as she climbed over feet to get out of the room.

Outside of the meeting room, Liddy dashed down the hall toward her desk, where her purse lay hidden in a drawer. Hannah barely acknowledged her from her perch across the lobby. Dizziness threatened to undo Liddy. She pulled a bottle from her purse, unscrewed the cap, and swallowed one small pill with her spit. *Breathe, Liddy, breathe.*

As the pill, leftover from the days in between her diagnosis and subsequent surgery, slid down her throat, the chatter of her heartbeat began to calm. The tension near her temples lessened. She glanced around, relieved to find the lobby still empty and the bell captain thoroughly captivated by something on her iPhone screen.

Carefully, Liddy tucked the half-empty bottle of pills back into her purse and made a mental note to have her anti-seizure meds prescription refilled before it expired.

SHE LEFT WORK EARLY FRIDAY AFTERNOON, and after a stop at the mall, arrived home in plenty of time to get ready for her date with Beau. The little black dress, or LBD as Meg would call it, might be a staple for every woman's wardrobe, but

Liddy had never actually owned one until today. She had hoped it would hug her curves in the way that it should, but she had lost weight since the surgery, and as she looked herself over in the mirror she felt more like a hanger with fabric draped over it than a woman with hips and breasts.

She frowned. He would be here at any second. Maybe another perspective? With little hope, Liddy grabbed a second dress from her closet, dashed out her door, careful to note first whether Beau had arrived. She looked left, then right. He had not, so she stepped across the landing and knocked on the door across from hers. Her neighbor Brandon worked odd hours mostly, so she rarely saw him. But she knew he drove an Audi and wore suits, so he must have taste.

The door opened and a willowy blonde wearing turquoise heels and a slightly bad attitude assessed her. "Hey," Liddy said. "I was looking for Brandon, but maybe you'll help?" She stuck out a hand. "I'm Liddy, Brandon's neighbor, by the way."

The woman shook her hand, her eyes so narrowed Liddy had second thoughts about whether Brandon's friend would give her an honest opinion.

"This may sound weird but … I have a date tonight." Liddy looked over her shoulder and back again. "That's not the weird part."

The woman snickered just as Brandon appeared behind her. "Hey, Liddy."

Liddy's cheeks were growing warm. Maybe this was stupid. "Hey, yourself. I just met your … "

Brandon put a hand on the woman's shoulder. "Business partner."

The woman scowled so delicately that Liddy couldn't help but admire her. To be that beautiful when screwing up your face, well, not everyone could attain it. *Brava.*

Brandon laughed. "Kidding. This is my girlfriend, Felicity." He brought her limp hand to his mouth and gave it a kiss, all the while watching her with wide, upturned eyes. He wrapped her arm around his waist and kissed her ear.

She wanted to say "never mind" and zip back into her own apartment, but they both stood in front of her with looks of *well?* on their faces, so she inhaled and let it out. "I'm just wondering what you think of this dress I'm wearing." The statement came out like a question and she realized she was nervous. A man with good looks, charm, faith, and gainful employment wanted to take her to a fancy restaurant, and suddenly she had no idea how to behave, let alone what to wear. The fanciest place Shawn ever took her to had parts of dead animals on the walls and served steak with prices ending in ninety-nine. She hadn't had many reasons to dress up in a long, long time.

She held up the second choice to get their opinions. "We're going to a French place and—I don't know—something's just not right."

Both of Brandon's brows tilted downward until she wondered if he could see. His lips hung in mid part.

Felicity, on the other hand, was all over it. She shook her head at the dress on the hanger. "No, forget about that one. Follow me."

Liddy ducked into her neighbor's home, noting the plush white carpet that stretched across the floor's width. She sunk into every step. If this were her place, she'd never use the couch.

"Here," Felicity said as she emerged from a bedroom and began to wrap a belt around Liddy's waist. She stood back. "Yes, that helps. And put these on. They'll sparkle beneath your hat." She handed Liddy gorgeous silver earrings that shimmered under the lights.

"Oh. These are spectacular." Liddy glanced up at her new best friend. "Are you sure?"

Felicity leaned forward, enclosing the earrings in Liddy's hand. "Trust me. He won't be able to take his eyes off you."

Though she would never admit it out loud, Felicity's words were her aim: to make it perilously difficult for Beau to take his eyes off of her. There was a recent time when, at least somewhere in the recesses of her mind, she believed this not too difficult a task. But that was before the divorce, and the surgery, and all the *hats*, which covered up all kinds of evidence. Her hair had grown in dark and lush, and though it was still very short, she could—maybe—be persuaded to remove the hat sometime soon.

But not yet.

She thought about all this back at her apartment while admiring Felicity's earrings in the little mirror posted by the front door. Beau was nearly ten minutes late, but she couldn't complain. If he had been on time at church that first night they'd sat together, would she ever have met him? Punctuality, she had decided, was not a deal breaker.

Her doorbell rang. In the evening's fading light, Beau dazzled her in a navy cashmere sport coat and collared shirt, while wearing a smile that made her forget whatever it was that had thrown her into a tizzy only minutes before.

BEAU GESTURED WITH HIS FORK to the "petit plat" on the table displaying various starters. "Bone marrow?" he offered.

Liddy scrunched her nose. "I believe I'll stick with the artichoke. Thank you, though."

He laughed and speared some for himself. She was cute and laughed easily. Any stress over whether this French country bistro was the right choice for their first official date had dissipated. The food was fancy, but the atmosphere was not. He hated stuffy. Something told him she did, too.

"It's beautiful in here," she said.

Those big brown eyes captivated him. *You're beautiful,* he thought. "I'm glad you think so," he said. "I've always thought this place had character without being over the top."

"Always thought so, huh? You come here often, then?"

Beau held back a smirk. She left off "with other women." She was tricky, that one. He appreciated that. Not that he'd let her get away with it. He pointed toward the appetizers. "Try the escargot."

She ignored his invitation, and instead watched him with a wide-open expression while demurely eating her artichoke. Not an easy task.

The waiter arrived with their salads and Beau poured them each some wine. They discussed their favorite movies—chick flicks for her, dramas for him—and the types of music they preferred—eclectic offerings of country and pop for her, mostly jazz for him (he'd have to show her the light). So far they had both avoided talk about their previous relationships. At least he did, and he suspected her of doing so as well. Then again, they had pretty well covered those topics previously. Tonight, he hoped, could be about them—what they wanted, who they each were.

Sometimes he wondered if he still knew the answers to those questions about himself.

Their salad plates were cleared and for a moment a lull fell between them. But it wasn't an uncomfortable one. They immersed themselves in the silence, sneaking glances at each other in between sips of their drinks. He enjoyed taking it slow.

Then her chin tilted slightly, and her lips parted as if in a question. Her eyes smiled before her mouth did. Actually, those eyes of hers were dancing and she appeared to be watching something over his shoulder.

"Sir?" Beau turned to find a waiter standing by his side, something large and plastic in his outstretched arms. A bib. The waiter was holding a bib. "For you, sir." He proceeded to lean around Beau and tie the monstrosity around his neck.

Liddy placed both of her hands on the table and leaned forward, the laughter in her face taunting him. He put on his best winning smile, but he could feel the heat of redness stretching all the way to his ears. The trouble with light skin. Who was he kidding? This moment would have made *anyone* turn red.

The waiter left and Beau sat back, cognizant of the sound of thin strips of plastic rubbing together with every move he made. Liddy, for her part, hadn't stopped laughing.

"You really have been here before," she said, cracking herself up.

"Meaning?"

"Um ..."—she pointed to his bib—"obviously, they know

you're sloppy."

Beau shook his head, laughing back at her. He didn't dare look around to any of the other white-clothed tables. Hopefully, they weren't drawing attention. "You're kidding, I hope. It's for the bouillabaisse I ordered." He felt almost certain that this was the case. The waiter hadn't exactly said.

She shrugged, that laughter lingering on her full lips. "Sure. For the seafood soup. Whatever."

"You're too much."

"If it helps—it's really hot. The bib, I mean. It's a hot … bib."

Beau rolled his eyes and groaned just in time for the server to appear with her prawns and his bouillabaisse. What a tease. He found himself cracking up, too, though—while also making a mental note to avoid all foods that required bibs on future dates.

After dinner, Beau drove Liddy back to her apartment, their conversation never stopping to refuel. Their banter was unabashed and easy, and to his mind, he and Liddy were quickly moving from tentative to *what time should I pick you up tomorrow?* The thought awed him in myriad ways—both thrilling and frightening. Perhaps it was time to slow things down.

Once inside, Liddy kept her hat on but kicked off her shoes. He willed himself to avoid looking at the line of buttons running down the center of her dress, and at the way the silky black fabric hugged her body.

She padded over to the kitchen. "Can I get you some water?"

Beau told her no and slipped out of his coat to hang it over the back of one of the chairs around her dining table. He watched as she stepped over to the fireplace in her bare feet, and flipped a switch.

Voilà. A fire was born.

Liddy curled up on the couch, and he sat beside her. They continued to talk about nothing much until she reached for some silly little book on her coffee table. She flipped through it then, and he realized there were no words on the pages. It was a children's book about a big black dog that was both funny and wry and it amazed him how much the illustrations tickled her.

As naturally as the sun had set on his way over to pick her up that night, Beau reached toward Liddy. He found himself sliding one hand behind her back and pulling her toward him, kissing her softly at first, then without holding back. The hard spine of a book landed on top of one of his loafers. The fake fire crackled. He drew her closer, reveling in the sound of her breath on his skin, and how her body folded into his embrace.

Reluctantly, he slowed himself. Her eyes fluttered open, throwing him flashes of yearning, of affection. She didn't pull away. He took her in, then. Those eyes, the shape of her face, the short tendrils of dark hair peeking out from beneath that hat. Without a word, he gently lifted the hat from her head ... and let it fall behind the couch.

Chapter Fifteen

"So you're a couple now?" Meg asked.

"Well, I don't really know ..." Liddy was speaking to Meg through headphones while on her morning beach walk. She detected a hint of something in her friend's voice—trepidation, maybe?

"What ... didn't he say so?"

Liddy laughed uncomfortably. "He didn't give me his class ring or anything, but we spent hours and hours together and then ..."

"And then he kissed you like a man who meant it."

Liddy dodged around a couple of guys tossing a football. "Yes." Even to her own ears her voice sounded wistful. Beau had awakened things both primal and brand new in her. She didn't expect anyone to understand that; after all, Meg had known her when she was married to Shawn. How could a once-married woman realize feelings wholly different—and far better—from those she had experienced before?

Whatever the reason, Liddy was in deep. And she could hardly contain herself. Hence, the impromptu workout on the sand, albeit one that would, hopefully, not push her into the abyss of fatigue. She needed this mental break, especially with another MRI appointment on the horizon soon. These days she found herself with one foot on cloud nine and the other sort of dangling over the edge.

Meg sighed. "Okay, well, I would like to see you two together sometime."

"Then we'll have to set up a double date."

Meg scoffed. "Okay, sure."

"Hey, there's always Thomas."

"I don't want your castoffs!"

Liddy laughed, glad for Meg's lighthearted response. "What was I thinking? Of course you'll have someone amazing with you." She paused. "Whatever happened to—what was his name again? Jim? Jess? Jak—"

"He's long gone. No worries. Of course, I'll dig someone up. Little black book, and all of that." She lowered her voice, suddenly sounding distant, distracted. "Listen, I have to run. Conference call in fifteen. Talk later?"

Liddy nodded, a spritzing of sea spray landing on her skin. "Sure, of course. We'll talk soon."

She continued on, the jeweled path of sand and pebbles and seashell remnants laid out before her. Growing up, Meg had been the first to divulge the details of every crush and sideways glance directed her way. While Liddy had met and married the only boy who'd ever shown interest in her, Meg had a seemingly unending supply of maleness from which to choose. She hoped it wasn't her marital status that had kept Meg from telling her more about the guy she'd dated last year—and abruptly stopped seeing. Had she not shown enough interest? Or was there something more?

With no answer forthcoming, Liddy blew out a sigh. She

switched on her Pandora app and called up some music to keep her motivated and continued her way down the beach.

In the distance, a camera crew of five scanned the ocean, perhaps a news station with an open time slot. Liddy veered around them, eager to keep up her pace, but also curious about whatever it was that seemed to be intriguing the crew long enough to keep their cameras on. As she passed by, she realized that they weren't with the local news station at all, but with a network she'd heard of called Blast.

As she passed by them with the song *Happy* playing through her earpiece, she couldn't help but notice that as the small crew gazed out to sea, they were all, each and every one of them, smiling.

WHEN THE DOORBELL RANG, she was still thinking about the barrier that had been annihilated between them last night. Beau stood on the stoop wearing that sexy grin much like he had less than twelve hours ago. Only this time, instead of well-fitted jacket and slacks, he wore shorts, a tee-shirt softened by a dryer's tumbling, and a Rockies baseball cap.

She, for her part, wore a Dodgers cap.

He grimaced, presumably at her choice of head wear, but kissed her on the lips anyway.

Apparently, no barrier had grown back overnight. She caught herself noticing the way the soft cotton hugged his torso, then forced herself to glance away.

"I brought you something," he said, bringing her blinking gaze back to him. He held out his palm and displayed a nickel-sized drop of sea glass.

She let out a tiny gasp, and plucked it from his hand. The fragment reminded her of the jelly candy she'd loved as a child. The glass looked ruddy ... almost orange, its surface satisfyingly rough, like sugar.

"Ready to go?"

Liddy looked up. "What?"

"To the picnic?"

She closed her hand around the gem. "How did you know ... how much I like sea glass? Because of the inn?"

He watched her with a kind of smile in his eyes, and she tried not to think of the way those same eyes held her spellbound the night before ... on the couch ... mere feet behind them ...

"The bowl."

She tilted her head, trying to understand his words while simultaneously trying to calm the overzealous thump of her heart.

He pointed to the small bookcase in the corner, the one bearing her collection of sea glass, mostly green, white, and the occasional blue. She tossed the pieces in there whenever she'd managed to find one in the sand, carrying it home in the pocket of her hoodie, listening to the pieces jangle together like so much spare change.

"Of course. Well." She looked up from the apricot-colored glass shimmering in her own palm. "Thank you. It's gorgeous. I've never seen this color before. I think it must be fairly rare."

He chuckled softly. "You're welcome. So ... are you ready to go?"

"I am." She grabbed her bag and they headed down the stairs and into the sunshine.

Last night, before he had torn himself away from her, Beau had invited Liddy to a picnic for a local physician's association. His light skin blushed slightly at the invitation, as if he understood that a day of networking—even though the setting was a park abutting the beach—didn't exactly sound romantic.

But he had already RSVP'd, and so it had touched her that he wanted to, well, be seen with her. Not that she wouldn't tease him about it, at least a little.

"Well, I don't know," she had said. "Will there be food?"

"Absolutely. And plenty of first aid," he had quipped.

She remembered how the laughter between them made her feel—like a girl without a worry. Another rarity in her life lately. "You sure do know how to court a gal."

He had wiggled his eyebrows at her then, sending another rather shocking thrill darting through her.

As it happened, the park was close enough to walk from her apartment. It had the best of the both worlds: the sea on one side and plenty of grills and green grass on the other.

He tucked her hand in his as they strolled the half mile or so to the park, and she wondered if he would notice how short her strides had become. When he'd asked her to join him at this "office" picnic of sorts, she'd been surprised by the invitation, but not unhappy about it.

Only now she wished it were just the two of them out for a romantic picnic. Greedy girl. She didn't want to share him.

At the park, visored women poured mimosas as men with deep crevices in their cheeks flicked Frisbees back and forth, their Hawaiian shirts opened to reveal vaporous clouds of grey hair. Keeping her expression from faltering as introductions were made was no easy task. By contrast, several families towing young children and wagons full of towels and buckets also milled about.

Through all the weaving and smiling and hellos tossed around, Beau continued to hold Liddy's hand, the feel of it warm and safe around hers.

"Hey, Beau!" A broad-shouldered man threw a "think fast" pass Beau's way. "Pick-up football game on the field," the guy said, still holding the ball in his throwing arm. "You coming?"

Beau hesitated, sliding a glance at her.

"Go on. I'll get some food and watch what you've got."

He spurted a laugh. "Oh, really."

Liddy shrugged, giggling. "Don't disappoint me." Then she gave him a gentle shove toward the game.

Two lines had formed at the food tables, and, quickly, Liddy could see why. This event had been catered, and instead of mismatched potluck bowls of potato salad partially covered by foil and buzzing flies, aproned servers stood behind steaming trays holding fixings for gourmet tacos. Not a hot dog in sight.

After loading up her plate, she gathered up napkins and utensils and reached for a bottle of water.

"Liddy? Is that you under that hat?"

A woman with unblinking eyes peered at her. She wore an association badge proclaiming her a Board Member.

"It's Mary. You may not remember me, but I work in Dr. Grayson's office."

"Oh yes." Liddy nodded. "It's been awhile. Nice to see you again."

"Oh, honey, I could say the same thing about you." She continued to stare into Liddy's face. "We were all so worried—

the other office ladies and I—but, well, look at you now. Why, you're … walking and everything."

Liddy tried to hide a wince, and she forced herself not to glance at the others in line who may have overheard Mary.

She took a step toward leaving. "Thank you, Mary. You're right … I'm all healed up."

Mary smiled and shot a look around. "Wonderful. And what brings you here?"

"My, uh, my friend Beau invited me." Without a spare hand, she couldn't exactly point, so instead Liddy gestured toward the pick-up game with her chin. "He runs Physician Marketing."

Mary's mouth popped open. "Yes, of course, we all know Beau." She pinned her with a question in her eyes. "Didn't … didn't he lose his wife to cancer recently?"

Liddy bit her lip. "Last year, yes, he did."

She straightened, a bewildering number of lines on her forehead jostling together. "Surely you and he are not… dating?"

A boy smelling of teenage years reached for a can of soda, bumping Liddy's elbow. She gave him a "sorry"—though clearly not her fault—and turned back to Mary. "We're … we're friends."

How could she say any more than that when she didn't actually know the status of her relationship herself? In high school, though drama abounded, dating was cut and dried. He asked you out, you went—bam!—you had a boyfriend. As an adult, a divorced one at that, the nuances of relationship were not so clear.

Still, she had felt something electric last night with Beau, a wild mix of adrenaline that had made her both giddy and fearful. Mary's question, still hanging between them as she filled her plate, brought the latter to the forefront. What, exactly, had Mary meant? That, because she had been ill herself, no way should she and Beau be together?

The teen bumped into her again. Liddy gave Mary a tight smile and shifted toward the exit. "Guess I'd better go. Blocking the line. Nice to see you again."

She hustled away from the food area, her heart beating unusually fast, a dismal drop in her belly. People could think what they wanted. All she knew was that she was fine. Beau was fine. Still sad, she felt quite sure of that, but fine. This ... this relationship with Beau was all new and fresh, and she hated that the slightest comment from someone who likely meant well had managed to sink this otherwise carefree moment in time. Maybe she was being too sensitive.

If not for the cheers coming from the football game, Liddy might have wandered along the sand for a while. Instead, she climbed an ice plant-dotted dune where several others had already spread out blankets and knelt down. From her perch on the slight rise she could see the ocean on one side and the field of players on the other.

"Excuse me, miss?"

A woman with brunette flyaway hair shooed her young son away from the corner of the blanket they were sitting on. An older man sat on the other side of her. "Please," she said. "Sit with us. There's plenty of room."

Liddy smiled and scooched over. "Thanks."

The boy, his lips outlined in Red #40, sucked on a lollipop and said, "We're watching my dad!"

"You are?" she answered.

"Yeah, he's in a red Spiderman shirt."

Liddy cracked up.

"Who you watchin'?" he asked.

Liddy cradled her plate in her lap. She scanned the field with her eyes, then pointed at Beau, the red hair on his arms glistening in the sunshine. "That's my friend, Beau, right over there. In the black baseball cap."

The older man spoke up. "You Beau's girl?"

Liddy swung a look at him. He resembled the woman on the blanket, and she wondered if he was the boy's grandpa. "I'm with Beau. Yes." She hoped her answer was sufficient.

The man nodded. "I see, I see." He seemed to look her over then, not in a creepy old guy way, but as if his wheels were turning and he had more questions than answers. "I'm Peter Acero."

"He's a doctor!" the boy said.

The boy's mother shushed him.

"Nice to meet you, Dr. Acero."

"And this is my daughter Lucy and my grandboy Teddy. My son-in-law Ace is out on the field."

"Well, then, it's a pleasure to meet you all." The heaviness that had momentarily settled on her flitted away on the ocean breeze. "And thank you again for sharing your beach real estate with me."

Teddy scrunched up his face. "Real estate?"

Lucy laughed. "She means the blanket, mijo."

They all laughed together, and settled in to watch the game. Down below, a cheer went up. Then a groan. At one point, seven guys joined in on a tackle ... was that even legal in flag football? Rowdy shouts from the sidelines turned into catcalls as two sweaty guys ripped off their shirts and tossed them out of bounds.

One of them was Beau.

Be still my rapidly beating heart.

Peter chuckled. "Seems your guy is showing off for you."

Under her breath, Lucy whispered, "Well if ya got it, flaunt it … that's what I always say."

Her father gasped. "I did not just hear my daughter say that."

She slapped him good-naturedly on the shoulder. "I was talking about Ace, Papa."

Liddy expected to hear another chuckle from Grandpa, but instead, he was giving her that once-over again. "You know," he said, his face thoughtful, "you could be Anne's kin."

Anne's … *kin?* Dr. Acero knew Beau's wife? And he thought that she and Liddy were … that they somehow looked alike?

Lucy slapped him harder this time. "Oh, Papa, she does not. Where do you get those thoughts?"

He shrugged. "All I'm saying is that Liddy and Anne—God rest her soul—could pass for cousins. Both lookers … although she was a brunette."

A lull settled between them. Liddy gave him a vague smile and turned her attention back to the game. She didn't bother mentioning that she, too, was a brunette. It's no surprise that Peter thought she was a blonde—the only hair that could be seen peeking out beneath the baseball cap had been bleached. If she were to yank that hat off her head, they'd all see the truth: a close-cropped covering of soft, loam-colored hair. Then she'd have a whole new story to tell them.

But at this moment, she'd rather keep quiet the rest of the day.

LATER THAT DAY, AFTER THEY'D eaten their fill, teamed up in a variety of team sports like horseshoes and croquet—not to mention Beau's shirtless game of flag football—and fulfilled some obligatory networking requirements, they walked back to Liddy's place. She'd planned to throw together a light dinner for them, but Beau suggested they head back to the beach and watch the sunset. So while he carried a couple of low-slung chairs out to the sand, she traipsed behind him, holding a basket of towels and two bottles of Perrier.

They watched the surf in near silence, the sun having moved closer to the sea, yet still offering plenty of warmth.

"I could sit here all night," Beau said.

"Yeah?"

"With you to keep me warm, that is."

"Aw, I hope you don't say that to all the beach girls ..."

He laughed. "Well, not *all* of them."

"Nice."

Beau laughed again. "Seriously, Liddy, we're lucky people to live here. When I was a kid growing up in Colorado, I used to watch the Rose Parade on TV and I couldn't believe that somewhere in the world the sun was shining. I always told my parents that someday, I would move there."

"And you did."

"Yes. For a kid who hadn't seen the ocean for the first twelve years of his life, it still astounds me that I can see it every day now."

"Ever think of living here?"

Beau glanced at Liddy, his brows raised.

"I mean, here, down by the beach."

"What are you saying? I do live by the beach."

"Okay, but you're like, what, five or six miles inland?"

Beau shook his head, laughing. "Honey, when you've grown up in rural Colorado, the entire state of California is on the beach!"

"Okay, okay. Laugh all you want, hotshot. I was just wondering …"

He hooked an arm around her neck. "I forgive you."

She gasped in mock disapproval and attempted to pull away from him, but he cinched her closer.

"I'm seriously glad you spent the day with me today."

She stopped, her heartbeat erratic. "Yeah?"

His eyes crinkled at their corners. "Yeah."

"You had so many admirers at that picnic," she started. "You must help a lot of people."

He released his grip and sat back. "I try. It's not hard to, really, when you have respect for the people you're working for. Some people think of marketing as a four-letter word, but it's really just coming up with the best way to connect people with someone who can help them. Hard to do these days with so much noise in the world. But when that happens? It's the best definition of a win-win situation."

"And you can pay your rent."

He smiled and gazed at her. "And I can pay my rent." He cleared his throat. "Or mortgage soon, hopefully."

"Oh, had no idea you were planning to move."

"Just started looking."

"And … do you have a place in mind … that you'd like to buy, I mean?"

"The general area, yes."

"Anywhere I know?"

"Not around here, but if you want, sometime I'll take you by the area I'm considering."

She blushed. Of course she wanted to see the kind of house Beau was thinking of buying—if it was even a house, could be a condo for all she knew—but she didn't want him to think she was prying into his life. Into his future.

And … what did he mean not around here? Hadn't Beau just shown her how fully ensconced he was in this community? In his business? Surely he couldn't be thinking of relocating.

"Sure. Why not." She tried to sound as nonchalant as she could. "Although, I hate to break this to you, but people living in, say, Bakersfield, don't actually believe theirs is a beach community."

"Ha. True. But don't worry your pretty little head." He plunked a kiss on her nose, as if they'd known each other for years and this kind of banter was normal for them. "It's not that far from here. In fact, it's close to where I live now."

"But not at the beach."

He shrugged. "Close enough. I'm not in a huge hurry, though. Still looking around, taking my time. When the right place comes along, I'll know it."

She'd noticed this about him. Beau wasn't a guy in a hurry. He'd taken his time asking her out, for instance. And when he had finally asked her—that Wednesday night after church— he'd had to work himself up to it. Or so it seemed to her. And he hadn't actually considered it a date. That moniker had been saved for their first "official" date—as he called it—several weeks later.

She could hear Meg's voice in her head. *Why are you in such a hurry?*

Truthfully, she didn't know. In some ways it felt like she'd been wasting time over the past few years. Her marriage to Shawn had never felt right, even on her wedding day. But she was so young and for reasons that only a shrink could someday reveal to her, she had become attached to him. She specifically remembered being nineteen years old and holding a mental debate in her mind over whether she should go through with it. In the end, she had decided that if she didn't marry Shawn, there would be no one else.

Looking back, that would not have been the worst-case scenario.

"You look pretty far away, Liddy."

She blinked. He was speaking to her, his forehead tense. Had he said something and she'd not responded?

"You ready to go in?" he asked. "Are you tired?"

Or maybe ... he was concerned. Like the woman from her doctor's office who she'd run into at the picnic today, the one who'd seemed quite surprised by the progress of her recovery. The thought brought her to the present, and the very real MRI appointment she would be going to later this week. She wanted to erase the snapshot of her calendar from her mind.

It occurred to Liddy then that maybe she was in a hurry to find the right guy and settle down for the same reason that Beau appeared not to be: fear of the unknown.

The sun had not yet set, and she shook her head at Beau's

question, determined not to let the sudden onset of doldrums spoil a perfectly pleasant day. "Sorry about that. No, not yet. Let's wait a few more minutes. Until the sun goes down."

He took his towel and wrapped it around her shoulders, then kept one arm lazily about her. "You got it."

The golden globe grazed the surface of the sea.

"Beau?"

"Mm-hmm?"

"Dr. Acero said that I reminded him of someone."

"Really?"

The sun's descent had accelerated, its rays disappearing into the ocean. Suddenly, she wished she hadn't brought up the subject.

Beau broke into her thoughts. "Who did Doc say you reminded him of?"

She swallowed back her hesitation and cut him a look. "He said ... he said that I look like your wife."

BEAU HADN'T LAUGHED THAT HARD IN ... well, not in a while. Dr. Acero's comment that Liddy looked like Anne's "kin" was strangely comical to him. There were some things you just didn't speak about in professional company, such as politics, religion, and oh, yes, the idea that a guy's date looks like his late wife.

He had laughed out loud again, the sound nearly swallowed up by a resounding wave. Acero was a good guy. Sadly, the man probably didn't really remember what Anne looked like—he hadn't seen her more than twice, if that.

Liddy's reaction to Beau's take on the incident puzzled

him, though. She hadn't looked angry, exactly, more like shocked. Or perplexed.

"It's not true," he'd said to her, hoping to quell the good doctor's curious pronouncement and its obvious effect on Liddy.

She shrugged. "Wonder why he said it then."

"Who knows? Maybe just to make conversation."

Her forehead wrinkled. "He also thought I was a blonde."

"Aren't you?"

Beau had made the quip with a smile on his face, but she'd slugged him anyway, with a force that surprised him. Of course, he'd known all along that she was a brunette; he'd noticed her before word of her illness had spread like wildfire through the church. And he'd been privy to seeing her up close—without that hat. He'd removed it the night of their official date, and she had not offered an ounce of protest when he'd let it drop to the ground behind them.

Now that he sat in front of his flat screen, his feet up on the scuffed coffee table, a heady reality faced him. No, Liddy didn't remind him of Anne. Not really. He missed his wife more than he admitted openly. He thought of her more than he could say.

But with Liddy, something altogether new was forming, and taking hold far faster than his comfort zone allowed. And this was the reason he had talked her into watching the sunset tonight. They had already spent a full day in the sun, and truthfully, he would have preferred staying inside.

But he couldn't trust himself. Not as a man, and not with her. His heart and body had already tried to take over once where she was concerned, but when the heat of the moment had passed, he wondered how wise that would have been.

And so, while she puttered around her kitchen in her bare feet, tempting him after hours of beach play with that slip of fabric molding itself to her, he'd spun her around.

Her eyelashes fluttered. "What are you doing?"

He leaned in for a kiss. Just a quick one. Then pulled back. "Let's go sit on the beach."

She had looked momentarily stunned, and even then he wondered if she was tired. Even if she hadn't had surgery a couple of months ago, she should have been tired.

But he hadn't relented. Still felt guilty about that.

"C'mon. I'll take the beach chairs and you grab the drinks," he had replied. "I won't make you talk to another soul, I promise."

She nodded her head, a tiny smile forming. "Okay, sure. Let's do it." She was a beach girl, after all.

Now, as he sat in the comfort of his own living room reliving the day, he grabbed the remote and released a sigh into the silence. He pointed it at the screen, and pressed "off." His mind might not be able to rest much, but his body needed the sleep.

Chapter Sixteen

SHE ARRIVED AT WORK mid-morning Tuesday to find Trace sitting behind the concierge desk, filing her nails. Trace looked up. "Something's different."

It was true. On her way in, Liddy had slipped in to see Missy at Shear Dreams.

"It's about time you let me lop off that blonde hair," Missy had said.

"I was hoping for something a little less drastic sounding."

Missy laughed. "I just meant that you have enough hair here on the other side that I think I can match it all up."

By the time she left her hairdresser's place, all trace of curls had been removed. In its place soft, dark hair covered her head, so short that if she were to go without a hat—which she was not yet prepared to do—she might have been able to join the military and skip the boot camp haircut.

Trace peered at her. "You cut your hair. Either that or you pinned up the blonde curls."

"No, I cut it. Wanted to see how it would look with both sides the same length."

"And?"

"It looks short."

Trace cracked up. "I'm guessing you had a good weekend?"

Flush with all the memories, the good and the strange, Liddy nodded and answered, "Great weekend, yes." She slipped her purse into a drawer, snapping a look at it to make sure she had pulled the zipper closed.

She sat down, rolled forward in her desk chair, and glanced around. For a Monday, the hotel remained eerily quiet. Usually the inn would be bustling with guests checking out about now and needing directions or last-minute reservations for various types of guided tours before heading on to their next destinations. Today, however, the lobby was quieter than a classroom full of students taking their SATs.

"Good," Trace said, dropping her emery board into a drawer. " 'Cause you look pretty tired."

"Do I?" She hoped her response sounded surprised enough. Truth was, she was exhausted. Liddy woke up so tired that her feet hurt. How could that be so after being curled up, dreaming of romantic sunsets, for eight-plus hours? A slight bout of dizziness had also caught her by surprise this morning, so she'd taken an anti-seizure pill with her coffee—just for good measure.

Trace surveyed her with narrowed eyes as if not quite buying Liddy's casual reply. "Just be careful," she replied. "We can't have any relapses, okay?"

The phone rang, and Liddy reached to answer it. She gave Trace an apologetic little smile and said, "Good morning, concierge desk, this is Liddy."

The next hour or so dragged until Housekeeping arrived in full force to, as the supervisor Clarice announced, give the place some "extra sparkle."

"Shoulda thought of that years ago," Trace sniffed. "There's more dust under that bell desk than a hoarder's garage."

Liddy opened her mouth to point out the irony in her treasure-hunting friend's words, but shut it quickly.

Meg breezed in through the double front doors, wearing a perfectly fitted dark chocolate suit with touches of cheetah in all the right places: on the cuffs, lining the pocket flaps—even a folded cheetah hanky peeked from her breast pocket.

A catcall sliced the air, followed by a couple of dorky high-fives over at the bell desk.

"Shoot," Liddy said when her pal approached. "If I weren't straight, I'd make a pass at you."

"You're such a loser."

Liddy smiled. "Love you, too."

"Is he here yet?"

"He who?"

Meg eyed her from beneath thick, straight bangs. She licked her pink-frosted lips and darted a look around.

Liddy tilted her head to the side. "Did you get a haircut?" She almost added "too."

Meg swung her gaze back to Liddy, her forehead wrinkled. "Does it look all right?" she whispered.

"It's actually perfect for you. I love the way it frames your teardrop face without hiding it, you know?"

Meg let out an aggravated sound.

"Is there something wrong? Who are you looking for?"

"Jack … is in town today. I received an early morning call that he wanted me here for a meeting. Didn't you know that?"

"Jack?"

"Jackson Riley, VP."

"He's coming in today? Oh … no wonder Housekeeping is all over this place."

Meg scowled. "I guess I'm early. Darn it."

Liddy hadn't seen Meg so antsy before. Well, not since they were in high school and the prom king ditched the queen for her and made a big show of it and … oh! "He's the guy you dated last year!"

Meg grabbed Liddy's arm, her grip like a vise. She yanked her forward until their faces were inches apart, and hissed into her face. "You did not just say that!"

"Ouch."

It was all making sense to her now. When Liddy still lived in the desert, Meg had met someone special—although she had been oddly evasive about the man. Before Liddy had the chance to meet him, though, the relationship had fizzled, and except for a few vague comments, Meg had not brought him up again—even when prodded.

And now at least one of the reasons was clear: she still had feelings for him. Liddy was certain of it. You can't know a person for most of her life, including the teenage years, and not know when your friend's heart hung in tatters. For the past several years, Meg had become the epitome of professional, much to Liddy's surprise and admiration, with perhaps a bit of envy thrown in. But the way she had said Jackson's name moments ago—or better yet, "Jack's" name—the more Meg reminded Liddy of her old self.

And she wondered. If Liddy had not followed Meg to the coast, would she have ever learned the identity of her best friend's old flame, namely, Jackson Riley, the hotel management company's vice president?

Hans sidled up behind her friend. "Hey there, Meg. Going to a party?"

Liddy gave the man a daggered look. "What are you saying, Hans? She's dressed to take over this place."

Meg, having collected herself, shot her an expression of gratitude.

Hans gave her a grim smile. "Hopefully she won't start with my job."

"I think you're safe," Meg said, now looking more composed than when she had approached the desk. "For now."

Nervous laughter sounded all around as a phone rang in the distance.

It rang again.

Hans nodded toward the desk. "I think someone's purse is ringing."

Liddy looked at Meg, then at Hans. "Sorry." She opened the drawer and pulled her phone out of her purse, chagrined that she'd forgotten to switch it off earlier. She looked up to say, "I have to take this," but Meg and Hans had their heads together, no doubt comparing notes over the VP's impending arrival.

"Liddy Buckle?" the caller asked. "This is City Hospital calling about your MRI appointment on Wednesday."

"Yes?" Although she hated the thought of having to undergo the test which stirred up claustrophobic nightmares in her, she was ready to hear the doctor tell her that, without a doubt, all was well.

"Unfortunately, the machine is in need of repair so we are going to have to reschedule your appointment."

She shut her eyes momentarily and held her tongue, the only way to hold back a knee-jerk response. In her most professional and pleasant voice she asked, "How long will it take to be fixed?"

"Oh, we expect it to be up by the end of the week."

"Great. I think I can rearrange my schedule."

"So our next opening is … three weeks from tomorrow. Ten a.m. okay?"

"Three … weeks? I thought you said the machine would be fixed this week?"

"Unfortunately, we are all booked up this week."

Liddy shut her eyes again, and bit her bottom lip. She'd already loaded music onto her phone and mentally prepared herself to be stuffed into that metal tube for the duration. But this was beyond her control.

She nodded once. "Fine. Three weeks. I'll make a note of it."

"See you then," the woman said in a sing-song voice.

Trace reappeared after her break. "What's got you in a snit? Boy troubles?"

Liddy grimaced at her, then allowed herself one exasperated laugh. So she'd had to change her appointment? In some ways she was relieved not to have to face it anyway.

Trace squinted toward the front desk. "What's going on over there?"

They both turned. Hans, Meg, and now Clarice, were huddled around a computer.

"Apparently the VP is on his way in."

Trace's hand flew to her face. "No!" She grabbed her purse after just setting it down. "I have to take a break."

"But you just took—" Liddy watched as Trace speed-walked to the nearest restroom.

When she returned, her hair had been twisted into an up-do and evidence of fresh blush tinged her cheeks.

Calmly, Trace sat, keeping her eyes downcast. "Is he here yet?"

Liddy shook her head. "For heaven's sake, you'd think the president was on his way in."

"Jackson is better. Powerful and hot." Trace began to fan herself. "I forgot you hadn't met him yet. Trust me, Liddy, you'll be shaking like a fan girl when you get a load of the chiseled awesomeness of that man's face."

As if on cue, the sliding glass doors parted open, and in strolled a man wearing a European-cut black suit and a decidedly determined grin on his face. His brown hair was combed in waves, and the I-don't-care stubble on his face somehow solidified his rightful place as boss.

Poor Meg.

Ignoring the crew that waited for him at the front desk, he strode right up to the concierge with laser-like precision. He held out a hand. "Jackson Riley."

She took his hand. "Liddy Buckle. Pleased to meet you."

Trace rushed forward and thrust out her hand, too, her expression unmasked and swooning. "Oh, Mr. Riley, it's wonderful to see you again. You look marvelous. Have you been vacationing? Time off really looks good on you." After a second's delay, she added, "Sir."

He nodded to them both and spun around to make his way to the front desk where the others stood at stick-straight attention.

Liddy hoped her face did not reflect how ridiculous the staff looked to her.

Then again, how must Meg be feeling? Despite the frenzy in the air, a heaviness began tugging at her heart and she felt for her friend. Why hadn't she known more about this man in her life—for however short a time it was? Maybe she had been far too caught up with her marriage problems and health issues to notice the pain Meg was in.

Later that night after work, she thought about this as she curled up on the couch and pulled a throw around her. Her fatigue from the morning had only gotten worse during the day. No second wind ever appeared. And so, as she drifted off for an evening nap, she tried to think of ways to make it up to Meg.

THE RING OF LIDDY'S CELL PHONE startled her. She answered it, dazed.

"Did I wake you?" Beau asked.

"No." She looked around, her vision blurred from slumber. "What time is it?"

"It's six-thirty." He paused. "Were you really asleep?"

She lay back, sinking deeper into the couch cushions. The hitch in his voice, like he was surprised, rattled her. "I must've dozed off."

"Guess I wore you out yesterday." He lowered his voice now, the sound of it smooth and inviting, like dark chocolate. "It won't happen again."

Liddy swung her legs around and planted her feet on the ground. "It had better happen again."

"How about now?" he broached.

She frowned. She'd slept more than the recommended twenty-minute power nap and now her mind felt murkier than a backed-up sink.

"Unless you have other plans …"

"No other plans, but I'll need a few minutes to pull myself together."

"You got it."

She threw off the blanket and padded upstairs to her bedroom where she had strewn her work clothes every which way. Shucking off her sweats, she wriggled herself into a pair of jeans and threw on a lacy empire blouse with three-quarter sleeves.

What she saw in the bathroom mirror pleased her. She didn't look as haggard as she had felt much of the day, so the nap must've done her some good. Liddy ran a brush through her hair and added a bit of liner to her eyes.

Downstairs, she slipped into a pair of flat sandals she'd left there the night before just in time to answer the door when Beau knocked.

"I come bearing a gift." He strode in, planted a kiss on her cheek, and stuck a cup of coffee into her hands, watching her with eyes that held a question.

The warmth of the cup soothed her nerves and she gave him a small smile. "Just my size, too."

"Listen," he said, wrapping his arms around her waist. "I was hoping you'd take a little drive with me—not far—but if you're too tired, we can do it another time."

She waved him off. "I'm fine. Long day at work is all it was."

"Sure?"

She smiled into those attentive eyes of his. "I am."

"Great. Grab a sweater and I'll take you by the neighborhood I'm thinking of moving into. It's not oceanfront, but it's not far from here either. If you're feeling up to it, we can grab a bite afterward. Sound okay?"

Liddy took a sip of the hot coffee laced with cream, gathering strength from the liquid as it traveled through her body. "Sounds perfect."

BEAU HAD MET TAYLOR FOR LUNCH countless times, but not ever in an official capacity like this. And it felt odd. Not because he had any qualms about divulging his personal financial secrets to his longtime friend—he knew he was in good hands—but because he was doing it as a single guy.

He'd been married to Anne for five years, and though he had accepted her death as well as could be expected, a guy didn't forget a fact like that in a blink.

Beau pushed the door open to the offices of Sky Mortgage.

The receptionist smiled at him. "Hi there, Beau. I didn't realize you were coming in. Are you here to meet Taylor for lunch?"

"Amanda. Hello. Actually, I'm here in an official capacity."

She furrowed her forehead and glanced down at her calendar. She looked up again with a slight raise of one brow. "I don't suppose you are also known as Bob Clemente? Because if you are, you're right on time."

He threw his head back in laughter. "I believe so."

She smirked and led him to Taylor's office, all the while shaking her head. "I won't even ask."

Taylor stood to greet them. "Hey, Beau. C'mon in."

Beau took a seat, while Taylor sat behind a monstrous desk and leaned back.

"Bob Clemente?" Beau said.

Taylor smiled wide and folded his hands behind his head. "Roberto … Bob … it worked, didn't it? Kept your secret safe all morning, didn't I?"

Beau shook his head. "Apparently no one else around here watches old pro-baseball footage. Besides, I don't have any secrets. I'm an open book."

"Yes, well, you can't be too careful with your information. What if some other mortgage guy happened to hear you were coming in and snagged your business right out from under me?"

"That would only happen if he gave me a better deal."

Taylor unlocked his hands. "Not going to happen." He slid a letter on company stationery over to Beau. "This is all you'll need to buy the house of your dreams. Guard it with your life."

Beau peered at the letter, which stated the amount of loan he qualified for. "This is all I need, huh?"

"That and a down payment, of course. But you're golden, Beau. I ran this through several lenders and they're beating down my door trying to get your loan. All you need to do is find the right property."

He nodded. "Great. Appreciate it."

"So … you find the place yet?"

"Maybe. Liddy and I drove around last evening to look at a few available homes for sale."

"Liddy? That's great. Did she help you?"

Taylor was perceptive enough not to question him about

taking his new girlfriend to look at houses. "It was eye-opening. She saw all kinds of things that I didn't, like bedrooms in the front of the house instead of the back—she doesn't love that—and lack of big windows. I'd been planning to drive around and check out the neighborhood, but she encouraged me to park the car and walk around."

"And?"

"And we had a nice time together."

Taylor squeezed his eyes shut and shook his head, a goofy grin on his face. "But did you find a house?"

"Right. Yes, I think I did. Narrowed it down to two and now that I have your official letter"—he picked up the mortgage document—"I will likely make an offer on one of them soon. Maybe even tomorrow."

"Wow. That's fast for you."

Beau shrugged. "My accountant tells me I'd better do something or Uncle Sam will be making more money off of me than I will."

"And that, my friend, is why I'm in business."

Later, as he walked out of Sky Lending, gratefulness settled in his gut. This was the right thing to do. He'd started this business with two dimes to spare and had finally reached a point in it where investing wasn't just recommended—it was required. It gave him hope to think of all that he'd accomplished, even as he and Anne fought against her illness, and that, somehow, he'd managed not to be swallowed up by the deep tide.

He drove away with a lingering contentedness, yet oddly aware of thunder rolling in the distance.

Chapter Seventeen

"TELL ME ABOUT HIM."

Liddy and Meg had snuck away from work to Skipper's Brew, a place in the harbor preferred by old sea salts and tank-and-flip-flop-wearing locals. Despite Meg's short grey coat and black skirt combo with knee-length boots, and Liddy's plain resort uniform, they were left alone to sit on an overstuffed couch toward the back of the store. To the scruffy crew scattered around in various corners of the well-weathered place, they might have well been invisible, which was fine by them.

"He's old news, Lid—very old news," Meg replied.

Liddy touched her friend on the wrist. "Meg."

"Fine. There really isn't much to tell, but we went out several times last year, and then it was over. Unfortunately, I still work for the company, so that means that, on occasion, we have to see each other."

"What was it like, I mean, seeing him on a more personal basis?"

"He was shyer than I thought he'd be." She blew out a breath, looking off into the distance. "I've worked with him in various locales, and his confidence could shake even some of our most experienced crew."

"But not you."

"Not really. I've always respected him. I've seen him sell the world to corporate heads, and do it without being arrogant. People would come in thinking they were going to put on the best dessert social their little company had ever seen, and he'd talk them into quarterly events topped off with a yearly five-course meal extravaganza." She laughed, albeit a small one. "I'd always walk out of those meetings exhausted."

"Do you ever talk?"

Meg held her cup of coffee close to her chin with both hands. She shook her head. "Only by email."

Just like the rest of the world.

"I'm sorry."

Meg wrinkled her brow. "Why? You didn't do anything."

"I'm sorry for not being there for you when all this went down."

Her friend twisted her mouth into a rueful smile. "You've had enough to deal with, girl. I really am fine. You know that."

"How was the meeting yesterday?"

Meg shrugged. "Oh, you know. He was cordial, even charming at times. Has all kinds of big ideas to make this place a world class resort."

"Really?"

"Yes, and if anyone can make that happen, it's Jackson."

"He does seem bigger than life."

Meg leaned her head against the leather cushion and seemed to stare off into space.

"I hate to ask this but … any chance …?"

"Then don't. Like I said, he was charming and cordial, but completely professional. We talked about what it would take to add a spa to the premises, and he wanted my opinion on whether such an addition would make a difference for me as I solicit conferences for this property. I told him it would, of course."

"But no small talk."

"None."

"Shoot."

"Although … at one point, he seemed to lose track of his thoughts in the meeting. I've never seen him do that. In fact, he's always been frighteningly en pointe with his ideas—and his criticisms, I might add."

"Hence the staff running around this morning like the Secret Service."

"He doesn't really scare me, you know. I just wish I could read him better."

"For personal reasons? Or as a boss?"

Meg's eyes grew wide, but she looked away, a tell-tale sign that she'd been hurt more deeply than she would admit.

Liddy was sorry she had asked.

THAT NIGHT, AS SHE SAUTÉED PEPPERS in a pan on the stove and sipped her wine, Liddy relayed her thoughts to Beau. "I met him, and he was both handsome and quite whimsical, really. He was wearing this amazing suit—the kind a Londoner might wear, with tapered pants—but his shirt pattern was this crazy red plaid and the tie was just as colorful."

Beau pressed his lips together, as if thinking hard about what she could possibly mean.

She waved a spoon at him. "Don't give me that look. He

strolled into the hotel like royalty, ignored all those who were waiting for him, and instead approached the concierge desk and introduced himself to me and to Trace." She stopped. "Although, come to think of it, he'd already met Trace. But he didn't act like it."

She continued, "It just really bugs me that he went out with Meg—and she's obviously not over him, but pretending like she is—and he goes about his day all business-like. What's his problem anyway?"

"Maybe he's just not—"

"Into her? I mean, shouldn't he at least acknowledge that they'd gone out a couple of times? He could have asked about her cat or something."

"With all her traveling, she has a cat?"

"I'm just saying—*if* she had a cat!"

"Well, I don't really know—"

Liddy set down the spoon, peering at him. "Sorry. I've been dominating this conversation, haven't I?"

He smiled at her.

"I'll take that as a yes." She sighed and gave her head a tight shake. "You talk now."

"You were doing fine. I don't have any complaints."

She leaned her forearms on her kitchen island and looked at him sitting across from her. So handsome. A thrill shivered through her. They hadn't known each other that long, and though there were no guarantees, she would miss this if he chose to end it.

Reflexively, she pressed her eyes shut at such an unwelcome thought.

"Are you all right?"

Her eyes popped open and she straightened. "Yes, of course," she said. "You were going to tell me about your day."

He breathed in deeply. "Well, actually, I met with Taylor today and he provided me with a mortgage letter."

"For a loan, you mean?"

"Yes, exactly. Now all I have to do is wait."

"Wait? I don't understand. You mean to find the perfect house?"

"To see if my offer has been accepted."

Her mouth dropped open. "You made an offer already?"

Beau nodded, and though he smiled, it didn't quite reach his eyes.

"Which one?"

"The blue one with the large picture window."

The one she had told him was her favorite. Not that she would mention that. Instead, she walked around the island and pulled him into a hug. "Congratulations."

He melted into her, whispering "thanks" into her hair, but there was something melancholy in his voice.

She leaned back and took in his face. "Aren't you happy?"

This time he was the one to press his eyelids together. He sighed. "Of course. I've wanted my own place for a long time—and now it looks like I'm about to realize that goal. It's just …"

She leaned her head to one side, still holding onto him, waiting. When he didn't continued, she prodded him. "What is it?"

His lips twisted. He didn't look at her.

"Beau?"

His eyes grew cloudy. He looked at her, blinking away the

tears. "It's Anne."

She nodded, although not quite sure what he meant. "Anne," she repeated.

"She'd always wanted us to have a house of our own, especially one with a garden."

"Oh … oh." She nodded. "I'm sorry."

He pulled away from her, folded a fist onto the island, and looked up at the ceiling, as if searching for a way to rope in the tumult of feelings rumbling through his head. "What am I thinking? Anne doesn't care about this now. She's happy. I know she is. And she's well now, too. Finally." He hung his head, shaking it fiercely now, and expelled a groan. "She doesn't care about a stupid house."

Liddy didn't know what to say. A battery of advice paralyzed her … the kind warning people about uttering the wrong words to those who grieved. She knew he was right, that heaven was far better than anything humans could hope for on earth. But was it her place to say that?

Part of her wanted only to reach for his hand and tell him that she believed Anne would be happy for him. But Liddy kept that close to her heart, too. She contemplated whether to deflect the moment and give the veggies a quick stir or to lightly kiss his cheek.

Beau didn't wait. He cradled her waist with his hands and pulled her close, crushing himself against her. "What you must think of me …" he whispered into her hair again, his voice thick with tears, some shed, some that never would be.

Her mind fled back to her week at the hospital. All those roommates, some hopeful, some resigned, all emotional. And the men who fussed over them, their aged bodies moving from chore to chore in an effort to keep themselves from folding under the relentless pressures of time and diagnoses. She swallowed against the memories, a sharpness deep in her throat.

What had happened to those women? To Bonnie? And Marie? And Cissy and Elizabeth? She wished she had attempted to stay in touch with each one of them.

With their faces and their stories rolling through her mind, Liddy held on tighter to Beau, telling him with her touch what she couldn't seem to find the words to say out loud.

Beau pulled away from her and peered into her face. "You asked me a few minutes ago if I was happy." He rubbed her arms up and down with an intensity that matched his emotions. "I want you to know that I am, Liddy. There are just some things that are going to take a while to overcome."

She nodded, fully aware that he had one foot in this relationship while the other one hovered above the ground unsure of where to firmly land. The thought created an ache in her chest. And yet, her own unfathomable experiences had brought her an understanding of sorts. If she had not faced her own brush with death recently, would she have been able to accept where he found himself at this moment?

Liddy leaned forward to give him that kiss on the check. "That's to be expected." She took his cheeks in her hands then, her smile pushing back her own tears. "Ready to have dinner with me?"

He found her lips and kissed her fiercely. Then he wrapped her in a hug. "Always."

Chapter Eighteen

THE SEA BLUE MICHAEL KORS BAG slung over Trace's shoulder shifted, and she winced while carefully setting it on the concierge counter. Despite her care, it landed with a heavy thud.

Liddy leaned her head to one side. "What's inside ... day-old bagels?"

"Ha. You wish. No, my friend, inside here is an old-fashioned library."

"Library ... you mean books?"

Trace blinked. "You've heard of them?"

She played along. "Vaguely."

"Well, phew. I was worried for a second that you'd forgotten all about them. E-readers just don't have the wonderful ol' smell of paper, and they definitely don't have covers on them that show just how loved they are."

"Or aren't."

Trace stuck out her tongue, but the mischief in her eyes betrayed her. "Ha ha ha," she finally said.

"Trace, you are an old soul. So ... what are the books for?"

She shrugged. "There's been so much talk about upgrading the inn, I don't know, I thought maybe I could put some books on those empty shelves in the lobby. I could create a little sign encouraging guests to take a book to the pool or their room during their stay."

Liddy nodded. "I like it."

Trace straightened. "You do?"

"Guests first. Isn't that what management is always saying?"

Meg strode through the lobby for the second time, her brown hair brushed smooth, every loam-colored strand neatly clinging to the one next to it. Determination set her mouth and lined her forehead.

"Meg."

The sales dervish stopped abruptly at the sound of her friend's voice, and made her way to the concierge desk. She raised an eyebrow at Liddy as if to ask, *Why are you bothering me right now?*

She considered pointing out Trace's bag full of reading material, but the intense set to her friend's jaw made her think better of it. Instead she asked, "Lunch today?"

Meg shook her head tightly. "I doubt I'll have time. Meetings all day. A proposal to get to a client." She pushed out an exasperated sigh and surveyed the lobby, allowing her eyes to settle somewhere north. "For heaven's sake, when was the last time anyone cleaned those windows?"

"Probably last time it rained."

"Well," Meg huffed, "that's a problem."

Liddy opened her mouth to suggest her pal take a break when, as if in slow motion and in choreographed sync, the entire valet and bell staff straightened. Shoulders back. Hands at sides. Eyes forward.

Jackson Riley entered through the sliding entrance doors

wearing a suit the color of silver ice, a bright blue tie, and an air of royalty. He approached the bell desk and shook Hannah's hand, his smile a unique combination of warm and winning. It occurred to Liddy that Jackson had the enviable ability to charm anyone and everyone around him. And yet she herself felt less than charmed. No doubt his skill boosted his business holdings, but from what she had heard about the way he'd brushed off Meg, his personal life likely suffered from such superficiality.

At least she hoped it had.

Not that she cared.

Beside her, Trace sighed. "He's lovely."

Liddy watched in dismay as Meg's chiseled expression melted like pudding in the sun. She leaned forward and hissed, "Meg."

Her friend's right eye twitched, then she looked toward Liddy, those curvaceous brows of hers knit together in an impatient question.

Before Liddy could say another word, Jackson zeroed in on their band of three and marched toward the desk, his face now a mask of professionalism.

"Good morning, ladies," he said.

He gave them all a look in turn, but did anyone else notice that his gaze lingered ever so slightly on Meg's?

Jackson squared his body with Meg's. "I trust you will be joining us at noon."

An expression equivalent to wheels slowly spinning appeared on Meg's delicate face, but only for a moment. "Noon, yes. I'll be there."

"Plan to work over lunch," he added.

"Of course."

He flashed that white smile again, this time at all three of them. "Good day, ladies," he said, then headed for the office corridor.

So much for calming Meg's nerves at lunch. Perhaps it was selfish, but Liddy had also hoped to get her friend's input on how she was feeling lately. Plus there was the issue of Beau's confusion from last night that created in her a need for a sounding board ...

Meg righted her shoulders and began to walk away, but Trace's voice stopped her.

"Wondering if you ladies would like to grab sushi with me tonight."

Meg opened her mouth quickly, as if to refuse, when something like resolve softened her eyes. "I would love that, Trace. Lid? Can you make it?"

Between climbing herself out of a monetary hole her divorce had created, and the brain surgery that had set her back for several months, Liddy relished the idea of a girls' night. So sushi wasn't her favorite? Relaxing with friends somehow made the thought of downing a California roll worth it.

She smiled. "I'm in."

"TAKE THESE SUSHI ROLLS," Trace said, holding up a hunk of seaweed-wrapped fish and veggies. "Usually I prefer to buy mine at Costco, but for special occasions like this, I'm willing to shell out a little more for the same food."

Liddy shook her head and laughed. "Shell out. Good one."

She wagged her fork toward Liddy. "You know what I

mean."

This time Meg cut in. "You really think that the raw fish at a big box store is as fresh as this?" The platter in front of them displayed more tantalizing colors than a rainbow.

Trace shrugged. "Hope so. Anyway, we're paying for the ambiance of the place."

They shared a small table and a tokkuri of saki in the darkened lounge of Sushi Love, a trendy restaurant at the tail end of the lineup of beachside eateries. Low background music with just enough base volume gave diners the impression that the outrageous menu prices were worth it. When Meg suggested the upscale place, Liddy expected Trace to balk. Surprisingly, she agreed. A good thing, too. They had survived several days with the big boss in town, and by the expressions of relief flittering across the ragtag group's faces—and in Liddy's heart—they needed this break.

Besides, maybe here, away from the inn, Meg would feel more comfortable about filling them in on her discussions with Jackson. At least the professional ones.

Meg interrupted Liddy's thoughts by pointing to Trace's MK purse. "You're full of all kinds of surprises these days. That's gorgeous."

Trace's brows rose. "I bought it at the outlet, and just so you know, that fact doesn't make me feel worse about this bag."

"Well, now I do," Meg quipped.

The group erupted in laughter.

"Hate to bring up shop talk, but since we're all together, what kinds of changes should we be expecting at the inn?"

Meg sat back, a wry smile curling her lips upward. "Lots

and lots of upgrades. More green, more luxe, an addition that will take advantage of our spectacular views without blocking the neighbors much ... we'll be the jewel on the coast, and it's about time. Riley Holdings has the funding, and my clients have been begging for a destination spot—not just a hotel with a pretty view."

Liddy nodded. "It's good to see you smiling."

"Thanks. It's been ... it's been a trying week so far."

Liddy knew her friend was choosing her words judiciously. They both loved Trace, but no sense saying more than was necessary—especially about a personal relationship that fizzled before it had a chance. She hated that Meg was forced to come face to face with that fact this week—and likely, again in the future.

"So," Meg said, segueing from all things Riley, "you haven't said much tonight, Liddy. How are you and Beau doing?"

"Great. We had dinner last night. He ... well, he put an offer in on a house and we made it a celebration." And really, they had. Why bring up his misgivings?

Trace frowned for the first time all day. "He bought a house without you?"

"He asked my opinion, if that's what you're wondering."

Trace waggled her head back and forth, like a scale weighing fruit. "I guess that's good, but I don't know, I would've thought he'd wait until you two were, you know, married to make such a big decision."

Meg set down her fork. "For heaven's sake, don't rush them. They barely know each other." Her protector, the friend who knew how hard she'd taken the failure of her marriage, rushed to her aid ... unnecessarily, but still.

"Shush, both of you," Liddy said. "His accountant told him he needs to buy a house, so he's doing so. I just wish it was closer to me, but I'll survive."

Trace speared another silver dollar-sized piece of sushi. "If you say so."

"Exactly how far away is the house?" Meg asked.

Liddy wrinkled her nose. "Inland. About three miles."

Meg leaned forward and cracked up. "You're just mad he didn't buy a house on the sand!"

"Ha ha ha. Whatever."

Trace snickered and gave her a big-eyed, fake pout. "You know it's true, Liddy."

The smiles continued as they teased each other even while splitting the bill three ways "down to the penny," as Trace put it.

Meg led the way toward the exit just as someone from the outside held the door open. She stepped forward, and stopped, nearly causing a Three Stooges-like accident from behind.

"Good evening, Meg." Jackson held the door open, a willowy Photoshopped woman grazing his other arm.

Okay, maybe she just knew how to apply makeup. Or had stopped at a Mac counter on the way to the restaurant.

Whatever.

To her credit, Meg breezed through the doorway as if completely unaffected by the woman—large-bosomed and pretty, if one liked that sort of thing—standing close enough to Jackson that he no doubt could call her Gucci perfume his own.

BEAU CALLED HER LATE THAT NIGHT. "Tell me about your

evening without me," he said.

She smirked. "Jealous?"

"Something like that. Unless this is a case of what happened at the sushi bar, stays in the sushi bar?"

Liddy lay on the bed and rolled over, phone pressed against her ear. The knotholes in the ceiling's rafters stared down at her. "You are a funny man."

"I missed seeing you today."

"Same."

"And ... you're feeling okay?"

Why did he sound so unsure?

Then again, there has been the dizziness ...

Silence sat between them like an expectant lover. Finally, she said, "I feel fine. And I had a good time with the girls tonight, except ..."

"Except?"

She sighed. "All was well until we were walking out and ran into Meg's ex with a centerfold model."

Beau whistled into the phone.

"Excuse me?"

"What? No, I was just thinking."

"And I don't even want to know what you were thinking!"

He chuckled, then quieted. "That must've been hard for Meg. How did she handle it?"

"I think she was just, you know, so shocked. All the way to the car she kept saying, 'He doesn't even like fish.' Of all the restaurants in town, I don't think she imagined Jackson showing up there." She let out a growl. "I, for one, wanted to smack that debonair face of his."

"Liddy ... don't tell me you pummeled the guy and lost

your job."

"I wish I had. It's not like me to take so long to act!"

"Well, in this case, I'd say your delay saved you."

"Maybe." She blew out a breath and stroked a hand across her forehead. "Poor Meg. She showed plenty of bravado, but I shudder to think how she really felt. Unfortunately, Trace had left her car at the hotel, so I had to drive her back. Never really had a chance to parse it all out with her, and by the time I got home she had already turned off her cell."

"Hmm."

"What?"

"If my clock is correct, you arrived home pretty late."

"Yeah …?"

"Sounds like you ate a lot of sushi."

"Yes, well, what was that you said? That what happens at sushi, stays at sushi?"

"Liddy…?" He said it like Ricky Ricardo in an old episode of *I Love Lucy*.

Blast her for staying up so late watching Nick at Night … "Okay, fine. We stopped in at the hotel restaurant and took a seat at the bar—I didn't drink any more alcohol, in case you were wondering."

"I was, but go on."

"I texted Meg, but she didn't answer, but then the funniest thing happened. A group of people were carrying on at one end of the bar over the tapas. They looked familiar. Anyway, Chef was there, serving them all sorts of things I hadn't remembered being on the menu."

"Sounds like a good time."

"I guess."

"Still worried about Meg?"

"I can't help it. She's ... she's never fallen so hard before. I can tell that she's been hurt and it kills me. I just can't believe that of all the places Jackson Riley could show up for sustenance, he would choose Sushi Love."

"Liddy, maybe none of this is what you think. The guy could have been doing market research. You said yourself that he's been talking about upgrading the hotel. And I seem to recall that there's been some talk of changes in the restaurant, right?"

"Yes ...?"

"Well, then, isn't it possible that the poor guy might have just been checking out the place for himself? Sushi Love is very popular right now."

Another growl escaped her, right into the phone. "You ... are ... defending him? That's ridiculous."

He chuckled for the second time during the phone call, although with less confidence than before. "I'm just offering another possibility."

"Why do men always stick together? You don't even know him."

"True, I don't. Let's talk it over tomorrow over lunch. Say, 11:30? It is your day off."

"I should say no."

"Give a guy a chance."

"Fine. Okay. Lunch tomorrow. I'll *probably* be there," she said, a smug smile on her face as she hung up the phone.

Chapter Nineteen

"YOU SURE YOU'RE OKAY?" Meg asked.

Liddy cradled the phone in one ear, while slipping into her shoes. Why did everyone seem to keep asking that? She spied her purse on the bed where she had left it after cleaning it out during a late-night frenzy, darted across the room to retrieve it, then abruptly sat. The room spun … well, her mind did. Her to-do list overwhelmed her. "After last night, I should be the one checking up on you."

"Forget it," Meg said. "Please."

Liddy snapped a look inside her purse to make sure her wallet was safely inside. "I worry about you, though," she was saying. "Listen, I've got to run some errands before meeting Beau for lunch, but can we do coffee later?"

"Liddy, take a breath. Enjoy your day off—and don't worry about me!"

"Impossible," she said with a huff. "Okay, maybe we can catch up tonight."

"You got it."

Ten minutes later, her grocery and incidentals list opened on her phone, Liddy made her way through a store aisle, tossing items into her cart. The bright lights inside the warehouse-like building did a number on her vision, blinding her enough to make her squint. She wished she could slap on a pair of sunglasses like some Hollywood celebrity, you know, because that would look normal.

A twenty-something woman moved toward her on the opposite side of the aisle. One of her children, a dark-eyed boy with waves of chocolate hair, leaned far out of the cart, straining toward some unnamed treasure on a shelf. The other child, a girl she guessed by the tiny red bow tied to a wisp of a hair spout, snuggled against the woman's chest in a sling. Liddy slowed as she passed the scene, taking in every messy detail, like the wad of wrinkles on the woman's sleeve, and the aroma of ground-up graham crackers on little hands.

At the sight and sounds of the party of three, an ache carved at her insides and worked its way toward her mind causing her to envision all kinds of dreams she'd never known she carried within her. Maybe they'd been there all along, locked up in a loveless marriage with no viable reason to be set free. Or maybe that curious voice she'd heard in the hospital, the one promising her a family, had provided the key.

The baby in the woman's sling let out a cry, a sound like a bleating calf, and Liddy shook her mind free from her musings. She smiled at the little family and turned toward a shelf of pasta, pretending to search out the perfect noodle, all the while hoping she hadn't been mistaken for a stalker.

She wasn't exactly sure when the row of shelving in front of her began to shrink, as if pulling away from her like the back end of a car. Instinctively, Liddy reached for a shelf, ignoring the box of pasta that fell to one side before sliding almost in slow motion, to the scuffed linoleum floor, the noise of it shaking her senses. She shut her eyes, willing away the sense of pressure in her head, then reminded herself to breathe.

Breathe.

Like she'd done that day at work when she'd been unable to respond to anyone around her.

Breathe.

Slowly she let her hand drop away from the shelf and, surreptitiously, she glanced about. The mother and children rounded the corner, away from her. Calls for assistance at register number one went out over the loudspeaker, as usual. The general din of the grocery store had the same dullness, but sounded louder somehow. More grating.

Liddy dug a hand into her purse and searched for the bottle of medication that had been her lifeline, especially right after her diagnosis when she'd had to continue working. She would have loved to stay home back then to nurture her fearful self, but starvation had not been a desirable option. She checked all pockets and came up empty, then allowed her fingers to poke along the bottom lining of her bag.

On her bed. The medicine bottle must be somewhere on her bed, most likely buried beneath a taut sheet. So much for learning from a young age to always make her bed! If she had a nickel for every time she had pulled the sheets and comforter over her phone, her wallet, her keys ...

She pressed her lips together, stifling a sigh. When she'd arrived home last night, she couldn't sleep. Her mind had been poring over the events at both the restaurant and hotel—and some from the evening before with Beau—so she'd stayed up and dumped the contents of her purse onto the bed, hoping to reorganize it all.

And then Beau had surprised her by calling to check up on her.

Liddy glanced around. If she hurried, she could pay for her items, run home for medicine, and still meet Beau around noon.

When she arrived at home, she yanked away the covers of her neatly made bed, but the medicine bottle wasn't there. Neither was it on the bathroom counter or in her nightstand drawer. Strange. She usually kept it close, like a tube of lipstick, always there and ready to give her what she needed—and quick.

She retraced her steps from the night before, starting with the front door. By the time she'd wound her way like a lost dog through her small condo, it hit her: when she'd cleaned out her purse, she had not come across the bottle. Think, Liddy, *think!*

No, it definitely hadn't been there. So where was it? Maybe she'd left it in the drawer at work where she kept her purse.

She glanced at the clock. It was already quarter to noon. Not enough time to stop by the hotel before lunch. Her heart raced in her chest, but not from dizziness. Instead a creep of dread began its ascent, winding through the knots that had already formed in her stomach.

Liddy reached for her phone, and her thumb hovered over the call button. Instead, she sent Beau a quick text: *Sorry. Have to cancel lunch. Will make it up to you!*

She added a happy face emoji, and slowly laid the phone on the table.

"YOU'RE DISTRACTED," BEAU SAID that evening. "Everything

all right?"

Liddy nodded at him, a lightning-fast flash of something in her eyes. "Yes, fine," she answered, but something was off. He'd seen that expression before, but he could not recall when, and therefore had no reference in which to frame it.

Beau eyed her for a few seconds more before returning to his meal.

Plenty of light still poured from the sky as he and Liddy sat outside, protected only by hazy blue netting hung like a tarp from each corner. Since they had not been able to meet up for lunch, they had decided to have an early dinner on the pier. Beachgoers, their feet slapping against weathered planks, and territorial seagulls provided entertainment enough to fill the pockets of silence between them.

Liddy's phone rang. He watched her glance at the screen, hesitate, and when she saw his eyes on her, quickly turn off the ringer. Then she speared a shrimp, ate it, and took a long sip of sparkling water while gazing at the expansive body of water that fanned out behind them.

Something was definitely bothering her, but it wasn't his place to pry her loose like a soldered oyster. He'd long learned that a woman would share what was on her mind often—and when she cared to. Besides, though he and Liddy had grown exceptionally close in a relatively short amount of time, neither had made a long-term commitment to the other.

Long-term. He mulled that over for a few seconds. The idea didn't scare him like it once might have. Maybe it sucked a few liters of air from his lungs at rapid fire pace, but fear? Not really.

Liddy's phone rang again, and this time her eyebrows knit

too closely together for his comfort.

"Go ahead and answer it. I'll wait here."

Her body barely reacted, but he could tell by a shimmer of hope in her eyes that she was glad he had encouraged her.

"I'll be just a second," she said, then quietly slipped out the gate and entered the fray of tourists milling about. She kept walking, head down, until she reached the pier railing. She leaned into it while continuing to talk, one hand holding the phone against her ear, and the other rolled into a fist.

Though he knew he would never interrogate her over that intense phone call, Beau could not tamp down the desire to stroll over there, take her fist into his hands, and kiss each finger free.

LIDDY SHUT HER EYES, but the warm breeze did nothing to cool her. "I don't understand why I'm getting bumped again."

The woman on the other end, the hospital's MRI scheduler, said, "I'm sorry, Liddy, but we've had some emergencies and it's created a domino effect. I've been asked to reschedule those whose MRIs are just routine."

"Routine? A brain tumor is … routine?" Her voice had begun to rise. She hated the feel of it scraping through her throat.

"I understand, but you had it removed. Right?"

She sighed. "Yes, yes, of course." It hit her that if she was being bumped, it was likely for someone who had been in her position months ago. The memory of those days and hours waiting to learn her fate rendered her without an appetite. "Listen," she broached, "I understand that there are more dire cases in front of me. It's just … I've been experiencing some weird symptoms lately—"

"In that case, you should really make an appointment to see your doctor."

"Oh, but I was hoping that this MRI would prove that all was well …"

"If you're having symptoms, your doctor may want to order a more involved test. Shall I hold off scheduling you until you can get an appointment with him?"

"No, no. Please." She bit her lip, hoping she hadn't sounded too desperate. "Let's just leave it as is for now."

Liddy made her way back to the table with a pasted-on smile. Seeing Beau waiting for her helped to quell the unease churning her stomach until another thought broke through: What if he asked her about the phone call? Did she really want to tell him about the follow-up MRI? And what if he learned she'd been dizzy lately? Would he prod her for more information? He'd already asked her how she was feeling far more than was comfortable for her.

She slid into her chair, resolved.

He eyed her with concern. "Everything okay?"

Liddy smiled. "It is. Now what were we talking about?"

"You've actually been pretty quiet today. Unusual."

"What do you mean?"

"Just that you're not your usual chipper self."

A wave crashed in the distance, sending a goose bump-inducing breeze through the patio. She forced a smile. "Didn't realize that was a requirement." As soon as the words left her mouth, she wished she could call them back.

He crossed his forearms and leaned them onto the table, his

eyes imploring her. "Are you feeling well?"

She straightened her back and reached for a napkin, rolling it in her hand. Again? Why was he pressing her? "Of course. I wouldn't have come to dinner if I didn't."

"You haven't told me why you missed lunch."

She scrunched that napkin into a ball. "Really, Beau? Are you accusing me of something?"

Beau's right brow rose as he scoffed. "Well, I wasn't, but now I'm starting to wonder …"

"Wonder what?" she snapped.

This time his brow lowered, concern marking his face. Beau reached across the table for her hand. "Hey, wait. I'm sorry."

His touch seared her fingers, sending a dart of passion through her. The sensation comforted her. She wanted to cry, but held herself in check and looked away, pretending to examine the sea.

What would he do if he knew how scared she was right now?

Could he handle it?

And how would she handle it if he couldn't?

Warmth continued to flood her body at his touch, and she pulled her gaze back to his, finding safety his eyes. If only this sense of calm had the ability to drive out the deep fears that had rooted in her weeks ago, the ones that had bloomed in unwelcome glory earlier today.

He played with her fingers, but slowly she untangled her hand from his. She swallowed, a sharp knot of emotion lashing the base of her throat. "I'm sorry for being so crabby," she said, wicking a look at him. She attempted a small laugh. "I'm really tired from last night, I guess."

He smiled, and though it reached his eyes the corners turned down slightly—as if carrying a weight of sadness. "Partying with the girls can do that." He hesitated, then said with a spike of a laugh, "Or so I've heard."

That night, she kissed him goodnight on the landing outside of her condo. As she locked the door behind her, she could not shake the ominous cloud of fear that had followed her home.

Chapter Twenty

AT WORK THE NEXT MORNING, Liddy checked every drawer, behind every knick-knack that Trace had somehow wrangled approval to leave up, and every inch of carpeting under the desk, but she came up empty. The medicine bottle was nowhere. Lost. Gone.

So she ducked out to call her doctor, even though she had barely started her day.

"Dr. Grayson's office. This is Mary."

The woman from the picnic. "Hello, Mary? This is Lydia Buckle."

"Lovely to hear your voice. Are you calling to make an appointment?"

"Uh, no. Not exactly. I realized this morning that I'd lost the bottle of Dilantin that Dr. Grayson said I should keep with me at all times. Would it be possible to refill that prescription?"

"Well, let me take a look. Just a moment. Hmm. It says here that the doctor hasn't authorized any refills."

"I know, but like I said, I lost the bottle and …"

"And from what I can tell, this is not an active prescription."

Liddy pressed her lips together, shut her eyes, and took a

deep breath through her nose. Should Mary even be reading her chart? *Aren't there HIPAA laws or something?*

"At least that's what I can tell from your file, although I haven't worked as a nurse in years. Tell you what. Dr. Grayson is in surgery all day, but I can have his nurse look over your file when she's free and advise me. If she gives me the go-ahead, I'll call in your prescription for you."

And Liddy let the breath she was holding back out.

For the next hour or so, she kept busy answering calls and making dinner or show reservations for guests. Once or twice it crossed her mind that she hadn't received a text from Beau. He knew she was at work, though, as was he, so that's likely why.

Hopefully she hadn't scared him away the night before.

Trace leaned in next to her. "Something's going down at the O.K. Corral."

"Excuse me?"

She gestured with a flick of her chin toward the bell desk. Yep, Hans was on a tirade and the poor bellmen and valets were stuck dealing with it.

Though she knew it wasn't the most mature move ever, Liddy rolled her eyes. "It's too early for this," she whispered.

"Don't I know it. I've still got a hundred phone calls to make and won't that be distracting if Hans decides to raise his voice at exactly the wrong moment?"

"Well, you make your calls. If a client hears Hans, it'll be his fault!"

Trace pulled back. "Whoa. What's got you in a snit?"

"Yeah," said Meg, as she sidled up to the concierge desk, "you look like Shawn just asked to borrow your car."

Liddy almost cracked a smile at that.

"Seriously. What's up?" Meg asked, her eyes zeroing in on Liddy's.

She shrugged. "Nothing. Overslept this morning and didn't get enough coffee. That's all."

Meg pursed her lips.

Liddy waved her away. "Go on now. Don't you have some million-dollar client to book?"

Slowly, Meg nodded. She began to walk backward, and Liddy fought off a twinge of envy over the perfect cut and fit of her friend's sleek cobalt blue suit. It was like she had stepped into a glove. How fun would that be to do every day? She glanced down at her plain-Jane wardrobe, as outlined in the employee handbook.

When Meg pointed a two-finger V-sign at her as if to say "I'm watching you," Liddy laughed out loud.

It was late afternoon before Mary called her back. "You're all set," she said, adding that Liddy really should make an appointment to see Dr. Grayson soon. She would, of course, but not until after she had undergone another routine MRI, which was now more than two weeks away.

A niggling worry from earlier in the day had evolved into one of epic proportions. Grabbing her phone, Liddy turned to Trace. "I'm going to run outside for a break."

"Good for you. Sea air is good for the soul."

"Agreed. Be back soon."

The short walk to the water's edge brought a noticeable drop in her blood pressure—not like it was ever really high—but tension eased out of her neck and shoulders as the cloudless sky beckoned her. Seated on a bench overlooking the surprisingly calm sea, a gaggle of boats bobbed on the water. She punched in Beau's number.

He picked up on the first ring.

"Hey," she said.

"Hey," he answered. Was there a moment of hesitation?

She licked her lips, and rubbed them together. "I wanted to ... I wanted to apologize for my crankiness yesterday."

"Are you better today?"

"Yes. Much. Work has been crazy, but I ..."

What could she say? Her mood was lifted now that her meds were waiting for her at the pharmacy? Or now that she had not experienced a moment of dizziness all day long?

"I guess I just wanted to apologize."

"No need. We all have bad days."

She nodded. He spoke the words she expected him to, but somehow they lacked enthusiasm. Perhaps he was just busy. She pictured him sitting behind his paper-strewn desk.

"So ... so I guess I'd better let you go, since you're at work," she broached.

"I need to ask you something, Liddy."

She hesitated. "Of course."

"How are you? Really."

"I'm good. Happy. Meg had me laughing today, even. Hans is on the warpath for some reason, but even that's fairly comical. So, all in all a good day."

"Mary mentioned you today."

A sixty-something man on roller blades wove down the sidewalk in front of her, his tie-dyed shirt lifted on the breeze, giving her way too much information. But even that did not fully distract her from Beau's statement.

"Mary from my doctor's office?" Did her voice just rise in

pitch?

"Yes," he said evenly. She imagined him sitting in his office, his hand raking over the gristle growing on his cheeks.

"And?"

"She mentioned something about you calling in a prescription, and I wondered—"

"Are you kidding me? Isn't that illegal?"

It took him several seconds to answer. "It is. She shouldn't have said anything, but now that she has all I can do is wonder. You've seemed tired lately. And last night you were definitely not yourself. Now I learn you need more medication. Liddy? Are you ... is there something you want to tell me?"

She stood up. A flag on a sailboat whipped flat against the sky, hailing from its mast. "I'm fine. I can't believe she divulged my personal information. That's unbelievable."

"It's wrong. But she knows you and I are close. She likes you, by the way."

"Don't butter me up."

"I'm not. But I'm concerned, Liddy. I can't deny that."

"Well, don't be."

"But I am. I don't know if ..."

"If what?

Silence.

Liddy stood there in the afternoon sun, waiting for Beau to fill in the silence, and knowing the likelihood was rare. He didn't know if he could take dating someone like her: a woman whose future health was unknown.

"Maybe we can meet to talk," he finally said.

She shrugged, although there was no one there to witness it. Her surgeon had said the tumor was gone and there was little chance of a recurrence, but the fact remained that weird symptoms continued to persist.

Oh, dear God, let it not be so.

"Liddy?"

At his voice on the line, Liddy startled. "Sorry. I was ... somewhere else for a moment."

A phone rang in the background. "On second thought," he said, distracted, "I really should work tonight. Okay if I take a rain check?"

She wagged her head at the sky. How could he take a rain check on a date that they hadn't yet agreed upon? Liddy looked out to the sea, half wishing she could hop aboard a sunset-bound cruise. Any one of them would do.

"Sure," she finally said. As they said their goodbyes and clicked off the line, Liddy couldn't help but sense her rebuilt happiness ebbing away.

SHE COULDN'T SLEEP. At two a.m., long after respectable people had gone to bed, Liddy pulled on a fleece hoodie and went for a walk. The narrow lane winding along the beach stretched out before her like one long gang plank. Dozens of beach houses illuminated her path, most of them modernized and standing tall, like narrow stalwarts, blocking the late night breezes.

The hotel staff had been on edge all afternoon, and though she had hoped to hear some breaking news about the mysteries surrounding the restaurant, even if it had come, she would likely have been too busy to stop and listen.

"Something's up," Trace kept saying, and sniffing the air as if the action could conjure up some news.

In the end, since a writing organization was due into the hotel, and many of their officers had checked in a day early to set up, she'd been swamped. From the moment their president arrived, Liddy had been called upon to offer assistance in everything from making dinner reservations to helping with last-minute administrative tasks. By the time she'd left the hotel, the writer's conference board had transported more than three hundred convention packets to the ballroom reception area and settled in for a round of Chardonnay.

A second-story window slammed shut and Liddy stopped. She peered up, the sky clear and starlit, and tightened the drawstring at her neck. Apparently, someone else couldn't sleep.

Wind chimes jostled in the breeze, the lightness of their song keeping Liddy moving. Physically, she'd felt well all day. After work she had picked up her medication, then carefully zipped it into a pocket in her purse, but not before taking out some spares and stashing them in a cabinet. Just in case.

Emotionally she was all tapped out, but not enough to cause sleep to come. So she walked along the darkened street, unafraid of strangers and ghosts, marveling at how loud the waves crashing sounded with nothing but a mostly quiet night as a backdrop. Yet the sounds of water onto shore soothed her, made it easier somehow to hear her thoughts, to voice her worries in her mind.

Though she did not feel ill physically, a kind of apprehension enveloped her. And that alone scared her. Before the divorce, and certainly before the tumor had appalled her with its sudden appearance, the emotion of fear had been ill-defined in her life. Fear meant encountering a black widow while wiping down windows in the desert or the slither of a nearby garden snake, neither of which could not be overcome.

But this new fear, the kind that carried with it endings that could not be revoked, gripped her in a startling way. She was twenty-five, and she had officially crossed over the divide between idyllic childhood dreams and adulthood, with all its neuroses and unwelcome realities.

And then there was Beau. If she were truthful, she would admit that he had not originally fit her idea of a "dream" guy. She'd always been attracted to men with ripples and girth and dark, jet black hair. How shallow was that? When she found herself admiring Beau, talking with him and caring about what he said to her, and when her heart began to race at the caress of his gaze, the smooth texture of his voice, she worried. *You'll grow tired of him*, she told herself. *You'll start something you cannot finish.* Meg had said as much as well.

But Meg was wrong. The opposite had come true—she couldn't get enough of him. Smitten was an understatement. Perhaps this is why her fears hurt so much: she had something to lose. If there were to be long-term debilitating side effects from surgery, or—God forbid—a recurrence, she couldn't stand to drag down Beau with that kind of news. And that would mean losing someone, who in a very short time had come to mean the world to her.

An uncomfortable chill rankled the skin on her arms and she once again cinched her hoodie tighter. By the time she rounded the corner toward home, the foghorn at the harbor's edge had begun sounding its call. A haze had blown in rather quickly, like a flimsy sheet pulled across the sky, catching Liddy off guard.

Hurriedly, she reached the stairway and took the steps two at a time. Her mind was as awake now as it had been when she'd left, but thankfully, her body was not. Once inside, Liddy stripped off her hoodie, stepped out of her slip-ons, and crawled into bed without removing another stitch.

Chapter Twenty-One

"ARE YOU UP?" Meg was on the phone, her voice tentative, almost motherly.

Liddy peered at the time with one eye open, then spoke into the mouthpiece. "Sort of. What's up?"

"You're on the later shift, right?"

"Ten to seven. Why?"

"Good. Then you can meet me for breakfast."

"But—"

"No, buts. See you there in half an hour."

Liddy set the phone down with a groan. "Well," she said to the rafters, "that was rather ominous."

She reached the place they always met—The Breakfast Bar—and Meg was sitting outside, looking chic and well-coiffed. As usual. Oversized and heavily tinted sunglasses camouflaged her face.

Liddy took a seat opposite her friend. "You know I love you, but what in the heck?"

Meg smiled, briefly. "Can't I invite my BFF to breakfast?"

"OMG, JW."

Meg slid those crazy huge sunglasses down her nose and peered over the top. "JW?"

"Just wondering."

"Ah."

The waitress brought them each water and coffee, and Meg said, "I already ordered you an omelet. You're welcome."

Liddy nodded once. "Gee, thanks," she said.

The waitress clucked a laugh and moved on, swinging her coffee pot toward the next outdoor table.

"So I'm guessing there's more to this breakfast than food. Right?"

"I wanted to warn you that Jackson's sister, Pepper, showed up this morning."

Liddy's lips hovered just above her coffee cup. "Jackson has a sister?"

"Yes. And she's an angry woman. You know that their father used to run the hotel chain, right?"

"I'd heard that."

"Well, anyway, they have a strange arrangement in that they are co-owners of the properties, but since Jackson's the creative extrovert and Pepper's more of a money whiz, they usually stay in their respective corners."

"I take it they aren't close."

Meg shook her head. "Not at all."

Liddy finally took that sip of coffee, then sat back, thankful that the haze from earlier in the morning had slipped away. The sun shone warm enough that she wished she had remembered sunscreen. "I take it you know Pepper pretty well then from your relationship with Jackson?"

As was becoming more and more the case, Meg's expression stiffened at the personal question, like shutters snapping shut.

Liddy changed her line of questioning. "Well, thanks for

telling me. Good to be on my toes. What was the staff's take?"

"She swept in late yesterday, demanding spreadsheets and updated budgets on her desk ASAP." Meg smirked. "She slid into the only empty office, as if she'd always been there. Sally didn't know what hit her."

"Do you think this has anything to do with the restaurant rumors?"

Meg leaned her head to one side. "You know what? That's an interesting observation."

"How so?"

"I saw Chef wander in there shortly before I left to meet you. He was all poker-faced, but"—she shrugged—"who knows? Maybe something's about to go down."

Their waitress delivered two omelets in record time. Liddy surprised herself by devouring the entire egg, mushroom, and cheese concoction without much of a struggle. That walk from the night before must have made her hungry. Or maybe it was the worry that had done so. Whatever the reason, she ate enough to cover breakfast and lunch for the entire day. Maybe even dinner.

When it was time to leave, she stood, and Meg touched her elbow. "Hey," she said.

Liddy squinted. "Something wrong?"

"C'mon," Meg said, flicking her chin toward the street that meandered along the ocean, the same path that Liddy had walked toward the harbor in the wee hours of the morning. "You still have plenty of time to get to work."

They made their way past the morning bustle of residents pulling out of their driveways, ostensibly to head to work, and surfers arriving to catch a wave before the swells became overcrowded with tourists and their unwaxed boards.

Liddy bit her lip. "You haven't told me everything, have you?"

Meg pressed her lips together and shook her head. "Oh, Liddy. I have something to say and I'm ... I'm just wishing I didn't have to."

Liddy stopped and turned toward her. "Well, whatever it is, just say it. Nothing shocks me anymore."

Meg pulled off her sunglasses, the sunlight causing her to squint. "I saw Beau walking with a woman last night."

"Last ... night?"

"Yeah. They were wandering down by the pier. I had worked late—kind of had to after all of Pepper's demands—and I decided to stop at Kincade's for a glass of wine, and that's when I spotted them."

Liddy's heart knocked uncomfortably in her chest. "Maybe it was a client. He said something about working late."

"He did?"

"Yes. We talked about getting together, but then he said he couldn't after all because he had work to do."

Meg's face was anything but closed off now.

"What ... what kind of woman?" She tried to keep the suspicion out of her voice.

Her friend sighed and looked away from her, as if searching for words. "I didn't recognize her."

"Okay, so it could've been anybody. Maybe even a relative. We haven't talked since yesterday ... I'm sure he'll even mention her to me." She hoped he was planning on calling her sometime today, although there was no promise of that.

"I guess that makes sense. She was talking-talking-talking."

Liddy leaned her head to one side.

"I mean, I wasn't close enough to hear anything, but her mouth was moving constantly and she was gesticulating every which way. She even leaned a hand on his shoulder more than once, laughing about something." Meg demonstrated by pressing down on Liddy's shoulder, and laughing nonsensically into the air.

"Well, I'm sure he'll mention it." She hoped he would, anyway.

Meg let her hand fall away from Liddy's shoulder. She wound her hair into a ponytail as they walked, then let it flop down again onto her shoulders. So unlike her. "Sorry if I scared you. I guess—I guess I'm just sensitive to things." She paused. "Well, you know, after all that went down with you and Shawn."

Liddy peered at Meg. A flash of something—like a wince—crossed her friend's features, and she wondered if some other unwelcome memory had surfaced in her mind.

"Yes, so, like I said, I was just relaxing with a glass of wine, and the next thing you know, I see this woman jabbering on and on to Beau, dropping a familiar hand on his shoulder like they were old friends. If I hadn't been two floors up and only a quarter way through my wine, I might have chased after them and introduced myself." She laughed then. "How hilarious would that have been?"

Liddy cracked a smile, but that's as deep as the emotion went. This ... *this* must be why she hadn't slept much the night before. Deep down, she had sensed something shifting beneath her already shaky foundation.

"So ... you're not mad that I brought all this up, I hope."

Liddy gave her friend a sad smile. "No, of course not. I'm just ..."

"Sad?"

"No. Distracted. I'm really, really distracted these days." She blew out a breath and looked away from Meg before the tears came.

"Yeah, me too," Meg said, her expression equally sour. "Me too."

SHE HELD OFF CONTACTING HIM, hoping Beau would call her first and have a good explanation. A *really* good explanation. But the closer it came to the start of her workday, the more she knew that would not be happening. Her anger simmered all the way to work, which thankfully was not that far. No matter; she was still seething when she reached the parking lot.

She found a spot in the employee lot, threw the car into "Park," and yanked the keys from the ignition. How could he do this to her? She grabbed her phone from her purse and stared at it. What good would doing something rash bring to her? No good at all. Reacting out of sheer emotional trauma—she considered this to be in that category—would solve nothing. She had learned this one sad and lonely day when she mouthed off to Shawn's girlfriend and received nothing but more heartache in return. She'd told her to return his photos, the ones she inexplicably left behind.

And had she ever. Something inside her still wept at the sight of her memories cut to shreds in the FedEx package she received one lonely night last winter.

Still, Beau had told her he would be working last night,

and apparently it wasn't true. Unless walking along the pier with some woman who felt comfortable enough to publicly fawn all over him could be considered work. She weighed that. Perhaps in some circumstance, it could.

Liddy had a long day ahead of her. In a short time, the inn would be overrun with creative types who found a story around every corner. Oh, to be able to retreat from reality like that! Anger, no matter how justified, would not help her serve hotel guests today. So she compartmentalized. She folded up her indignation, slid it into her pocket, and began making her way across the long parking lot with her chin up.

She almost made it, too, until encountering a puddle just deep enough to infiltrate her flats when she accidentally stepped into it. As the water flooded her favorite trouser socks—the ones Meg had given her last year from the Kate Spade outlet store—something inside of her flared.

Liddy pulled her cell phone out of her pocket, and typed a missive to Beau.

BEAU'S PHONE BUZZED. He pulled it out of his desk drawer and read the screen:

Working last night? Really? Of all people, I thought you were honest.

He blinked and read the words again. The text from Liddy landed like a punch to his midsection. Bile oozed in his gut. She'd seen them. She must have seen them. The gasp he heard was his own. He shook his head, disgusted with himself. *I thought you were honest …*

Wendy had called him, right after he'd told Liddy he had to work. And he really *had* planned to work. He owned a home now. The proposals were piling up, and if he didn't do something soon to convert them from the proposal stage to the active stage, he would eventually have trouble with his mortgage.

True, that was a long while away. Still, when he'd sensed Liddy's indecision over seeing him last night, it seemed easier to hole up in his office and get some paperwork done.

Or maybe he had been practicing avoidance.

Then Wendy called. Said she had something she wanted to discuss with him. They had ended their relationship amicably—not that they'd spent enough time together to consider anything between them all that serious. At least in his mind. He'd run into her in church on occasion, too. Sometimes with Liddy by his side. She had always been pleasant, friendly, never showing any sign of animosity toward him.

So when she'd called asking to meet for a brainstorming session about a business venture, he'd said, "Sure."

They met on the boardwalk just outside of the Java Cafe. Two hot coffees and five minutes later, they began walking. She loved art and knew how much Anne had loved it, too. He was always too busy coloring inside the lines to be considered artistic, but he'd grown to appreciate fine works. Anne had taught him that. Besides, he'd built a good business for himself. Wendy knew that about him, so it hadn't surprised him that she'd asked to meet to talk.

"I have an idea to open a wine bar that features both local and out of the area artists," she'd told him. "My plan is to rent wall space to the artists for a nominal fee."

A light breeze rustled his shirt collar as he considered her venture. "Or you could charge them commission."

"Hmm, yes, that's an idea. That way starving artists could be featured next to those who have marketing money available to them."

"True." He sipped his coffee. "How do you plan to vet the works you display?"

"Well, I haven't formulated all that yet. I do think it would be a good idea to organize some kind of panel with local experts—and maybe even those with more of an appreciation of artistic forms, rather than only those who create it themselves."

He nodded.

She stopped. "Someone like you."

"Me?"

"Yes, of course. What a beautiful way to honor your late wife."

He considered her earnest expression. "Yes, I think Anne would love that. If she could, she'd likely laugh about it, too, but in the end, it would make her happy to see me using what I've learned to honor her."

Wendy gripped his shoulder then. "Thank you so much, Beau. I've made business mistakes in the past, and I really, *really* needed your expertise." She paused. "I knew you wouldn't let me down."

He smiled back at her. This was one of the first times he could remember smiling when thinking about Anne. He had despised her suffering, and often when he thought about their time together his mind drifted to her pain-filled last days until the memories wrenched his insides. This time, however, he recalled all she had taught him about her love for art, and all he could do was smile.

Wendy kept walking along the pier, talking non-stop about her ideas. He thought more about her business venture, too. Her idea would bring something new to this beach area. In fact, he could see the idea taking off in all kinds of venues, such as restaurants, doctor's offices ... even Liddy's resort.

Liddy.

His heart constricted. She had grown distant lately, quiet. Did she ... was she ... he shook away the questions. He knew what she had been facing when he began dating her. Her prognosis had not only been good, but excellent. Surely if she were facing some challenge, she would tell him. He wanted to believe this. He'd confided in her often, especially in recent days, and she had allowed him his misery with open arms.

"Can I buy you dinner?"

Wendy's question pulled Beau out of his deep thoughts. She watched him, her eyes wide and imploring.

"Please? It's my way of thanking you for being my sounding board." She paused. "I'm very grateful to you."

He cradled the coffee in his hand, suddenly noticing that it had grown cool to the touch. A million conflicting thoughts battled in his brain, but one of them—the one that told him he was hungry—won out.

"Sure. Let's grab dinner."

Now that he sat here in his office, staring down at Liddy's text, Beau knew he'd made a mistake.

Chapter Twenty-Two

LIDDY MADE HER WAY INTO the inn's bustling lobby, a thin thread of triumph buoying her. In only a few characters, she had told Beau what she knew and how she felt about it.

Her phone rang, but Liddy ignored it. When it happened again, she switched the ringer to off and buried her phone deeper into her purse before shoving it into the concierge desk drawer.

"You can answer that if you want," Trace said as Liddy pinned her name tag onto her blouse.

"It'll wait. Busy day ahead."

"Suit yourself."

For the rest of the morning, guests continued to check out of the hotel as a slew of writing conference attendees streamed in. Liddy was being asked for everything from names of restaurants that could seat large and lively groups, to information on an infamous, decades-old crime scene in the town to the south for a curious bunch of mystery writers. Thankfully, additional concierge staff had been called in for the day.

"Oh, hey, did you hear?" Trace asked in a lowered voice. "The big boss's sister's in town and she's ordering all kinds of people around. Little brother's none too happy about it, either."

"That bothers me to hear about family members feuding, especially publicly."

"Yeah, well, the more money that's involved, the more it happens," Trace said. "My uncle's a lawyer, and sees all kinds of disputes and misunderstandings all the time."

"Those two things aren't the same."

"Precisely. Half the time if people would only talk—and listen—to each other, they wouldn't have so many problems."

Liddy looked up from her computer, half-expecting Trace to be staring into her soul. Instead, her co-worker held the phone in her hand, ready to make a call.

"Have a question for me?" Trace asked.

Liddy shook her head. "No, sorry. Just thinking."

Trace smirked. "If I had a nickel for every time I caught myself staring into space."

Despite the ringer's silence, Liddy's phone vibrated in the desk drawer.

"Sure you don't want to get that? My calls can wait."

Liddy swallowed. "Maybe I should." She grabbed her phone from the drawer just as it stopped ringing. One glance at the screen told her that she had missed three calls from Beau. "Um, I think I'll take a quick break outside. Be back in a sec."

She reached a bench in a sunny but secluded spot near the water, clicked on voice mail, but all Beau said was, "Please call me."

She twisted her lips, biting the inside of her mouth. Obviously, he had read her text—and he didn't deny any of it.

This morning when Meg had reluctantly given her the news, Liddy didn't cry. She held it together, knowing that she'd been through worse than this, and besides, crying about it wouldn't change a thing. But now, hearing the voice she had come to love, and painfully aware of his lack of explanation, she had to fight harder against the threat of untethered emotion. A fissure had begun in the wall she had built.

She listened to the voice mail again, and huffed out a sigh. Calling back now would only complicate her day. *And Beau's.* She stood, took another glance out at the calm water, and swallowed the tears. She made her way back to the resort, to the guests waiting for assistance, and stopped.

Beau was waiting for her by the entrance, his face somber.

A tear tickled her eye, and she swiped it away.

"Liddy," he said when she approached.

She shook her head, her voice low. "Not now."

He nodded. "I understand, but we have to talk. Take a walk with me."

She nudged them away from the hotel entrance where valets and bellmen circulated. "I've already taken my break and I need to get back now."

He reached out and touched her wrist. "I want to explain, if you'll let me."

"Then you're saying there's something to explain."

He didn't reply.

She glanced around, hoping no one had spotted them. "That makes it worse, in a way."

Beau lowered his head, as if examining the stone pattern on the ground, then glanced up at her. His eyes—those gorgeous hazel-brown eyes—implored her. "Wendy called me ... she wanted to talk. That's all it was—talking."

Liddy shook her head tightly, remembering the petite

woman from church. "It's pretty immature to … to blame this on *her*."

Beau dropped his hand from Liddy's wrist and stepped back, assessing her. "I want to talk about your text. You wouldn't answer my calls."

"Because I'm working!"

"I called you seconds after receiving it."

Liddy raised a hand. "Please. I-I really can't do this now. We're really busy in there." She glanced nervously toward the hotel's massive sliding doors.

Beau closed the space between them, his breath landing on her cheeks. "Then when?"

He smelled amazing. Like cedar and cardamom. She could hardly pull herself away, and yet a part of her didn't care to hear whatever it was he had to say. She'd been lied to before, why give him—or any other man—even an inch toward doing that again?

"I don't know."

He blew out a sound laced with exasperation and melancholy. She was making it hard on him. She knew this. Deep down, she did not—could not—believe that Beau would purposely lie to her.

But he had.

Or at the very least, had led her to believe they were exclusive, yet had spent what looked like some intimate time with another woman.

She wanted to slap him.

Instead, she speared him with a look. "Is it true? Was she leaning on your shoulder?"

His mouth opened, but no words came out. Beau's face was

still inches from hers, but he tore his gaze away. "Who told you that?"

"Doesn't matter."

His Adam's apple bobbed and his eyes found hers again. "It wasn't like that," he finally said. "I know what it must have looked like, but she was just happy for my advice."

The thought made Liddy ache. Till now, Beau had been good for her—sweet, kind ... sexy. Every fiber of her wanted him, and wanted to believe that this was all some sort of stupid hiccup that a couple of deep breaths would wash away. They'd laugh about it later, maybe even over a glass of wine by one of the hotel fire pits.

But truthfully, she had sensed a subtle change in Beau lately, as if he had been analyzing her, watching for signs of, well, weakness, maybe. Maybe that's why he so easily accepted Wendy's invitation last night.

"Forgive me," he said, as if he could read her inner conflict.

Her voice was a whisper. "What would you do if I told you I had been ... if I had been feeling dizzy lately?"

He gave her a quizzical, tentative smile. "I don't understand."

She grew bolder. "What if I said I was worried that I don't feel as well as I should in this stage of my healing?"

She noticed the way he pulled back physically as realization washed over him. His eyes began searching her face, and he swallowed back whatever words had suddenly come to his mind.

Slowly, but with steely deliberation, Liddy pulled herself away from his embrace. She blinked hard at the puddles building in her eyes and nodded with finality. "That's what I thought."

"I haven't said anything."

"You don't have to, Beau. Your silence says enough."

He reached out to her. "Liddy."

No doubt she would have a ton of explaining to do when she finally returned to her post at the concierge desk, but at this moment she didn't care. This needed to be said.

She kept herself away from his reach, and her voice low. "Really, I don't blame you for seeking comfort somewhere else, Beau. If I were you, I'm not sure if I'd be able to handle a relationship with me either."

Beau's jaw clenched. "That's not true. At all."

"No? Are you sure about that? You said last night that you were working, but ended up strolling the pier with Wendy—"

"We *weren't* strolling the pier—"

"And when I told you how I've been feeling lately, you nearly fainted."

Beau raked a hand through his hair. "You have got to be kidding ... Liddy, promise me we can sit down and talk this out tonight. Will you do that?"

Liddy's lungs tightened, the very breaking of her heart keeping her from breathing. She wanted this to go away, but how could it? She shook her head. "I'm sorry, Beau, but I can't. I don't want to walk on eggshells around you anymore. I think ... I think we need to ... take a break."

"WHERE'VE YOU BEEN?" Trace asked, a bead of sweat on her forehead.

Liddy stashed her purse inside a drawer, steadying herself as she did. "Terribly sorry. Got caught up on a … on a call."

"Well, thankfully you're here now. These writers are driving me crazy! They're party animals, every one of them."

Despite the clump of tears that could unravel at any moment, Liddy smiled at her co-worker's description of the creative types milling about the lobby. She blew out a determined breath. "Let me help. What needs to be done next?"

Well, for one you could call this one back." Trace handed her a message with a name and number. "She wants to take a group to see *My Fair Lady* at the Conch Theater *and* she'd somehow like us to finagle a way for them to meet the cast backstage. She specifically requested that the playwright be there."

"The dead one?"

Trace gasped and pointed at her. "That's what I said!"

Liddy nodded, thankful for the distraction. "I'll call her right now."

"And after that, would you want to make sure that the bell desk is sending people over here for reservations? You know how those guys like to horn in on our commissions! I'd like to give that Hannah a piece of my mind …"

"Gladly."

"You're the best. Now I'll just sit here and wade through this stack of requests while Lilly and Pat—wherever they went—handle walk-ups."

Liddy arrived home later than usual. She was supposed to leave at seven, but a flurry of last-minute restaurant reservations and Uber calls kept her there until nearly eight. The medicine flowing through her veins had made her exceptionally tired—she had taken a pill sans water during one extremely brief lull in the afternoon. So she planned to eat, take a shower, and go to sleep. If she did all that without breaking down, Liddy could say she had accomplished something extraordinary today.

Her cell phone rang, and the big knot in her throat grew with every ring.

"I need to talk to you!" Meg said when Liddy answered the phone.

"About?"

"I was at Sally's desk today, giving her my travel schedule for the next three months when I heard a brouhaha brewing between Jackson and his sister. Suddenly the door opened and she marched out and glared at me, wanting to know where I was planning to fly off to and when."

Liddy curled her lip. "Really."

"I wouldn't let her scare me, of course."

"Of course."

"But Sally's scared to death of her, so she handed over my itinerary and I swear that woman turned three shades of red."

"I'm wondering ... do you think the inn's in trouble? Financially, I mean."

"I don't really think so. I'm privy to the sales budget and it was increased this year. We always hit our numbers—even if it takes a bit of travel from yours truly to do it."

"A bit."

"Come on, I'm not gone all the time."

"But a lot. Not that your work doesn't pay for itself, but I need you to be around more." Liddy sniffled, wishing she could keep her emotions in check.

"Oh, Liddy. Oh, no. I'm so sorry ... I got so caught up in my story that I haven't asked what happened when you talked to Beau about ...”

"The woman?”

"You did clear all that up, right?”

"I did.”

"As in ...?”

"We ... we're taking a break.” Her voice cracked, sending forth the flood of tears she had been holding at bay for hours.

"I'll be right there,” Meg said, and clicked off the line.

Fifteen minutes later Meg showed up with a pint of Ben & Jerry's and her own tear-streaked face. She threw her arms around Liddy. "This sucks, Lid.”

Liddy stepped back and shook her head. "It's fine ... I'm fine.”

"Bull. Here.” She thrust the pint into Liddy's hands, then dug something out of her pocket. "Spoons.”

Liddy released a ragged sigh. "You think of everything.”

They sat on the couch, surrounded by pillows and blankets and the remnants of quick work of that ice cream.

Meg approached Liddy tentatively. "I can understand not fully trusting men right now. Shoot, I'm still open to keying your jerk ex-husband's car. You name the time.” Her voice softened even more. "But Beau.”

But Beau.

"He did say that this was some kind of misunderstanding, right?”

She nodded.

"What did he say?”

"What does it matter?”

"I'm not suggesting that you let someone lie to you again ... but why not let him tell you everything? I couldn't see him all that well from my perch, but from his body language I could tell he wasn't in to her. There was a lot of space between them."

"It doesn't matter anyway. This was going to happen sooner or later, so why not now?"

"And you think that why?"

Liddy looked away.

"Wait a second. It's you, isn't it? You wanted this breakup."

"'Wanted' isn't exactly the right term."

"But it was your idea—and for more than the Beau and Wendy show from last night. Why?"

Liddy huffed a sigh. She flipped a sober look at Meg. "I've been dizzy lately."

"I don't understand."

"I've had this weird pressure in my head lately, even a few headaches. And the other day at the store, the place began to spin and I had to grab onto a shelf for support." Liddy bit her lip. "Scared me."

"So you think … it's back?"

Liddy threw aside the blanket covering her legs and stood up. She pressed a hand to her head. "No idea. Whenever I feel something strange coming on, I pop a pill. I still have plenty left over from before the surgery." She didn't mention that she had recently refilled the prescription.

"What does the doctor say?"

"Again, no idea. I'm supposed to have an MRI, but the hospital has rescheduled my appointment twice."

"Are you seriously going to tell me you haven't seen a doctor? What's wrong with you?"

Liddy put her hand on one hip and her mouth dropped open.

Meg raised a palm. "And wait, wait, wait … what does all this have to do with …? Oh. I see, I see. You think Beau's going to hear about this and bolt."

"Doesn't really matter what I think. I've been afraid to tell him about any of this for fear of shaking him up, but he suspected something anyway." She crossed her arms, her voice turning to a harsh whisper. "It's just … it hurts so much. I had no idea how deeply I'd fallen …"

Meg rushed toward Liddy and pulled her into a bear hug, which wasn't easy to do considering their differing heights.

"Listen to me. You have to stop jumping to conclusions—about your health and about Beau. This is likely just some kind of residual effect from your surgery. And don't forget—it hasn't been all that long since you experienced a trauma of a different kind. Liddy, if the roles were reversed, I don't think I could've handled it with the type of gusto that you've shown."

"Not true."

Meg nodded vigorously. "It *is* true. I would've folded like a pop-up tent in the wind. Promise you'll call the doctor tomorrow and get the heck off that medicine now."

"I'm afraid."

"Of what?"

Liddy hiccuped before speaking. "What if it did come back?"

Meg squeezed both of Liddy's arms. "Then you'll face that with the same audacity that you've shown all year."

"SO YOU JUST WALKED AWAY?" Taylor stared at him over a platter of tacos.

Beau looked to Ginny for some support, but she frowned back at him.

"What were you doing at the pier with Wendy anyway?"

He shook his head. "She just wanted to talk to me about a ... a business venture. I was giving her advice."

Taylor raised one eyebrow. "Sounds like she wanted you to give her something else, bro."

Ginny slugged him, her expression fierce.

A knife twisted in his gut. Clearly they both thought this was his fault, that he'd run Liddy off. "Look, I asked Liddy if I could call her after work, and she said no."

"And you believed her?" Ginny said.

"It's been years since I've had a new relationship to deal with, but yes, I believed her. She made herself clear: she wanted a break from from us. And if nothing else, marriage taught me well."

Ginny continued to press him. "Meaning?"

"If a woman doesn't want me around, I won't force the issue."

Ginny leaned forward. "Beau, you've been through so much in the last year. I wish it wasn't so, but it is. Which is why what I'm about to say to you is so difficult." She paused. "You are a stupid man."

Taylor grinned, his mouth full of taco. "Listen to her, dude. She knows her stuff."

Beau sat there, dumbfounded. He had never seen this side of Ginny before.

Ginny slid out of her seat and stood. "Sorry to have to be

blunt with you, my friend. I've seen you and Liddy together, and there's something there. Don't give up on her—or yourself—so quickly." She sighed and bent to give her husband a peck on the cheek. "Gotta run, love."

Taylor watched her sashay away. Lucky idiot. The guy had fallen for Ginny on their first date and that was it. He was in. All in.

But that wasn't Beau's way. Life for him was a series of direction signs. Green meant go, and red? Stop. Halt. Do not proceed. When he'd attempted to smooth things over with Liddy the other day, he definitely saw red, and he had taken that as a sign to walk away.

"So," Taylor said, broaching the subject again, "are you going to go after her?"

Beau flicked Taylor a glance. "There's more."

Taylor sat back. "You didn't … take it too far with the Wilkes woman, I hope."

Beau shook his head. That thought hadn't even entered his mind, and he took an odd sense of satisfaction in that. "No. But Liddy said something strange to me the other day. She said she hasn't been feeling that well lately, that she'd had dizzy spells."

"Was this the same day she broke up with you?"

He swiped a hand across his grizzled face. "Yeah. She was rather in my face about it, like she wanted to see how I handled it."

"And how did you handle it?"

Beau snapped him a look. "How do you think?"

Taylor wagged his head, a telling look on his face. He leaned forward, his arms clasped together onto the table in front of him. "Aha."

Beau crushed his napkin and pitched it onto his uneaten plate of tacos. "Aha nothing. She surprised me, that's all. I just needed some time to take in what she was saying, and to ask questions. But she never gave me the chance. Just said she was walking on eggshells around me."

"Maybe she is."

"So this is my fault? I take a meaningless walk with a friend—"

"That involved some inappropriate touching."

Beau set his chin. "Not on my part!" He sighed. "I may have been a little surprised when Liddy suddenly announced that she's been dizzy lately. Out of the blue."

A waiter came by and wordlessly removed their plates. A woman carrying a pitcher of water filled up their glasses.

"Admittedly, it's a tough spot you're in. I like Liddy, and my gut tells me she's good for you, but dude, if it were me, I'd be a little nervous, too. I know Ginny thinks you should offer some kind of grand gesture to Liddy, but I don't know. Not sure you're ready for that."

Beau sighed and took in the colorless day that surrounded them. Truthfully—and painfully—he found himself agreeing with Taylor: he wasn't sure if he was ready yet, either.

TODAY, SHE RAN. Not a fast walk, and certainly not a jog. No, today after work, Liddy laced up her running shoes and ran as fast as she could down the beach, bounding over incoming waves and fighting against the rising pressure in her lungs. It was the good kind of pressure, the kind that presented her with a goal, and then another. Sweat poured from her, dripping off her chin, the droplets occasionally landing cold on her warm skin. She wanted to hit the wall, then leap right over it. She needed to do this for herself. It had been days since she had spoken to Beau, and she had been surprisingly calm about it. She'd had to be.

Her cell phone rang the second she entered her condo after a brief cool down. She sneezed, then flopped onto the floor, her chest still pulsating. She pulled off her shoes, and hit the answer button, putting her phone on speaker. "Hi. What's your news?"

"How did you—wait. What news?" Meg said.

"Too sweaty to talk." She grabbed a magazine and began fanning herself with it. "Haven't seen you at work in two days, so I figured you had news. Spill."

"I've been in So Cal—awful traffic. I stopped by the hotel on my way back into town today, though, and you're gonna die when you hear ..."

Liddy stopped fanning herself. "Really."

Meg paused for longer than usual. "Oh, you know, Sally was all worked up again. Face was red. May have been a few tears." She chuckled unevenly. "The usual, but enough about my day. Anything from the doctor?"

"Whoa, no way. You told me I was about to die. I think you at least owe me an explanation."

"Seriously, it was nothing. Something about unapproved restaurant expenditures ... I think spreadsheets and receipts were being demanded. Forget it. I want you to keep me informed about your health. You know that!"

"Yes, I do. But I don't know ... I feel like you have more to tell me."

Meg sighed. "Fine. Whatever. Jackson and Pepper were at each other's throats in the office when I walked in. Another reason Sally looked the way she did."

"Hmm. Any word on why they were fighting?"

"Their battles are nothing new ..."

"What does that mean?"

Meg sighed. "It means that during our brief relationship, Jackson may have mentioned things he doesn't want me remembering now."

"You can't stop there, you know ... unless, well, unless, it's all pillow talk or something."

Meg laughed. "You goof. Fine ... he told me once that his sister is his father's daughter from another relationship. He didn't find out about her until he was nearly an adult, and the news rocked him. His relationship with his father until his death was nearly non-existent."

"Wow." Liddy thought back to the revelations about her own marriage, and how Shawn's betrayal shook her deeply. For months, she had wondered how she had missed the signs that a relationship she had taken for granted had crumbled almost overnight. As the days wore on, though, she knew better. She had seen the signs, but hadn't recognized them for what they were. She held her breath a moment. The diagnosis of her tumor had been like that, too. She'd felt strange and weak for months, but played down the rumblings in her mind. Had Jackson really not known about his half-sister for that long?

She cleared her voice. "And apparently their father's holdings were left for both of them to handle. That's one way to force your children to get along."

"Or not," Meg said. "Enough about all that. Please tell me you've heard from your doctor."

Liddy stood and bent over to one side, hoping to limber up after her run. "I had an MRI late yesterday," she said, exhaling. "I'm supposed to hear something this week, but I keep hoping it'll be tonight before the doc's office closes."

"What?! And you didn't tell me?"

Liddy gave her friend an exaggerated little laugh. "I was getting to it."

"What'd they say?"

"Honestly, I didn't tell you because I was worried that at the last minute I would get bumped again. Although, I have to say, my doctor pretty much made sure that wouldn't happen. As for results, I'm waiting for them. If I suddenly cut this call short, you'll know why."

"This is great news, or at least it will be soon. I know it. Can I ask ... how's the dizziness?"

She grimaced. The dizziness had dissipated. Her breaking heart? Not so much. "Honestly, I haven't had a bout with it lately."

"Good. What did your doctor say about the pills?"

"He said to keep them on hand, and if I found myself needing to take them, do so, but that I should also call him."

"I suppose he's being cautious until the MRI results are in."

"Yeah."

"Yeah, so ... anything from Beau?"

"Like I said, we're not together right now." When she had told Beau she wanted a break, Liddy half-expected him to show up anyway. But he didn't and that was fine. Probably even for the best.

"You okay? Really?"

Liddy nodded, hoping to shake away the tiny lump forming in her throat. "Yeah, fine. I just came in from a run, in fact. I think I'll grab a warm shower and read for a while."

They said their goodbyes and clicked off the line, Liddy keeping her phone close as she made her way out of the room.

Chapter Twenty-Three

AT WORK THE NEXT DAY, the morning hours dragged on and on. So at the first opportunity, Liddy stepped outside for a break, taking a walk behind the hotel to the path that overlooked the shoreline. The ocean glimmered in the late morning light, offering up soothing colors of spring and shades of blue, but the spectacle did little to buoy her mood.

She leaned against a railing and let go of a sigh, the release softening her shoulders, as if they had been caged since daylight. Beau hadn't called. Neither had the doctor's office. She felt herself sinking into the depths of wallowing—and hated herself for it.

Pull it together, Liddy.

She fought off the hover of a grey cloud, and instead offered up a broken prayer, her failures fresh in her head. Shawn, his girlfriend … their son. She swallowed, hard. That reality was never far away from her mind but she had to let it go. A child, a new life, had risen out of the ashes of her crumbled marriage. How could she be bitter now?

I have loved you with an everlasting love.

The words swirled on the breeze around her, loving and rich, blanketing her with warm hope. Where had she heard them before? And why did they pierce her so deeply now, especially when love, the kind that ran deep as the ocean, seemed elusive.

I have loved you ... an everlasting love.

Once again, the words reverberated, the shudder of the sea a longing companion. Comfortable, gripping. In a way the words she clung to reminded her of the voice she had heard in the hospital, the one she had not questioned.

She saw the words in her mind this time, letters like silk flowing across a page. A measure of peace settled her as she repeated them softly in the wind.

Her gaze wandered to the end of the path, where a guy in striped shorts dug a deep hole flicking shovelfuls of sand haphazardly behind him. A girl in a yellow sun dress sat next to him, egging him on, her laughter infusing the sea-laced air with a kind of dreaminess that she longed to emulate. The salt air tickled her nose. Her eyes watered, and she blinked it away. Trace would be sending a valet out soon to check on her. She laughed quietly at the thought.

Liddy glanced at the couple again, longing to be carefree. Water pricked her eyes, but this time, not from the sniffles. She couldn't stay out here forever, hiding from her truths. The thought of being apart from Beau hurt so much more than she ever thought it could. She'd thought she would never recover from the loss of her marriage, but the truth struck her with alarming clarity that this time, she had so much more to lose.

She went back into work, knowing the stakes were higher than they had ever been.

"LIDDY BUCKLE?"

Liddy lifted her gaze to the women who had appeared at the concierge desk, seemingly out of nowhere. She'd been so entrenched in the manual in front of her, she had not heard the approach of footsteps. "Yes, may I help ..."

"We've met briefly once." She paused. "Do you remember me?"

Wendy Wilkes stood in front of her, her hair pulled up into clip, her face free of makeup. It had taken a second or two for recognition to set in, but the woman who seemed to have more than a passing interest in Beau had showed up at the hotel. For what, she couldn't imagine.

"Beau suggested I speak with you."

An uncomfortable heat filled Liddy's cheeks. "I see. What can I help you with?"

Wendy blinked a couple of times, then set a binder on top of the counter. "Actually, first it was Beau, and then a Mr. Riley, I believe?"

"Mr. Riley?" Liddy said. She could sense Trace's stillness, as if her co-worker had leaned in to listen.

Wendy flipped open the book. I presented an idea to him over the phone about holding an ongoing art show at the hotel. Well, actually, Beau suggested it first—that's why he told me to talk to you. But when I called, the secretary had me speak to Mr. Riley. He thought the idea had merit and that you could show me where we might put our displays."

Liddy nodded, finally able to think, to speak. "I see, I see. Okay, well, maybe Trace would be the best one to talk to. She's been here longer than I have."

Trace stood and peered over Liddy's shoulder at the open binder on the desk. "Hi, I'm Trace," she said.

Wendy smiled, tentatively. "Hello. Thank you. It's a pleasure. But if you don't mind, I'd like Liddy to show me. Would you?"

Their eyes met. Liddy saw something like challenge in them, and maybe a little resolve. She swallowed.

Trace whispered. "I suggest the library."

Liddy nodded once, meeting Wendy's eyes. "Certainly. Why don't we head across the lounge area, and I'll show you an area that you might want to consider."

As they walked along, Wendy said, "This place is nicer than I remembered it."

"Has it been a while since you've been in?" Liddy asked, keeping up with the small talk.

"Yes, I grew up in the area, but this hotel was pretty run-down back then." She glanced around. "There have been some improvements."

"And hopefully there will be more soon." Liddy stopped inside the area that she and Trace had recently begun referring to as "the library." "As you can see, we've added some classic books to the shelves. I'm not sure what Mr. Riley had in mind, exactly, but I could see this area being a start for you. Do you think the artwork you're planning to install would work here? Are the walls and lighting right?"

A full smile broke out on Wendy's face. "I do. Wow … yes, this would be awesome."

"Of course, depending on how many pieces you're planning to show, I suppose you could use some of the hallway space around the corner." Liddy suspected that no one would miss the plastic-framed paintings that had hung on those walls since the 80s.

Thomas wheeled a cart full of luggage by. He threw a lopsided grin at Liddy and a rather obvious leer at Wendy.

"He's cute," Wendy said.

"Well, he likes to think so anyway." Liddy shook her head. "Anyway, I think you could—"

"You know Beau and I had dinner together the other night."

Wendy's interruption startled Liddy, but she managed not to react. "I heard that."

"All he did was talk about you."

Liddy blinked, trying to measure the tone of the young woman's voice. "That's right. You mentioned he told you to talk to me about your art show idea."

"Not that so much. Yes, he said that, but he kept lapsing into stories about how funny you were, and how you talk a lot but he likes hearing your voice." She shook her chin slightly. "It was kind of annoying."

Liddy raised her brows but said nothing.

"Anyway, I tried to find you at church to tell you all this, but our paths never crossed."

"It's a big place."

"Sure." She slid the binder she'd been holding in front of her beneath one arm, and held out the other to shake Liddy's hand. "Well, I've taken up enough of your time. Thank you for showing me this area. I will get a proposal to Mr. Riley within the week."

"You're welcome."

"And Liddy? You should talk to Beau. He looks like hell."
Then she pivoted away.

"I HAVE SOME PAPERS FOR you to sign, but by the looks of that
avalanche on your desk, I should've brought my own pen."

Beau glanced up to find Taylor leaning against the doorway
to his office.

Taylor smirked. "Jill let me in," he said.

Beau sat back and rubbed his face with both hands. How
long had he been stuck in here, mired in paperwork? "Didn't
realize you'd be here already."

"Jill warned me that you've been pretty preoccupied these
days, so I told her I'd go all tough love on you for her."

Beau crossed his arms. "She'll be getting a pink slip tomorrow."

Taylor plucked a page from a disheveled stack. "Man, what
is all this stuff? Don't you know this is the age of machine? No
one should have this much paper scattered across his desk."

"Says the man who's about to ask me to sign a stack of
legalese."

"Ah, but this is a very important stack, one that, if you
sign, will bring you lots and lots of money."

Beau groaned. "Well, considering I've got a real estate
agent breathing down my neck with her incessant checklists, I
suppose I can take a break from this right now. Have a seat."

Taylor grinned. "I don't think so. Come on." He waved
the thick envelope he was carrying toward the door. "Let's get

out of here."

"Really, Tay, I can't. Too much to do."

Taylor kept that grin on his face. "Come on."

The look on his friend's face told Beau he wasn't about to waver. Beau released a deep breath. Fine. The guy wanted coffee, and Beau needed money to close the house deal. He stood and grabbed his keys.

Taylor grabbed the ring of keys from Beau's hand and tossed it back onto his desk. "You won't be needing these"—he glanced back at the messy desk—"although I might have to help you find them later. Let's go. I want to show you something."

Outside, Beau walked toward Taylor's blue SUV when he realized that his friend had veered elsewhere in the parking lot.

Taylor waved him over to a silver Porsche. He dangled a key in front of him. "Wanna drive it?"

Beau frowned. He turned back toward the SUV, noticing now that it was lighter in color than he remembered. The paint was faded in places, too. He took in the sports car again. It shined.

Taylor still held out that key. "Let's go."

Beau started her up, relaxing as the Porsche roared to life. Within seconds, he thought he heard it purr. "Who in the world loaned you this?"

Taylor laughed, a full-force, head-back kind of laugh. "I bought it, man. It's a 2005 Carrera."

"Does Ginny know about this?"

Taylor let out a gasp of incredulity. "You think I'm whipped or something? I can buy any car I want."

"Right."

"As long as she gets something shiny, too, of course."

Beau nodded, satisfied. "Now we're getting somewhere. How shiny did you have to go to get this baby?"

Taylor pursed his lips. He let out a sigh. "Just opened escrow on a hillside house."

Now it was Beau's turn to throw back his head and laugh like he hadn't laughed all week.

"Fine, fine," Taylor said. "Take this baby out on the freeway and you'll see that she's worth every penny."

Beau wagged his head. "She'd better be."

Getting to the coffee house by way of the freeway was about as out of the way as one could get. Neither of them cared, though, especially Beau. The sheer thrill of power rising in a breath of time, not to mention the risk of a massive speeding ticket, pulled him out of the funk that had been penetrating his mind and lonely days for the past week. He pulled into a compact space, reluctant to kill the engine.

"Woo-hoo!" Taylor said. "That was some test drive!"

The expression on Taylor's face had knocked ten years off his age, and Beau hoped it would do the same thing for him. Still smiling, he exited the car and handed Taylor the keys. "I don't know how you'll be able to control yourself. Not exactly the kind of car you can take to your daughter's ballet practices."

"Why not? I can fit a kid's car seat in it."

"I stand corrected."

Inside, they ordered their coffees—an espresso for Beau, a cold blended concoction for Taylor—and found a table outside. Taylor slapped the packet of papers onto the table and pulled out a pen. "Okay, some of these will have to be notarized, but I figured I could go over the bulk of them now with you." He looked up. "Who am I kidding? I just wanted to give you a go with my car."

Beau let out a short laugh. "Why's that?"

"Because you, my friend, have been miserable lately." Taylor was pointing the pen at him now. "It's a horrible thing to witness. Any change on the romance front?"

"I haven't talked to Liddy all week."

Taylor nodded once. "I get it—you don't want to know if there's something seriously wrong."

Beau shook his head quickly. "No, no, that's not it at all. I hope she does call me ... if she receives some bad news."

"Okay, so if you're ready to accept that, why haven't you called her?"

"She called me immature."

"Immature? As in too young or ...? I don't get it. Dude, you're older than her."

"She was angry about the Wendy thing when she said it. Can't blame her, though it stung."

"A little sting can be a good thing."

Beau blew out a long, low breath. "You're right. But I don't know ... losing Anne changed me. I'm less foolhardy than I once was."

"The way you flipped the gears out there on the highway, I am not inclined to agree."

Beau gave Tyler a reluctant smile. "Maybe I have been afraid. Anne's illness took me—all of us—by surprise. I never really got used to the idea, even up to the end. Frankly, I'd prefer not to ever go through anything like that again."

"And I'd prefer to spend all day on a surfboard."

Beau rolled his eyes. "You haven't surfed a day in your life."

"It was an expression, dude. What I'm saying is we prefer all kinds of things, but there's not one thing in this life we can control. Nothing."

"I know that."

"I'm going to ask you something, but you'll have to promise you won't punch me in the face if I do."

"I haven't punched another guy since high school. He did have it coming, though."

Taylor sighed.

Beau sat back, waiting. "Well, go on now. Ask away."

TAYLOR DROPPED OFF BEAU AT his office, but instead of heading back inside to his paper-filled desk, he pivoted around and set out for a walk. He couldn't get Taylor's question out of his mind, and he certainly didn't want to sit in his office, obsessing over it while avoiding his assistant's inquisitive mind. There were definite advantages to employing someone as fiercely loyal and skilled as Jill, but when it came to his love life, her presence and "advice" often caused him unnecessary bouts of stuttering and explanation—much like facing his mother's unyielding questions did when he was young.

So he chose the most appropriate maneuver: avoidance. His dress shoes clipped along on the sidewalk at a fast pace, the steady rhythm providing a gentle background to his thoughts. He admitted to himself that he was no stranger to avoiding the hard things. Not in work, per se, but in relationships, mostly.

Anne had wanted to get married long before he found himself ready to propose. He loved her; that wasn't the issue. But he wanted to make sure that he had made sufficient money and headway in his work before making a commitment to her.

At least that's what he'd always said.

Truthfully, he was never really sure he could handle the heady weight of supporting another person, not only financially, but emotionally. He'd had the best example of a marital relationship in his parents, but that didn't stop him from obsessing over the right time, the right place, the right ... everything. He sighed, remembering the agitation in his gut the night before he proposed in that park with the old trees that she always liked to walk through on Sunday afternoons. The closer he moved to that pivotal moment, the more his desire to be Anne's husband grew, yet at the same time a monster of doubt surged inside of him, taunting his confidence. His biggest foe was the worry that somehow he would let Anne down.

The memory of that day and those thoughts sliced through him. He swallowed them back, his throat slack with emotion long shed. Before the end, she had caressed his face and thanked him for being a husband who didn't bail when her illness began its daily ravage. "I will love you through eternity," she had said, her voice remarkably stable, considering.

He stopped at the edge of a park two blocks from his office, his chest heaving from gulping heavy doses of oxygen. He leaned forcefully against a wrought-iron railing, and found himself passively watching a boy and his dog. Leaves glittered in the sun, a blessed wind flowing through them, through him.

He glanced around. This idyllic spot wasn't much different from the park where he had proposed to Anne all those years ago. He rubbed his face, aware of the shadow forming on his skin. It had been good, his marriage. And right.

A man's voice interrupted his thoughts. The little boy was kicking a ball two times his size toward a gargantuan, tail-wagging dog. The older man, perhaps the boy's father, urged him on from a distance. The little boy kicked the soccer ball again, this time with enough force to send the massive dog running, ears back, tail flying. As Beau watched a perfectly normal event on an equally average day, he realized with startling clarity that despite all the pain, all the discouragement and shifted dreams, he knew, and had always known the answer to Taylor's question: He did not, for one moment, regret his marriage to Anne.

When the dog reached the ball, he somehow managed to sink his teeth in it and lift it high. The dog turned then and galloped, full force toward the young boy, that ball like an appendage to its snout. Beau groaned, certain the boy was about to be flattened.

Instead, the little guy ran with chubby arms open toward the barreling animal as if unafraid—and unaware—of impending danger. The dog stopped abruptly, dropped the ball at the feet of the child who was half his size, and began slurping the young boy's face. Giggles bubbled on the breeze. Beau could hear the boy's father laughing heartily.

Beau laughed, too, noting the steady, forceful pumping of his own heart, telling him he was much alive.

So was Liddy.

And ... he missed her.

Maybe … maybe it was time for him to face his demons. Head on. *Am I going to keep living in fear? Or do I have the guts to follow the path laid out before me?*

He pondered this while watching the man scoop up his son, slip a leash around the dog, and kick the ball toward the parking lot.

Chapter Twenty-Four

LIDDY HURRIED PAST THE line of cars at the valet station, weaving past writers who had formed small goodbye parties near the hotel's entrance. It was the last day of the week-long event, and though the creative storytellers who had filled the inn had provided plenty of entertainment, Liddy wasn't unhappy to see them go. Her files were in disarray, as were the concierge desk brochures, not to mention the supplies that had been depleted. She and the rest of the concierges had their work cut out for them if they were going to turn things over in time for the travel press trip arriving in a few days.

As soon as she hit the lobby, she paused. There was a stiffness to the staff, stern expressions replacing the usually jovial mood of the place. She, too, had been wrestling with her emotions lately, so she had welcomed the workday ahead. Staying home left too much quiet to ruminate, and Liddy had begun to rely on her friends in the hospitality industry to give her a daily dose of laughs.

"Why is everyone so glum around here?" she asked Trace while sliding her purse into a drawer.

"I don't really know. Maybe something in the water?"

Liddy glanced around. Everyone seemed to be all business

today. She shrugged and picked up the phone after it began to ring.

"Concierge desk. This is Liddy."

"It's me," Meg said. "Listen, have you seen Jackson yet this morning?"

"I have not. But I just got here." She turned away from the phone. "Trace, have you seen Mr. Riley?"

Trace said nothing, but shook her head while doodling directions on a notepad for a couple of hat-wearing women standing in front of her.

Liddy turned back to the phone. "Neither has Trace. Would you like me to give you a call when he arrives?"

"No, no. It's okay." Meg's voice fell to a whisper. "It's going to have to be."

"Sounds like something's up."

"You can say that again … you could do something for me, though. If a camera crew shows up, would you call me first?"

"Well, sure …"

"And stall them, okay?"

Liddy's forehead tensed. "Of course, but—"

"Gotta run!" Meg clicked off.

"What was that all about?" Trace asked after her guests walked away.

Before she could answer, Pepper Riley marched into the hotel, her long, white-blonde hair dusting the satiny fabric of her all-black pantsuit. Her creamy, line-less skin—the kind that can't move until the chemical wears off—stood out among the flushed and suntanned faces of both tourists and staff milling about the lobby. Guests unaware of Pepper's connection to the hotel likely wondered at their luck at happening upon someone famous—someone they could not exactly name.

"Oh, brother. Why is she dressed like a skunk?" Trace asked, before turning away to pick up the phone.

Liddy hid a laugh, thankful for a Trace-ism to lighten the mood—not to mention the ability to offer a wholly different perspective.

Pepper strode up to the desk, her eyes zeroing in on Liddy. She put out her hand, her nails manicured into sharp red points. "We haven't met," she said. "I'm Pepper Riley, co-owner of the hotel."

Liddy shook her hand. "It's a pleasure, Ms. Riley," she said.

"I am expecting a Mr. Nethering and guests to arrive sometime this morning," she said, her gaze moving about the lobby now.

Liddy nodded and slid into her seat. "Mr. Nethering … allow me to pull up his reservation."

"Mr. Nethering will not be staying at the resort; however, he will approach you and ask for directions to Chef's office." She leaned forward, her eyes impressively round and searing despite her frozen forehead. "You must not give him those directions. Instead, send him and his guests to me."

Though Liddy kept a poker face, a sensation like peach fuzz rose on the back of her neck. "I will see that I do," she said.

Pepper smiled, her lips so full that their edges had disappeared. "Excellent." She turned and strode across the lobby and down the hall.

Thankfully, as the number of departing guests continued to swell around the concierge desk, where she'd been left alone due to Trace's lunch hour, Liddy didn't have the time to focus on the resort owner's request. She had just said goodbye to a darling couple who wrote mysteries together, when her stomach grumbled, alerting her that it was nearly time for her own lunch. She sat for a moment, trying to decide between a walk to the marina where she could grab a smoothie or something more decadent like a burger from the restaurant.

A sudden fluster at the bell desk broke her from her musings, and she glanced up. Jackson had arrived, his expression more surly than she'd ever seen.

Quickly, Liddy dropped her gaze to her computer screen, hoping to avoid any kind of interaction with him. Her childhood kitten had often tried something similar—looking away in order to not be noticed—but it had never worked. Hopefully, unlike his sister, Jackson had no assignment for her.

"Liddy," Jackson said, suddenly appearing deskside. "I'd like to speak with you."

She stopped typing and looked up. "Certainly. How may I help you?"

"Before I forget—thank you for meeting with Ms. Wilkes when I couldn't be here."

"My pleasure." She hoped that didn't sound like a lie. She still hadn't decided what to believe about the personal things Wendy had said to her.

"Now," he continued, "it's my understanding that you have crossed the aisle, so to speak, and that you have taken it upon yourself to learn our reservation system."

She stared at him, speechless. Was he about to chastise her in front of the staff and guests? To tell her not to be so nosy? To keep her eyes out of other people's business? At some point she realized she was holding her breath and began to slowly let it out.

"I'm impressed," he finally said. "And I think it would be wise for us to sit down next week with HR to discuss new ways for you to integrate your knowledge about our systems."

She smiled. "Yes. Yes, I would be happy to do that."

He gave her a perfunctory nod, but she sensed the start of a smile as well. "I'll ask my secretary to set something up before I leave town for the rest of the month."

He was about to turn away, when, as if in slow motion, a group of five people dressed in black appeared in the lobby, sunlight highlighting their artful hairstyles. The entry doors slid closed behind the two women and three men, drawing attention to their sunglass-adorned faces, and the dolly of equipment being pulled behind them. There was something … familiar about them.

Their leader, tall and slender enough to tuck in his pants without causing his shirt buttons to become taut, approached the concierge desk. He knew he was beautiful, and Liddy sensed that he had never known the backside of a camera. "I'm here to see the chef."

Oh, no … the camera crew Meg wanted me to stall.

Liddy pulled her attention from Jackson, hoping the VP would continue on his merry way. "Allow me to help you. May I have your name?"

"Nethering."

Liddy's heart stuck in her throat. *Meg had asked to greet them first … but Pepper wants them directed to her.*

The man's smile was white, reminding her of French nail tips. He spoke again. "If you will direct me to Chef Franco's office, I have a special surprise for him."

Liddy took slow breaths in an attempt to keep calm. She

noticed, but did not acknowledge, that Jackson had barely moved away from her. "Yes, of course." She had to stall. "Perhaps I can call him for you." She picked up the phone, intending to call Meg. What she would say to her when she answered, well, she hadn't figured that out yet.

But the man put his hand on hers. "No, please." He flashed those teeth. "It's a surprise."

Jackson pivoted. "Perhaps I can help." He thrust his hand out. "Jackson Riley, VP of the resort."

The man's smile faltered somewhat. Liddy removed her hand from the phone and as stealthily as possible reached for her cell phone and texted "911!" to Meg.

BEAU HAD PICKED UP THE PHONE to call Liddy last night, but changed his mind. She would have sent it to voice mail anyway. Right? Now as he drove along the water's edge, he glanced over at Sea Glass Inn, the tourist spot looking especially regal today with its flag-flanked curved driveway and pristine, palm tree-lined grounds. The sun appeared overhead as if shining a spotlight on his chance. He could pull over and try her number. He tapped his thumb on the steering wheel over and over then froze. This was not a conversation for the phone.

Abruptly, he made a U-turn and pulled his car into the hotel parking lot, taking in the lack of vehicles in view. Thankfully, the lot was nearly empty. On the one hand, she probably would not be too busy to talk to him face to face. On the other, he did not want to say what he had to say in front of a lobby full of bored employees.

He pulled into a spot, exited the car, and made his way toward the hotel where several valets loitered in front. She may not be happy with him for showing up here, but if she wasn't taking his calls, he had no other choice. He wasn't about to just drop the matter and scurry away like a wounded animal. Beau slowed his pace, his eyes focusing on those gleaming doors. Hopefully, he was not about to make another big mistake.

A SMALL CROWD HAD FORMED around her and the others at the desk, including Trace, who had returned from lunch. Liddy had recovered from a bad marriage and survived brain surgery, but this ... this did not look good. She kept her eye on the office corridor, silently willing Meg to appear. *Come on, come on ...* Meg did not disappoint. She came skidding around the corner without allowing one strand of hair to rustle out of place. Liddy raised her brows, her eyes locking on Meg's, but she said nothing.

In a blink, Pepper appeared behind Meg, following after her at a fast clip. *How did she know ... ?* A barely perceptible glance passed between Pepper and Hannah, who stood stalwart at the bell captain's desk, one hand resting on the phone.

Liddy held her expression in check and turned, hesitantly so, to find Jackson scowling. She thought about interjecting something witty or stupid, since either one might break the taut strand of growing silence. But when she lifted her chin to make eye contact with Jackson, another man caught her eye.

Beau.

Wendy had lost her mind—Beau exuded strength. He looked strong, sexy, and vulnerable. She made herself breathe.

He stood off to the side, watching the spectacle silently, as if he could sense that this was no ordinary day at the inn. His presence both calmed and stirred up the tempest brewing within her, her reaction to him an unlikely mix. Still unable to make sense of where their relationship was headed—where it *should* be headed—she blinked away the tears.

Jackson's unmistakable voice punctuated the murmuring and broke Liddy's reverie. He pinned his gaze on Meg, and Meg alone. "Why didn't you tell me about all this?"

Meg made her way forward, her stance professional and unyielding. She stopped in front of the group, her eyes unreadable. She breezed a look at the faces of the camera crew, lingering a second longer on the host, and finally on Jackson. "Why don't we step into the back office?" she said.

Pepper cut in, waving her tanned bare arms, her metal bracelets rattling into the air. "Gentlemen ... and ladies. Of course, we can accommodate your request. But first, you"—she pointed toward the man with the camera—"turn on your camera and make sure that your assistant has me in the best lighting. Hurry now."

By this time, the crowd around the concierge desk had grown to include other members of the hotel staff. Pepper flashed a smile at the onlookers first, then at the camera.

Jackson spun around, and in one quick and impressive move he leapt on top of the concierge counter.

Trace gasped. She reached for a stack of fliers, her pencil holder, and a statue of a cat holding an "Open" sign in its paws, and cleared them all away.

"Hold on, everyone," Jackson said, his hands splayed in the air.

"Get off that desk right now," Pepper demanded. She crooked an arm into her side and proceeded to further solidify her prima donna reputation by tapping one pointy, high-heel-shod toe vigorously on the tile floor.

Jackson didn't acknowledge her except to say, "Quiet!"

The murmurs stopped.

"Now," he said, "will somebody please tell me what this is all about?"

Liddy teetered on the edge, her eyes shifting nervously toward Meg. The man had asked for the chef. Did this have something to do with the drug investigation? He looked more like a reality show host than a hard-nosed journalist, but it occurred to her that these days they were often one and the same.

Liddy sensed Beau's gaze on her cheeks and she flicked a glance at him. She didn't know whether it was possible to sense a gaze, but her cheeks had gone warm and not in a particularly bad way—which surprised her, considering the drama unfolding.

A murmur drew her attention. Chef Franco appeared in the midst of the crowd, as if from a secret passageway, his uniform uncharacteristically crisp and white. "I believe I know what's happening here."

Pepper clapped. "Turn on the camera," she shouted, while sidling up to the chef.

Chef beamed, his animated gaze commanding the camera lens. The bright grin on his face barely flinched as he stood his ground, holding off Pepper's battle for the camera's attention.

The crew moved into position.

Lights burst on.

The leader of the crew, Nethering, the man who looked as if he had stepped off the cover of a slick brochure, jumped in front of Chef and Pepper, his smile brighter than the pristine uniform cinched just below the chef's girth. He spoke into a microphone. "I'm Brian Nethering and welcome to the reveal episode of 'Best Chef'!"

Someone on the bell staff whistled. A passerby cheered, inciting a round of applause from inside the hotel lobby. Pepper kissed Chef Franco on the cheek, while never taking her eyes off the camera. She left a splotch of deep, dark red on the robust man's already rosy face.

Liddy's gaze moved away from the impromptu taping to Meg who returned a tentative smile. Jackson, however, stood out awkwardly, his face a riddle of confusion.

"Meg?" he said, glaring now.

Meg shrank back—out of character for her—but said nothing.

His mouth hung open wide, his eyes black and tiny. He gestured toward the TV crew, and shook his head. "You knew about this?"

Liddy leaned her head to one side. *Did she?*

"N-not originally." Meg tried to smile, but her cheek twitched under Jackson's glare. "I found out accidentally ... and was sworn to secrecy."

Jackson let out a sarcastic laugh. His words sliced the air. "I thought we meant more to each other than that."

Chins swiveled upward toward Jackson, as did the cameraman.

Meg pulled her shoulders back, and lifted her own chin. "Do we?"

Liddy swung a lip-biting look at Beau. He in turn watched her, a question in his eyes.

Meg and Jackson were at an impasse, and Liddy feared that pretty soon her best friend and her boss would be starring in a show of their own. Liddy raised a hand into the air. "Meg didn't mean to keep anything from you, Jackson." She paused. "Everybody knows that she's the best thing that ever happened to this inn."

One pencil-sharp brow attempted to rise on Pepper's lineless face. "Oh, really?"

Meg shook her head. "Liddy, stop," she hissed. "Why didn't you just call me when I asked you to?"

Liddy's mouth popped open but she hesitated. Was Meg blaming *her* for this fiasco?

Jackson scoffed. "Now you're calling on the staff to go sneaking around my back?" He pointed at Liddy as if she were Exhibit A. "Hasn't this woman been through enough after her husband's betrayal? You said yourself that the man she was married to even made a pass at you!"

It took a solid three seconds for Jackson's words to settle in Liddy's mind, and another three to drive them deep into her wounded heart.

Trace, who had held her tongue for the past several minutes, let out an "oh boy" under her breath.

Liddy set her chin, her thoughts severe, smoldering. After a long pause, she looked up. "Well, Mr. Riley," she said, evenly, "I've heard about your family troubles, too. I guess we both know firsthand about betrayal by those we trusted."

Meg frowned at Liddy, Jackson glared at Meg, and Pepper? Pepper managed to mug for the camera while surreptitiously darting unpleasantly wide eyes at her brother.

Liddy pivoted away from the fray and Beau's sight. She headed for the exit that would take her to the harbor, and once outside, drew in a clumsy breath as she raced away from the hotel. She needed to think. Had Jackson really just announced how pathetic she was to the hotel staff? And to the cast and crew of a TV show while the camera rolled? She flushed, embarrassed. All those times Jackson had spoken to her, he *knew* that her ex-husband had made a pass at her best friend.

Liddy shook her head tightly, her jaw set. Jackson knew something about her that she, until this very moment, had known nothing about. She swallowed a garbled groan and darted a look back. Any hope that Beau might give up and leave her alone was dashed when she noticed him following her at a fast clip as she marched past the marina, and all the way down to the beach.

When she heard him breathing, she stopped, and swiveled around. Strands of his hair fluttered in the breeze. "This is not a good time, Beau."

He reached for her elbow. "Will there ever be?"

"What's that supposed to mean?"

"You haven't answered my calls."

"Well ... I've been busy!" She waved a hand toward the resort in the distance.

He wanted to smile. She could tell by the way his lips twitched. He was laughing at her!

She bit her lip, forcing back a tide of emotion. "Beau," she whispered, "this isn't funny. I'd really ... I'd really like to be alone. Could you please leave?"

He stared at her, and for a split moment, she thought he

might comply. He shook his head then, his mouth falling into a grim line.

Her heart sank in her chest, sending her stomach into a tumble. She gulped fresh salt air and crossed her arms. "Is life ever *not* like a roller coaster?"

"Not as long as I've been alive. But I suppose that would be boring anyway."

She turned away from him now, willing herself out to sea. Even if she could catch a departing ship, would there be any way to control the roll of the waves? She sighed, giving up, then pressed into the railing that kept her from tumbling into sea water. "I have some news," she finally said.

He put a tentative hand on her shoulder and leaned into her back, lightly resting his chin on her. She kept staring at the ocean, not really seeing it. Instead, she pictured his expression to be much like a forlorn puppy dog. "I'm sorry," he said.

"Wait, I—"

"Shh. Please," he said. "Let me get this out."

From its spot low in her chest, her already damaged heart twisted, sending her stomach in an all-out assault on her equilibrium. She swallowed, and bit the inside of her lip. The chance existed that her time at the resort was swiftly coming to a close. Suddenly Beau's decision to say goodbye to her now seemed all that more appropriate ...

Beau's tentative touch tightened on Liddy's shoulder and he guided her to turn around and face him. He steadied her with a long, slow gaze and caressed her cheek. "I love you," he said, simply.

Liddy tilted her head into his palm, reveling in its embrace. She fought back another bout of dizziness, but instead of it being the sort that came from some kind of illness, this feeling came from something more serious—like a man's sudden and inexplicably-timed confession of love.

He closed the slight space between them. "I'm sorry for backing away from you, and that you haven't been feeling well ... it tears me up inside. But it doesn't change how I feel about you, and it won't. I can't stop myself from pursuing you." He kissed her lightly, then whispered it again, "I love you, Liddy."

Pursuing her? When had a man pursued her for anything other than the convenience of her presence? For anything ... lasting? Her resolve to resist him floated away, and she closed her eyes. Despite the drama she'd just run from, Liddy felt herself free falling now, like in a dream where there's no worry, just a sense of weightlessness. *I have loved you ... with an everlasting love.* The words that had drifted into her mind the last time she had run to this very spot sprang to life, releasing her from the fears that held her captive.

She opened her eyes, her own failings washing over her. "I'm the one who's sorry, Beau. I-I've been hiding things from you, hiding things from myself, too."

He watched her, but didn't move.

"I let my fears control me." She sniffled, tears prickling her eyes. "Never a good idea, you know?"

He nodded. "I know."

She searched his face, his eyes, seeing something in a man's face she had never seen before ... and it took her breath away. She inhaled, and said, "I love you, too, Beau."

Beau's strong arms slid around her waist, and she allowed him to mold her into him. The days apart from this man that she loved had been too much. She breathed in his scent, letting it fill every one of her senses, and then ...

She sneezed.

He drew back slightly. "Gesundheit."

She sniffled. And sneezed again.

He began searching his pockets.

Liddy ran the back of her hand across her nose and sniffled once more, letting out a giggle this time. "If only you were older," she said, finally.

He furrowed his brow, a quizzical half-smile on his face.

She pointed at his chest. "Then you'd have one of those little tissue packets in your shirt pocket."

A smile broke out on his face, and he reached for her again. "You're too much."

Her smile faded slightly. "Seriously, though, I have to tell you something."

His brows lowered, turning his kaleidoscope eyes darker, but his embrace never faltered.

Liddy lifted her chin, looked squarely into his gaze, and spoke, keeping her voice calm. "I have a deviated septum. A small one."

"Excuse me?"

"The dizziness ... I saw the doctor and it turns out it's a sinus condition." She allowed herself to breathe normally again, and stifled another sniffle.

"That's all it was?"

She shrugged, and gave him a little smile. "Or maybe I'm just allergic to you."

He let out a low whoop and pulled her body against his, hugging her so tightly that it was unlikely she could take a breath even if she needed to.

Chapter Twenty-Five

"LIDDY?"

Liddy stared straight ahead.

"Liddy?" Meg called, her voice rising. "Are you okay?"

Liddy pulled her eyes away from the vast and deep blue sea. She dug her toes deeper into the sand and rested against the back of her beach chair. "Of course I am. Just mesmerized by the beauty of it all."

"Well, don't *do* that!"

She laughed and hung her chin. "Sorry."

Meg huffed a sigh and returned to an old copy of *People* magazine. She thumbed through the pages, settling on one featuring last year's sexiest man alive.

"I'm guessing you haven't heard from Jackson, huh?"

Meg frowned. "Hardly, and that's okay by me. He took off as soon as the infamous taping was in the can, and I've only spoken to him by email."

"I'm sorry for my part in that."

"Please. I'm the one who should do penance for a year for all that I didn't tell you."

"You've already apologized for that." Liddy sighed. "I know that by keeping Shawn's advances to yourself you were only trying to protect me."

"Big mistake. I'm still sorry."

"I know."

Meg shrugged. "Just wish I could make it up to you somehow." She shook her head. "And also for telling Jackson things about you that I never should have."

"Forget it, please. What I wish, well, what I wish is that you and Jackson could find some way to talk through this strange relationship you have. I mean, since you have to work together ..."

"At least I still have my job."

"As well you should! You took that family fiasco and turned it into marketing genius ... concocting a plan for Chef to visit our other resorts around the country? Who else would've come up with that?"

"Anybody worth their salt would have."

Liddy scoffed. "Right."

Meg turned to her. "Don't forget, your man helped immensely. His knowledge of social media marketing is beyond! The resorts are packed—I'm lucky to have a room for myself. Anyway, please give him my thanks again for allowing me to harvest so much of his brain." She laughed. "That sounded odd, didn't it? I mean, considering ..."

"You can thank him yourself."

Beau arrived and plunked his chair in the sand next to Liddy. He leaned over and pecked her on the cheek before nodding at Meg. "Thank me for what?"

Meg tossed the magazine onto the towel stretched out by her feet. "For your marketing mojo. You're the bomb."

He chuckled. "Any time."

Meg stood and stretched, sighing deeply. She folded up her beach chair, stuffing her towel and magazine inside.

Beau looked up. "Don't leave on my account."

"Wish I could stay here and relax with you lovebirds, but I have a date with my carry-on and I still have laundry to do." She took another look out to sea. "May even have to check a bag this time."

"Do you really have to go for so long?" Liddy whined.

Meg peered at her. "Franco's pretty in love with himself, wouldn't you say? No, I have to go and keep that man in line." She cracked a smile. "At least the food'll be great."

"Silver linings," Liddy added.

Meg bent down and kissed Liddy on her head of fully grown-in hair. "Love you, girl. Talk soon."

"Please call. Love you, too."

Liddy and Beau sat together not far from where she'd met a drifter who created elaborate castles out of sand only to watch them destroyed by the tide. She thought back to her family's sporadic trips to the beach with friends and cousins, their tongues clamped between their teeth as they built their own castles in the sand. For the most part, whenever a rogue wave took their creations from them, they would hunker down in the sand and start again.

She watched a wave sputter onto the beach, leaving froth in its wake. There was something to be said for the magic that can happen when lives are rebuilt, especially by something stronger than sand and water.

"What's got ahold of you?" Beau asked, interrupting her musings.

She smiled at him. "You mean, other than you?"

He leaned to the side, kissing her shoulder. "I like how you think."

"I was just thinking about this past year, the bad and the good. I like how it's turned out," she said.

He gazed at her with those kaleidoscope eyes. "Me, too."

"Well, except for the fact that my boyfriend chose to move miles away from me."

Beau groaned. "This again."

"Just trying to make sure you know how much I miss you."

"Ah. I see. Well, you know, if you're ever able to tear yourself away from the beach long enough, you could come over more."

"I suppose."

"Tonight, even. I can put a couple of steaks on the grill for us, open a bottle of wine ... what do you say?"

She bit her lip. "I've been thinking."

"Uh-oh."

"No. Hear me out. It's your ... it's your guest bathroom."

He frowned.

"It needs some attention. Maybe I could run out and buy some towels and a couple of rugs. Oh, and a new shower curtain ... something more ... I don't know."

The proverbial light bulb moment lit up Beau's face and he reached for Liddy's hand. "Feminine?"

She laughed into the sea breeze. "Yes! It needs a feminine touch!"

Beau kissed her fingers, his smile wide as the sky is blue. "We'll see, beautiful. We'll see."

Epilogue

✹

BEAU WOKE TO A SLIVER of light unmasking the distinct shapes in the otherwise darkened bedroom. He lay there, blinking, as his mind took in the peaceful stillness. His eyes began to focus then, finding the framed picture on the wall, the dress sprawled across the back of the chair that sat beneath it. He sucked in a breath, and reflexively reached his arm across the empty space beside him, his hand landing on sheets of cotton, warm and rumpled.

As the white noise of dreams began to clear away from his mind, a wry smile tugged at the corners of his mouth, and Beau sat up, taking in the abundance of covers pulled over to one side of the bed. Her side.

His gaze adjusted to that sliver of light coming from the deck off of his … off of *their* bedroom. Liddy's and his. The memory of their wedding one month prior astounded him still. He'd asked and she'd said yes. They had married within a month. He had never moved on a decision faster.

He swung his legs off the bed, planting bare feet on the floor, and stood. Quickly, he padded across the room, retrieved his robe from the chair and slipped it around him. Her perfume reached his senses, and he realized that she must have borrowed his robe. Again. The idea filled him with something raw and welcome. Reaching for the door that stood ajar, Beau opened it wider, allowing a cascade of light to awaken him more fully. He found her sitting on the deck just outside of their bedroom, her head resting against an Adirondack chair, her features awash in moonlight's luster.

"Liddy?"

She startled. "Oh. Did I wake you?"

He reached for her hand, pulling her up to mold against him. He nuzzled his mouth next to her ear. "You not being there woke me."

"So sorry, love."

"Is something bothering you?"

"Nothing to worry you about."

He tugged her body closer to his, though that was nearly impossible. Her nearness took him to unimaginable places and he drank her in. "Well," he whispered lazily into her ear, "I'm here to take your mind off of your worries, Mrs. Quinn."

She smiled at him in the moonlight and gave the lapels of his robe a tug. "You do an amazing job of that, I must say ..."

He touched her face. "But you're still worried about something."

She sighed, rocking them both. "It's Meg. She ... she seems so unhappy these days."

He pulled back farther, taking in his wife's face. His wife. He loved the sound of that. "She seemed great at our wedding."

Liddy gave him a smile that said "silly man."

"What was that look for?"

"Of course she *was* happy then. I mean she was so happy

for us, Beau." Her smile turned sad. "I think she's not over Jackson, though, and that working for the inn is getting to her. She's traveling more than ever before, but she doesn't seem content like she used to be."

"Have you tried talking to her?"

She gave him that look again, like he was Captain Obvious. Then she sighed and looked back toward the moon's soothing glow. "You're right. I'll try again to talk to her. I just hope she'll tell me everything ... I'm not sure that she has."

Beau had no words for her. Instead, he rubbed his hands along her shoulders and down the sides of her arms to warm away her shivers. Then he stepped behind her and with her back to him, enveloped her in his embrace. Her hair tickled his neck, even as he fought to keep her close without offending her with his morning stubble.

After a while she spoke. "You know what I'm thinking?"

"Hmm. No. What?"

"We should re-do the backyard."

Beau shut his eyes, his eyelids cool in the night air. Wait. *Weren't we just talking about Meg?*

When he didn't answer right away, she shifted in his arms. "Did you hear me?"

"Well ..."

"What do you think?"

"I think ... that I've never met anyone like you."

She laughed lightly at his quick save and turned herself to face him squarely. She kissed him softly then, showing no sign of offense at the brush of his stubble across her cheek. "I have never met anyone like you either, my love, my all ... my husband," she laughed again, the sound of it like rain after a drought. "I adore you."

Her love for him had unleashed him to live with fearless passion, and by her response to his touch he knew that he'd had the same effect on her. It was as if they had each been given the gift of each other. "I adore you, too," he whispered.

And with a possessiveness made for a moment like this, Beau led Liddy back inside.

NOTE TO READERS

I hope you enjoyed *Walking on Sea Glass*, book one of the Sea Glass Inn Novels. My husband, Dan, and I met under circumstances similar to Liddy and Beau's—and like them, we made it! We are grateful to family, friends, and God—all who cradled us during the dark and the amazingly bright times we experienced back then. While Liddy and Beau may have been loosely inspired by my husband and me when we were (lots) younger, as their story unfolded, they quickly became their own people. This story is theirs.

I'd like to give a shout out to my thoughtful and thorough editors Kim Huther and Denise Harmer. Thank you both for your fine work!

Kudos to Roseanna White for another beautiful cover. Your patience with me will be rewarded someday, I have no doubt.

Thank you, too, mi familia—Dan, Matt, Angie, Emma, and my parents, Dan and Elaine—for your constant encouragement.

And readers, I appreciate you very much—you keep me writing (and daydreaming, but that's kinda like working, right?) As I write this note to you, the next story is already playing out in my head. Now to get it down on paper …

If you liked this novel, and any of my other titles, please consider reviewing them at your favorite online retailer and/or Goodreads. Thank you much.

Runaway Tide is coming soon!

Julie

OTHER TITLES BY JULIE CAROBINI

The Christmas Thief (A Cottage Grove Mystery)

Otter Bay Novels
Sweet Waters (book 1)
A Shore Thing (book 2)
Fade to Blue (book 3)

The Chocolate Series
Chocolate Beach (book 1)
Truffles by the Sea (book 2)
Mocha Sunrise (book 3)
The Chocolate Beach Collection (books 1-3)

The Spa at Winter Beach (A Seaside Novella)

CPSIA information can be obtained
at www.ICGtesting.com
Printed in the USA
FFOW03n0728160418
46278026-47739FF

9 780986 229299